FURTIVE RETRIBUTION

GARY D. MCGUGAN

Furtive Retribution

ISBN 978-1-0692808-1-7 (Paperback)
ISBN 978-1-0692808-2-4 (eBook)
1. FICTION, THRILLERS

Also by Gary D. McGugan

Fiction

The Multima Saga

Three Weeks Less a Day
The Multima Scheme
Unrelenting Peril
Pernicious Pursuit
A Web of Deceit
A Slippery Shadow
CONTENTION
When Power Fails

Non-Fiction

NEEDS Selling Solutions
(Co-authored with Jeff F. Allen)

What Readers Say About Gary D. McGugan's Books

"One thing is clear—Gary D. McGugan knows how to write top-caliber stories. Some authors write predominantly character-driven books, while others drive their stories through enticing plotlines. McGugan does both, and with equal excellence—no small feat, especially in keeping a series exciting and suspenseful with escalating intensity."
~ Sheri Hoyte for Reader Views

"What an incredible story. Exciting, suspenseful, and thought-provoking, *A Slippery Shadow* by Gary D. McGugan is one of the best stories I have read."
~ *Natalie Soine for Readers' Favorite*

"As is the case with McGugan's two previous novels, *Three Weeks Less a Day* and *The Multima Scheme,* the plot of *Unrelenting Peril* is tight and complex. McGugan has a gift for well-paced, well-blocked flurries of nail-biting action that all lead up to a surprising finale."
~ *Norm Goldman, Bookpleasures.com*

"The chapters in this fast-paced plot jump from character to character, all interlinked by the hand of fate—some scheming, some grieving, and some learning valuable lessons about how stuff really works in the world beyond the headlines."
~ *Barbara Bamberger Scott, Feathered Quill*

"Gary D McGugan writes in a way that is easily understood and believable in this exciting book. He introduces characters to the story that allow you, the reader, to form a mental picture of what is going on in each scene while we are flown off in private jets to different parts of the world where crimes are plotted and put into operation."
~ *Christopher Anderson for Readers' Favorite*

One

Atlanta, Georgia, Monday November 13, 2023

A third call rang on the mobile phone buried deep inside Suzanne Simpson's handbag.

Earlier, when she'd answered the landline in the room they shared at Stonehurst Place Bed & Breakfast, there'd been only absolute and haunting silence. Even heavy breathing would've been preferable to the eerie quiet.

Twice, she'd picked up the phone nonchalantly when it rang. It sat on a stand within reach on her side of the bed in the luxurious second-floor suite of the old building. Stonehurst was an inn for the affluent, and she'd always considered it a quaint, lovely spot to get away from it all in midtown Atlanta. Every previous stay had been uneventful, and she'd experienced no issues at all during her three preceding nights.

On the second series of rings, when she was again greeted with only morbid quiet, she'd passed the receiver wordlessly to her live-in companion, Serge, with a shrug of her shoulders. After listening to the continued silence for several seconds, he demanded to know who was calling and what they wanted. Only unsettling stillness hung in the air. After a minute, the caller had hung up, and a dial tone hummed annoyingly.

Serge noted that the second call had come almost precisely a half-hour after the first and muttered that rest would be impossible for either of them should it continue. Of course, sleep was already an elusive intention. Following the shocking murder of their colleague Gordon Goodfellow, president of her Supermarkets business at Multima Corporation, she still struggled to suppress tears and allow her body to relax.

Only hours earlier, they had visited Gordon's family to break the painful news. State police in Alabama had discovered his bullet-riddled body in a ditch beside a dead female police officer, near Interstate 20. It had been a traumatic time for everyone involved, but the mysterious calls were far more than odd and troubling.

En route from Gordon's home to their temporary lodging, Suzanne had also broken the sad news to several senior leaders within her corporation with brief phone calls. Meanwhile, Serge had contacted multiple state police officials in Alabama, others in Georgia, and even his former employer, the Royal Canadian Mounted Police. None of those chores was pleasant, but nothing seemed inappropriate either, considering the extraordinary circumstances.

Nor had anything seemed out of place during the first few hours after they'd arrived at the inn. Dim lighting from overhead chandeliers in the tiny reception area glowed warmly as usual. A charcoal-colored cat dozed on the dark brown sofa guests might use while waiting for a cab or chatting casually with the nearby receptionist. They'd climbed the carpeted stairs to a suite that spanned the entire second floor. At the top, she'd glanced at Serge. The subdued creaking of the ancient stairs brought smiles to both their faces.

She passed the keycard across the sensor. The lock clicked loudly before she pushed the door inward and stepped inside. The room smelled of orchids and was freshly cleaned.

It was late because they had stopped for dinner at a fast-food outlet, and both appeared drained, emotionally and physically. After a quick shower and a glass of wine, they'd retired to read for a few minutes before turning out the lights and hoping for sleep. Those unsettling calls had begun about a half-hour after they'd both settled into bed.

After that second annoying call, Serge called the inn's receptionist to see if she might intervene and block calls to their room. The woman apologized but claimed there was no way she could override the automated system to prevent it from receiving and routing the calls, though no calls had passed through reception, she'd assured them.

Did whoever was calling them know their room number? Did they also know enough about the inn's technology to connect calls directly to their room?

Serge put on his clothes once again and sagged back onto the bed, fully dressed except for his shoes. "My skin is tingling," he said. "I want to be ready should we need to leave here quickly."

"Let's not become too alarmed. They're probably crank calls. Maybe even a disgruntled former employee of the inn looking for some retribution," Suzanne offered with a sigh. "I really need some sleep."

Precisely thirty minutes later, they both bolted upright when her mobile phone rang. Once again, silence was the only response. Whoever was calling knew not only the room they were staying in but also her personal mobile number, which only a handful of her most trusted colleagues knew.

She pressed the speaker button and continued repeating hello, asking the caller to identify themself.

Serge leaped from the bed and reached down for his shoes, motioning for her to disconnect and do the same.

"What? Who are you? What do you want?" Suzanne screamed into the phone, but she heard nothing. The call eventually disappeared from her screen.

Now fully dressed, she heard Serge make two hurried calls to his bodyguards stationed outside the inn as she threw on the closest garments she could find. One call was to a subordinate on Multima's bodyguard team, the unit Serge managed as her company's chief of security, asking him to scour the area around the bed and breakfast.

The other call was to the head of the Atlanta Police Department. Serge apparently knew the guy well and used the phone's speaker feature. She could hear the ringing from her side of the bed. Only seconds after keying in the chief's personal phone number, Serge described the mysterious goings-on as only a former law-enforcement agent could. Then, switching his tone to be less professional and more polite, Serge asked him to check with his people in their cars outside the inn to see if they had observed any unusual activity.

The fellow put the call on hold for a moment. Less than a minute later, he reported that all looked normal from the outside, but he would intensify scrutiny of the blocks surrounding the inn. Serge shrugged and politely thanked the police chief as he crossed the room.

"Let's get out of here right now." Serge motioned toward the door as he stuffed the phone into his jacket pocket.

"Okay," she replied. "Grab my luggage. I've thrown in everything I brought, and it's ready, but first, please call the pilots and get them to the jet as quickly as possible. It may be two in the morning, but I'm uncomfortable with this entire circumstance. Let's get to the airport and onto the plane. We can decide what to do from there." She clutched her arms across her breasts with a shiver of discomfort.

From the corner of her eye, she watched Serge press a button as she gathered her computer, her handbag, and a jacket for the cool night air.

Before they reached the doorway, her mobile rang again. Though she handed it to Serge to answer, she still heard the caller clearly. He used only five words: "Leave now, or you're finished."

Serge grabbed Suzanne by the wrist and almost dragged her down the stairs, leaving their luggage behind. At the bottom of the stairs, the inn's reception station was vacant, with no one in sight. Outside, he tugged her toward the street and urged her to run, high heels or not.

They hadn't gone far when a roaring blast from inside the inn threw them into a disheveled heap on the pavement.

Two

Atlanta, Georgia, Monday November 13, 2023

When Serge Boisvert realized how narrowly they had escaped the explosion, he bounced to his feet and pulled Suzanne up from the sidewalk. He yelled for a parked company security car to approach, waving wildly to attract the driver's attention.

The vehicle screeched to a halt, and Serge opened the rear door and pressed Suzanne into the seat, shoving her toward the other side of the interior. She slid the rest of the way across the wide seat, and he, too, jumped in, yelling instructions into his phone. "Check inside for any others, if you can. Handle the police! Call me when the senior guy arrives."

As the car lurched away from the curb, he turned to Suzanne. "Are you okay?"

She nodded, still in a state of shock from the blast.

"I'm calling the pilots," he said while he keyed in a sequence of numbers, then spoke when someone answered on the first ring. "File a flight plan for Montreal. Get clearance for takeoff the moment we arrive at the jet. We'll decide if we want to change the destination when we get in the air."

As they sped down I-75 in the early hours of that chilly November morning, it took three quick calls to get the necessary security clearances from the airport. There was little other traffic at that time of day, and it took only about fifteen minutes to drive from the sidewalk in front of the bombed bed and breakfast to a poorly lit gate in the rear section of the airport. The authorities understood the need for secrecy so as not to telegraph where the bad guys might easily find parked multi-million-dollar jets. It also provided cover for the occasional extremely wealthy passenger who might use an aircraft for more than a simple takeoff or landing.

One flash of Serge's Multima Corporation ID was all it took to coax an instant, knowing smile from the attending guard and a thumbs up from the man's colleague on the gate. Serge took some satisfaction that his stature in the world of security remained high despite Suzanne's occasional tendency to treat him like a subordinate.

He loved almost everything about the woman with a passion: Her beautiful face. Her charming smile. That her mind worked overtime and at optimum speed. Her memory for details he barely noticed, let alone retained. It was easy to see why she'd risen to the position of CEO, even if her predecessor had been her father. Suzanne had all the tools not only to run a great company but also to draw in virtually everyone she encountered with her natural magnetism.

He found it frustrating when she treated him likc hircd help rather than her life partner. She didn't do it often, but sometimes, when she felt stress or annoyance, her tone of voice changed ever so slightly. That night, combined with her choice of words, her manner had signaled clear superiority, whether she'd intended it or not. And it grated.

Her reluctance to abandon the small bed and breakfast when he had first expressed alarm was a case in point. As a security specialist, Serge would have immediately bailed from the inn after the second call to take safe harbor in the corporate jet parked in front of them on the tarmac.

But he had to hand it to her: the woman had recovered quickly and worked with remarkable precision. While he'd made the calls for last-minute arrangements to take refuge on the jet, he'd overheard Suzanne arranging a meeting of her board of directors that would take place in just five hours. Her long-serving assistant, Eileen Lee, had protested at first, perhaps insisting that she'd be sending emails and making phone calls around the globe for the next few hours at a time most assistants would be sleeping. Suzanne had told her to do it anyway.

She had also roused Edward Hadley, her director of corporate and investor affairs, from deep slumber to get his people revising a media release she'd discussed with him only hours before she'd tried to get some sleep at the bed and breakfast.

As they drove up to the jet on the tarmac, Suzanne finished a call with Natalia Tenaz, the president of Multima's Financial Services division. He couldn't focus on what they discussed, but thought he heard Suzanne instruct the woman to get out to the airport in Chicago and fly to Montreal for an eight o'clock meeting at corporate headquarters.

He shook his head to clear the disbelief at how much Suzanne could accomplish in such a brief time. It was a trait he'd openly admired while she climbed the corporate ladder, and he'd worked toward the leadership summit of the Mounties after they'd reunited a few years earlier after a long period of separation.

It was her conditioning to that hectic pace and decisive manner that contributed to Serge's annoyance when she occasionally expected him to jump at her every command like everyone else. But lovers should be treated differently.

The pilots were already on the jet. When he'd first reached them, they were sleeping in a hotel room in the Renaissance Concourse Atlanta Airport Hotel. It had probably taken them mere minutes to walk over from their room. The lights were on, and the plane's heating system hummed quietly in the background as the pilots greeted Suzanne and Serge in the doorway.

"Let's get to Montreal as quickly and safely as we can," Suzanne told the chief pilot as she passed. He nodded reassuringly and stepped away to execute her orders.

"Serge, I'd like a quick word with you. In my compartment, before I try to sleep." Her tone was softer than minutes earlier, and her smile seemed to acknowledge a realization that she'd lapsed into her occasional tendency to prioritize business ahead of personal issues. She closed the door to her private space, put her arms around his shoulders, and gave him a long, lingering kiss. Her tongue was warm, but it lacked her usual inviting tease for more.

"Someone tried to kill us," she whispered as their lips parted.

Her eyes drew his attention. Rather than appearing damp or poised to gush tears as one might expect, they were stone cold. Still a brilliant blue, but more like the hue of an iceberg.

"There's also something terribly amiss with Gordon's murder. Why did that female deputy sheriff take him out of his cell at the county jail? Why did someone murder her as well? And why did they take them, dead or alive, to Alabama?"

"All good questions, Suzanne. But as troubling as they might be, we have no answers at this stage. It could take months for law enforcement in Georgia and Alabama to get to the bottom of this mess," he warned.

"That's what I fear, and I can't wait months to know the answers. Will you take charge and find out what's going on?" Her eyes narrowed, piercing his gaze as if trying to read his thoughts.

"What do you mean, 'take charge'? You know I have no authority in either jurisdiction. I can do nothing to directly influence the outcome of the investigation or the pace at which that investigation will move." He kept his tone soft but emphasized the appropriate negative word. Nothing. She needed to understand that she was asking the impossible.

"I understand the challenges, but I can't accept the premise that we're helpless. I'm convening a meeting of the board of directors later this morning for one specific purpose: I'm going to ask them to authorize up to fifty million dollars to create a special fund. I want you to use as much of that money as you need, with more available, if necessary, to launch a *private* investigation into what happened to Gordon."

Serge didn't know how to mask his shock at the request, so he stood silently, gazing at Suzanne, his mouth agape. It took several seconds for him to recover.

"When did this idea germinate?" He smiled to soften the words but looked directly into her eyes, probing.

"It's not as impulsive as you might think. When I first read about the arrest of a Japanese Yakuza leader in Thailand—the one suspected of trafficking in nuclear weapons—I wondered if there might be some connection to the mischief we encountered during the Jeffersons Stores acquisition. Yesterday, when I learned about the plane crash that killed Fidelia Morales in Europe the same day we learned about Gordon's murder, I sensed the events might not be coincidental. Now, the suspicious phone calls and a bombing attempt on our lives? Something horrible is happening around our company. And that something might ruin us if we can't figure it out soon."

He offered the hint of a smile again as he nodded. "You know I've expressed the same concerns using other words and examples. I absolutely get where you're coming from."

"Will you do it?" Suzanne asked, her eyebrows arched expectantly.

"Let's see if you can get the board of directors to allocate the fifty million first."

Three

Montreal International Airport, Monday November 13, 2023

Natalia Tenaz checked her long, dark hair a final time and swept it back before wiping away any wrinkles that might have formed in her business suit. She stood in the tiny restroom compartment on the Multima Financial Services' jet as it taxied slowly to a parking spot in the area reserved for private aircraft. She expected a car to be waiting there to drive her to the Multima Corporation's downtown offices.

She felt tired. Between the call from her CEO at a godawful hour in the middle of the night, her rushed trip to the airport in Chicago, and the frequent turbulence on the flight eastward, she'd squeezed in only a few precious minutes of sleep overnight.

It wasn't a total shock to her system. Since Suzanne had promoted her to the role of president at Multima Financial Services the previous year, she'd made frequent trips to Central and South America. Her plan to grow the profitable subsidiary she had inherited from James Fitzgerald sought several acquisitions of smaller competitor banks in those regions, and she traveled there at least twice a month.

So, she'd adapted to jet lag and sleep disruptions and was still young enough to recover quickly. But she thought the experts were right when they'd said that everything about the human body started to wane after the early forties. She might not be far past that magic marker, but it was clear only the intrigue of her coming conversation with Suzanne Simpson would provide a much-needed energy boost.

During that quick call a few hours earlier, the CEO had subtly mentioned her intention to discuss some increased corporate responsibilities after holding a brief meeting with the board of directors in the morning. Suzanne hadn't dropped a hint about what those responsibilities might include, but it was fun to speculate and dream a bit.

Natalia was also looking forward to attending the meeting of the board. Unlike the guy who preceded her, she wasn't yet a member of that exclusive club, and invitations to join the elite were rare indeed. She gathered up the files she'd studied before trying to sleep and stuffed them carefully into the compartment of a tan leather briefcase she used to store acquisition stuff. Then, she checked her phone for emails or messages one last time as she walked toward the front of the aircraft and down the steps.

Surprisingly, Serge Boisvert, Suzanne's beau, stood waiting at the bottom of the stairs. Behind him, a black Mercedes-Benz idled with a chauffeur standing beside it, gawking off into the distance. As she stepped out from the doorway, he waved, flashed her a broad smile, and gave her a cheerful hello. When she set foot on the tarmac, Serge, always the professional, reached out with a formal handshake—a hug was probably entirely outside of the realm of possibility.

"I brought you a coffee," he offered as she settled into the rear seat of the luxurious limousine. The door latches clicked, and she almost spilled her coffee as the chauffeur departed with a spurt.

Though still professional, Serge's demeanor lacked its usual higher-than-normal energy level. His shoulders stooped forward slightly, perhaps a nod to the lower ceiling height in the limo, but maybe also a sign of fatigue. He probably hadn't had much sleep during the night, either.

"Thank you. I can't think of anything I need more right now than a cup of coffee. I didn't get an agenda for the BOD meeting. Any idea what Suzanne plans to discuss?" She watched him closely, waiting for his reply.

His gaze darted immediately to the right, although he clearly held his face toward her. His forehead was creased, and his tone of voice uncertain, his discomfort apparent. "I didn't get a copy of the agenda either," he said finally, opting for a light response. This led to a broader, more relaxed smile. "She dropped occasional hints, but I learned a long time ago that it's better not to share info before the boss is ready."

Both laughed in understanding, but Serge's expression turned serious again. "You're probably wondering why I'm meeting you this morning, so let me get right to the point. Suzanne always raves about your ability to ferret out information others don't seem to have. What's your secret?" His face portrayed sincerity and genuine interest, although the compliments and questions both seemed odd. Odd enough to merit a probe before answering.

"Is this some sort of early morning test to prepare me for the BOD meeting or my conversation with Suzanne?" She laughed as she posed her question, but tilted her head enough to show that she expected an answer.

"No," he assured her. "I just need your help and whatever expertise you can share. You know your way around the dark web. Are you as active there today as you were before all your career advancement over at Financial Services?"

"Not at all. These days, my time is fully occupied with running the business. Working the dark web takes far more time than I have available."

He didn't seem to buy the quick dismissal. "Suzanne always maintained that you used the dark web to gain an advantage with your research and development and strategies."

"That's true, but now I use my research team to do the legwork. They're a good bunch. They've learned the dark web well and feed me the background details I need."

Serge nodded, still interested. "I expect one of the subjects Suzanne will discuss with you today is your willingness to share some of those resources. I wanted to give you a heads up before the BOD meeting and your meeting with Suzanne."

He continued to look her directly in the eye, seeking a response.

First, she needed more information. "Fair enough. I'm usually willing to share. What kind of specialist are you looking for?"

"I need someone you might use for fraud detection or money laundering research, someone who understands the criminal element, someone with an established presence in that world and an extensive network of contacts."

"All of my team has some presence in that environment. It's the only way we can stay one step ahead in the crypto world, and we need that kind of info to avoid getting trapped by the bad guys."

"I'll appreciate you giving it some thought before you meet with Suzanne. If possible, I'd like you to lend me your two best resources for the next three to six months. Suzanne will be looking for names when you meet, and I wanted to give you time to think about it. We need them urgently. Later today, if possible. And I would prefer it if they could move to Supermarkets' headquarters in Atlanta almost immediately. Any names coming to mind?"

She nodded. "I'll need to give it some more thought and have a conversation or two. I'd want to be sure they're willing to relocate, but I think I can help."

Serge's smile disappeared. "Why don't you start those calls right now?"

Four

*Multima Corporate Headquarters, Montreal, Quebec,
Monday November 13, 2023*

Suzanne swept into the massive conference room, which seated over forty people when all the leather chairs around the oval table and along the west wall were occupied. Today, they could all cluster at one end of the room, where she habitually sat to chair meetings.

Besides Serge and Natalia Tenaz, sitting opposite each other, only two other directors attended the meeting in person. Both lived in Montreal and had short commutes to the downtown office tower.

Eileen fiddled with a wall-mounted widescreen that displayed other meeting participants seated before cameras. The backgrounds suggested a variety of locations. Some appeared to be working from offices as the eight o'clock hour approached in Montreal, but her assistant had reported that the day's participants were calling in from Europe and South America, as well as from several cities across the United States and Canada. Then again, the backgrounds could be from anywhere, given Zoom's virtual backgrounds library.

Suzanne waved to the camera as she strode toward her usual chair. This morning, she dispensed with any effort to charm the crowd before starting. The subject matter was grim, so she pasted on the same dour expression she'd practiced in the full-length mirror tucked into a corner of her office a few yards down the hallway.

Moments earlier, that mirror had also served as her last-minute inspection of the suit she wore. She'd chosen a dark maroon jacket and black slacks. Beneath the jacket, she wore a simple white blouse. Today, there were no frills, little color, and no fashion distractions. She expected her manner would demand unquestioning respect from everyone attending the meeting, regardless of their role, gender, or location around the globe.

Suzanne checked her image on one square of the screen. The table in front of her chair was conspicuously empty, as she'd instructed—it should be clear to everyone that she carried no notes or cue cards. Everyone should know that she'd be speaking directly from her heart and mind.

After a brief, unsmiling, and more formal hello to the group, Suzanne got right to her purpose.

"Apologies for dragging you to a meeting of the board on such short notice. It's urgent and crucial that I share some information with you and gain your support. So, let's get started." She drew a deep breath as she scanned the images projected in orderly squares on the wide screen in front of her before looking directly into the camera mounted on the wall below it.

"Yesterday was among the most difficult days in my career. By now, you've probably read the shocking email I sent last evening about Gordon Goodfellow's sudden death and the media release Edward distributed early this morning with more details. Serge and I broke the horrible news of his vicious murder to his family yesterday." She paused for a moment to let the directors murmur their brief condolences or share grim expressions. Some shook their heads in disbelief. Others gazed into space, seeking answers.

"I've called you all together for a brief discussion this morning. Again, I apologize for the short notice, but I have essential information to share with you, and I'll share it with you as concisely as I can. Serge will help me fill in any blanks or address any questions and concerns you might have. Then, I'm going to ask you to authorize a significant company expenditure to root out what we believe are genuine threats to Multima Corporation's very survival."

The introduction over, Suzanne carried on uninterrupted for the next five minutes, explaining the odd sequence of events she'd recently observed and how they directly or indirectly impacted their company. Her tone was slow, deliberate, and forceful, displaying little emotion and never showing a trace of fear.

She described the evidence linking Gordon to organized crime in Japan and South America, then revealed his recorded agreement to actively participate in a major cyberattack against Multima Corporation. She recounted the news story that had broken a few days earlier about the arrest of a Japanese Yakuza leader in Malaysia, trying to acquire nuclear weapons. Finally, she revealed the evidence they'd received about a plane crash in Krakow, Poland, followed by the discovery that local authorities had identified Amber Chan and Fidelia Morales among the victims.

Both women had recently been involved in major plots to disrupt and damage Multima Corporation. As succinctly as possible, she drew the connection between Gordon, Amber, Fidelia Morales, and the organized crime outfits plotting a cyberattack against Multima Supermarkets, picking up the pace as she approached the end of her monologue.

"Within the next few days, I'll ask for two or three more meetings with you. Of course, we must discuss the great void left by Gordon and how I plan to fill that void. I expect to make recommendations about our human resources and corporate reporting structure to the board, and I'll ask you to consider and vote on those recommendations within another day or two. But first, today, I seek your approval to immediately allocate fifty million dollars to a special fund that I propose Serge Boisvert manage as part of our overall security budget."

Suzanne paused to study the immediate reactions of the board members on the wide screen. Predictably, every participant sat straighter in his or her seat. Several leaned in closer to their cameras, anticipating further information, and she didn't make them wait. "I know it's a huge amount of money, but I'm convinced the very future of our corporation is at stake. Do I have your support?"

Five

Multima Corporate Headquarters, Montreal, Quebec,
Monday November 13, 2023

Serge expected it took longer than Suzanne had probably hoped, and resistance was more substantial than she'd probably anticipated, but she got the fifty million, with only three directors dissenting. After she'd turned over control of the meeting to him, he first thanked the board of directors for their confidence.

"I'll make this my number one priority from the moment this meeting is over until we get to the bottom of this," he pledged. "I've warned Suzanne that I may not always be able to share specifics. Sometimes, our activities might draw us into unconventional circumstances, and we may have to use unusual methods to get information. But I've assured Suzanne, and I'll assure each of you, that our actions will be careful, deliberate, and legal. We'll work with law enforcement when we can, and we'll identify alternative legal means when we can't get enough support from the police."

Suzanne had wrapped up the session with a warning to the board that she'd need more of their time over the next couple days to discuss Gordon's replacement. As soon as the cameras shut off, she had also dismissed the two directors attending in person, offering them rides to their respective destinations, using Multima Corporation cars and chauffeurs. Both declined, but they got the message and scrambled off within a moment or two, leaving only Suzanne and Natalia with Serge in the conference room.

Suzanne wasted no time. She directed her first question to him: "Did you two agree on the people Natalia's going to share with you?"

Natalia answered quickly. "Serge made me aware of his needs and asked me to recommend a couple folks. I haven't been able to reach any of them to see if a temporary move to Atlanta will work, but I think I'll be able to get two good ones."

"Thanks, Natalia," Suzanne replied, "but I think the number Serge is looking for is a minimum of four, right?"

"Yeah, I want teams to work the dark web twenty-four hours a day. I've got four that I can move from my team in Montreal, and I know of four excellent candidates working on the Supermarkets' technology team in Atlanta. If you can provide the same number, we'll have the foundation in place." He looked at Natalia expectantly.

She acquiesced with a silent nod.

Suzanne shifted her attention back to her fully cooperative president of the Financial Services business with a warm smile. "I need a few minutes now with Serge to review some last-minute details before he heads out to Atlanta. Ask Eileen to find you a spare office, and see if you can get those four names for him before he leaves. Then, meet me in my office. I'd like to have our discussion there."

Suzanne started again before Natalia had left the conference room. "I know you're probably as tired as I am, but I assume you'll leave for Atlanta shortly, as we discussed?" She structured it as a question but left little doubt about the response she expected.

"Yeah. I'll head home and pick up some clothes after I meet with the resources I want to draw upon here. They'll all need a few hours to gather their personal effects. I'm guessing we'll take off around the dinner hour. You're still okay with me using your corporate jet for the next while?"

"Of course. Back here we can all share the Supermarkets' and Financial Services' jets. I'll just borrow one or the other from time to time if necessary. Did you get accommodations arranged for everyone?"

"Eileen hasn't messaged me yet to confirm it, but I'm confident she'll get it handled. The building I have in mind has lots of empty Airbnb apartment rentals, and I think we can take over the complex's conference facility. It should be perfect for our dark web research."

"What about the equipment?" Suzanne wondered.

"I got a text during the board meeting. The guys found all the servers and screens we need. By the end of the day, they should receive all the switching devices and software required to operate in the shadows."

"Did Alberto Ferer get visas?" Suzanne had insisted her chief legal officer manage all documentation for travel.

"Yeah. He reached the guy you suggested. So long as we pay everyone from the US or Canada, they'll issue tourist visas electronically. We should have them by the end of the day after we submit the passport information. Alberto's confident we'll have no issues at the airport or any time while we're there."

"Was he able to schedule a meeting for you with Đại Dang?" Ferer had called the Vietnamese Minister of Industry and Commerce after Suzanne told him about knowing the guy from university days.

"Yeah. Dang agreed to meet with me for an hour on Saturday. Alberto and I thought that would be my first full day after getting the team together in Atlanta tomorrow, submitting all the passports on Wednesday, and flying out late the same night. The pilots think we should refuel in Anchorage, Alaska, en route. It will probably be late Friday before we get there."

"I'm going to miss you," she said as she stood up and stepped toward him with her arms outstretched. She underlined her comment with the most passion he'd detected in a while. It was a shame her schedule didn't allow for one more romp before he headed out.

"Don't worry." Suzanne teased him with her finger on his chest. "There's lots more where that came from. Let me know the best place and time we might meet the first weekend you can take a break."

"Let's assume it'll be somewhere in Hawaii," he replied, winking as he formed a smile.

Six

Multima Corporate Headquarters, Montreal, Quebec,
Monday November 14, 2023

With what appeared to be a smile of empathy and a friendly wave, Eileen Lee summoned Natalia Tenaz from the vacant office she'd pointed her toward earlier. They walked down the short corridor together, making small talk. Suzanne's thoughtful assistant asked if Natalia wanted to pick up a coffee on the way, and she did.

Armed with a steaming cup of java, she entered the CEO's sanctuary and watched Suzanne lift herself gracefully from a leather sofa. The other times Suzanne had invited her to meetings, she had conducted them formally in the conference room, so the magnificence of the suite was overwhelming at first. Entering this corner of the building felt something like entering another world.

Suzanne pointed for Natalia to join her at one end of a large, comfortable, dark brown sofa. There were three huge matching sofas in the room, and Suzanne had them oddly arranged. The identical pieces sat perpendicular to each other, carving out a separate area from the rest of the office.

Each sofa was long enough for a basketball player to stretch out for a nap and looked both comfortable and indestructible at the same time. They appeared custom-made and must have cost a small fortune. As large as they were, those three pieces of furniture consumed no more than a quarter of the vast real estate of Suzanne's office. It was probably three times the size of the entirely comfortable space Natalia had inherited from James Fitzgerald over at Multima Financial. Large original oil paintings adorned each of the walls—some were beautiful landscapes while others were abstract, but they must have cost many thousands of dollars each.

Natalia entered through one of the four doors in the room. She supposed one of the others provided direct access from Suzanne's office to a separate, private meeting room. Did the others lead to a private toilet or workout area? She'd put her money on the latter; Suzanne surely appeared fit.

Then, Natalia noticed the carpet. The color was an unspectacular shade of medium brown, but it was plusher than any she had ever experienced, even in the finest hotels. The broad windows on two of the walls allowed a lot of natural light into the room, and the circulating air seemed to have a hint of either a fresh or artificial scent that felt welcoming and inviting.

"Have a seat beside me here, Natalia. I'd like to discuss the reasons I asked you to come to Montreal for the board meeting and chat in person," Suzanne began. "You didn't seem unduly perturbed at the information I shared with the board. Do you think I'm walking down an unnecessary path?"

Natalia straightened, crossed her right leg across her left knee, and leaned in as she replied, "Not at all! I'm shocked at the number of signs you detected, and I agree there may be someone pulling the strings behind all those disturbing events. I concur. We must determine what is going on and who is responsible. I share your assessment that the company's future might be at stake."

Suzanne studied Natalia intently. Was the CEO looking for some other, more specific signal of support?

"I know Serge appreciates you giving up your research personnel for a while, as do I. Please be sure to extend our appreciation to each of them when you speak next."

"I'm glad they were available to share," Natalia replied. "I think you know I try to encourage everyone on my staff to be a team player." It didn't hurt to slip in a personal plug with the boss from time to time.

Suzanne smiled, no doubt recognizing the brazen self-promotion. "James always spoke highly of your business outlook, teamwork, and exceptional skills. How have you enjoyed the role since you became the president at Financial Services?"

Was that a trick question? Was it okay to admit you loved almost every minute of every day, or was the highly successful CEO looking for something more profound?

"I find the role very gratifying," she decided to say. "James left me with a strong business unit and a powerful balance sheet. I enjoy the opportunity to leverage our financial and corporate strength to grow our business in markets like Central and South America. With my Latin American heritage, I hope to leave a positive legacy behind and help both our company and the customers we serve there."

Suzanne flashed a disarming smile. Natalia had passed the test.

"Allow me to share some information with you," Suzanne said. "I expect you to keep this entirely to yourself, but as all good executives must, I've started thinking about succession planning. I don't expect to leave in the short- or even medium-term, but I want to prepare and have a successor ready to eventually assume the role of CEO. Of course, who that successor will be is not entirely my decision. The board of directors will vote to choose the candidate they think best fits the corporation's needs at the time."

Natalia signaled her understanding with a nod but remained silent. There had to be more.

Suzanne took only a second to process her thoughts before she carried on. "Gordon Goodfellow's unfortunate death creates an interesting challenge for me. For some time, a few of the directors have suggested that I consider bolstering Multima's management team by recruiting established talent from our competitors. Talent that might step into Gordon's shoes in the event of a circumstance like the one we've just experienced or someone we might eventually groom for another role."

"Like mine?" It slipped out before she realized it, but there it was.

Suzanne smiled, but it was difficult to determine if the smile was meant to reassure or simply reflect her amusement at the outburst. "Yes, perhaps a role like yours, should a change become necessary, but also with an eye to eventually replacing me. Candidly, although I enjoy the support of a board chosen mainly by John George, my father, I still detect unease from some members. They haven't all moved beyond thinking it's an old boys' network."

Natalia nodded again, careful to say nothing and convey as little as possible.

Suzanne appeared satisfied with that posture and continued. "I'm thinking about asking you to move over to Supermarkets to become the president there." Suzanne paused, probably looking for an initial reaction, but Natalia displayed only genuine, silent surprise.

Suzanne continued, "In the grand scheme of things, Multima Supermarkets still represents almost sixty percent of the company's profits, even with the great potential and excellent progress your leadership is making with Financial Services. The board would probably expect any candidate who might eventually replace me to have some experience leading a major supermarket business, either Multima or a competitor."

Natalia nodded again but still chose not to comment.

Suzanne apparently expected as much and carried on after taking a quick breath. "There are already some good candidates to fill Gordon's shoes over at Supermarkets, but those who are ready are all women. I might get some push from the directors to bring in an outsider—a male outsider—if I propose someone from that current team. I'm not opposed to looking outside Multima for a successor to Gordon, but with all the distractions in the background, I'd prefer to see you move over to Supermarkets and ask James Fitzgerald to come back to his old role at Financial Services for a while. It would give you an excellent opportunity to establish your credentials in the Supermarkets world."

The strategy was brilliant. Natalia felt comfortable commenting, "And the board of directors loves James Fitzgerald, so you can use the same rationale with the board to shift me over to Multima Supermarkets while he holds the fort at Financial Services."

Suzanne smiled again. "James was right about your perceptiveness. Are you willing to give it a try?"

Within an hour, Alberto Ferer, had summarized the conclusion of their discussion in a legal document: the salary and bonuses they'd agreed to, the key priorities Natalia was to focus upon in her new role, and the timing and parameters of an agreed review.

Both women signed the document before Suzanne stood to offer her hand to Natalia. "Congratulations, and welcome to your new role. Now, get prepared for a meeting with the board of directors this afternoon at four. They'll need to ratify my decision. Then, work with Edward Hadley to prepare for a media conference at five. I want this to make the six o'clock news. In the meantime, I need to make a call to James Fitzgerald." She smiled confidently.

Seven

Multima Corporate Headquarters, Montreal, Quebec,
Monday November 14, 2023

Suzanne asked Eileen to set up a Zoom session with James Fitzgerald, her long-time associate, colleague, and friend. As she waited for her assistant to reach him and display his image on the wide screen beside her desk, she tried to remember and tally up the number of times she'd needed to seek help from the guy since she'd first fired him for his less-than-professional behavior four years earlier.

She shook her head as memories of potential disasters in each of the years since then flashed through her mind. In every case, James had brought wisdom and counsel to help her out of the jam, for which she'd rewarded him well.

Each time, new salaries and bonuses were more significant than the cumulative sums he had earned over the decades he'd reported to her father, the founder of Multima Corporation. James always made her work for his support, but she had absolute confidence in his judgment and faith that his loyalty to a corporation he'd worked so hard to build would once again prevail.

When Suzanne spoke with him in the hours following Gordon Goodfellow's death, James had taken the news hard. She couldn't be sure if his instant emotional response was due to the shock of it all or if James might hold some greater insight. After all, his latest assignment for Suzanne was to essentially babysit Gordon and keep him out of trouble until she decided how she would eventually shift the players at Multima Supermarkets.

That he'd audibly shed tears when Suzanne broke the news of Gordon's murder raised questions. She'd need to go there first to assess his current state.

When Eileen signaled she had James for the Zoom session, Suzanne took a deep breath and posed her first delicate question: "Have you had enough time to process it all, James?"

During the board of directors meeting, Suzanne had found him uncharacteristically silent. He hadn't commented at all, and he wore his unreadable poker face throughout the video session.

Again, his expression telegraphed no signal about where he might be in the grieving process, and he formulated his response slowly and carefully. "I think I missed all the signals, Suzanne. I can't tell you how sorry I am that it all turned out this way. He seemed, fundamentally, a good guy. I was certain we could mold him into a top-notch executive. Clearly, he must have veered off the path much farther than I realized to be the victim of a gangland-style murder like that."

Interestingly, James seemed to feel some responsibility for the gruesome outcome, but why?

"Serge agrees that Gordon's murder carries the hallmarks of an organized crime hit, but the police aren't so sure. What do you think happened?"

"I can only guess, but Gordon certainly seemed to still carry a flame for Amber Chan, that Chinese woman who seemed at the heart of it all. While I was shepherding him these last few weeks, he mentioned her name in a couple conversations. I got the impression that he kicked himself for being so gullible and falling into her trap, but he also showed some remorse about losing her. I found it curious."

"Did you detect him making any new contacts with the underworld after Amber disappeared?"

"Nothing. Gordon told me he wanted to stay behind in California rather than travel east with me on the corporate jet last week. He said he just wanted to get some rest. Jet lag was taking a toll on him, and there was no reason to spend his weekend back in Atlanta. I think his divorce proceedings were weighing heavily as well."

This insight was nothing new. It was about the same as what he'd shared with Serge on the evening of the murder. It was time to take another tack. "How is the morale around the office in Atlanta today?"

"Terrible. The guy was extremely popular here. When I gathered the staff together to be sure everyone had heard the news, there were dozens of people wiping away tears. The shock and sadness were palpable. For anyone who felt they needed time to process the news privately, I offered the option of taking the rest of the day away from the office. It looks like about half the desks and offices here are empty as a result. The office is functioning, but barely."

Productivity had no meaning that day, but it was so like James to worry about it. Reassuring perhaps, but it was time to try a different direction again. "I have an idea to bounce off you." Suzanne had learned it was always better to introduce an idea gradually to James rather than present it to him as a *fait accompli.* "I share your impression that we have no one on the Multima Supermarkets' team ready to assume the role of president, and you probably noticed at this morning's meeting that some on the board are already itching for a quick decision on a replacement."

"I agree. You could groom three or four good leaders for the role over the next few years, but I don't see a candidate ready at the moment. What are you thinking about?"

Always perceptive, James must have realized she already had a plan. With only the hint of a smile, she waded in: "If I don't move quickly, directors like Abduhl Mahinder will start pressing for me to look outside Multima for a replacement. I don't want to go there. Instead, I want to use the opportunity to groom one of those existing Supermarkets' leaders who need a little more time."

When she paused to take a breath, James immediately intervened. "Before you go on, Suzanne, let me warn you that I'm not a candidate to assume any role as a placeholder leader. I'm retired, and with Gordon's demise, I think my undertaking to keep an eye on him ends. I'd like today to be the first day of the rest of my happy retirement."

If James had any constant characteristic, it was his predictability. She hadn't expected precisely those words, but also had little doubt about the essence of the message he'd deliver, and she was ready.

"I know your preference is to retire. With almost every day in my current role, I gain a better insight into why you think that's such an appropriate idea." She paused and laughed to lighten her tone. "But the candidate I have in mind to become president of Multima Supermarkets is Natalia Tenaz."

Silence followed—a longer silence than Suzanne had expected—but she'd play the waiting game as long as necessary. Because Natalia had been his protégé almost from the day she'd joined the company, James needed to be the one to break the uncomfortable quiet.

It seemed like more than a minute passed before she heard the characteristic clearing of his throat, indicating he was about to speak. "That's an interesting proposal. I can see why you'd want to have one of your people in control at Supermarkets. I sensed where Abduhl Mahinder was heading during the conference call, but who do you have in mind to fill Natalia's role at Financial Services?"

The instant James ended his question, Suzanne pounced. "You. I want you to oversee the Financial Services business for two years. I'm prepared to pay you twenty million dollars each year, with the potential to double that with performance bonuses we will agree on. Can I count on your support, James?"

She hadn't expected an immediate response, nor did

she get one. It was a positive indication that he was at least thinking about her proposal and hadn't rejected it reflexively.

So, she broke the silence after what she thought was a reasonable time. "I know I didn't give you much warning about my idea, and I won't demand that you decide right now. However, I think you understand it's essential for me to announce Natalia's new role at Supermarkets today, before anyone on the board starts organizing alternative candidates. It's not a requirement for me to announce her replacement at the same time, but I think you understand that it's preferable for several reasons. I also think you realize that re-appointing you to the Financial Services role carries a ton of auxiliary benefits."

Suzanne left her additional thoughts hanging out there for him to mull over, along with the probable tsunami of other scenarios and personal issues he'd need to address. James knew her well and wouldn't feel pressure to respond before he was ready. Still, she needed to hear something more than an absence of "no."

"Any thoughts you care to share as you work your way through it?" She used a tone barely above a whisper, grinning silently at the humbleness she had conveyed in her voice.

He looked directly into the camera before speaking, but his face conveyed no emotion. One might have expected the same body language had she inquired about the weather that day. Then, the subtle nod and almost undetectable lean in toward the camera.

"You've learned to play the game well, Suzanne. Keeping outside resources beyond the inner circle is probably the correct strategy for Multima Corporation right now. If I don't accept your proposal, you've safeguarded access to the Supermarkets business, but you probably suspect the same unwelcome forces might simply pivot to gain influence in Financial Services instead."

He paused, wrung his hands together, then sat straighter, backing away from the camera slightly. His eyes seemed fixed on a spot just above the camera, so she couldn't read them as precisely. Then, he cleared his throat again, and his face relaxed.

"Your proposal is a generous one, and you know I want to help you despite my increasingly creaking bones and genuine desire to put the corporate life behind me. Tell me I can keep using the more luxurious Supermarkets' jet and let Natalia keep the one she's currently using. With that modest concession, I'll accept your offer for two years and two years only."

She pressed her palms together and bowed her head toward the camera, conveying humble thanks and appreciation. She held that position for a long, grateful moment.

Eight

Multima Corporate Headquarters, Montreal, Quebec,
Wednesday November 16, 2023

The temporary arrangement provided Serge Boisvert no
privacy all, but it was the only appropriate working area on
Supermarkets' ground-floor meeting room to accomplish all
he wanted in an extraordinarily short time. He had at least
managed to sequester a few feet at the head of the long
conference room table. By stowing his briefcase on top of
the table and a good distance from his chair, he effectively
carved out a small separation from all the others. And they
were engrossed with tasks on their individual laptops.

He felt relaxed enough to lean back in the comfortable
high-backed leather chair and gaze off as he processed it all.
Suzanne Simpson announced late on Monday afternoon
that Natalia Tenaz would become the new president of
Multima Supermarkets, Serge imagined no one was more
surprised than he. The young woman had completed little
more than a year as the president over at Financial Services,
after all.

Did she even know anything about the food business?
He scoured his memory for highlights of the in-depth
security check Suzanne had asked his team to perform
before promoting Natalia the last time. Still single, the
woman had no blemishes on her record that he could recall.
American-born and raised by immigrant parents, she had
been a stellar student through high school before
completing a master's degree from the Booth School of
Business at the University of Chicago.

She was a protégé of James Fitzgerald. He couldn't
recall all the positions she'd held but remembered that she

started in business intelligence, was promoted almost every year to roles with increased responsibility, and was Fitzgerald's only recommendation to fill his chair when he announced his retirement. She was popular among her colleagues and used a combination of good humor, sharp wit, and seemingly unlimited intelligence to sell her ideas.

If Suzanne had enough confidence to move Natalia into the Multima Supermarkets beehive at such a challenging juncture, it didn't take a genius to suppose his lover-in-chief had even greater plans for her on the horizon. He should pay a courtesy visit to congratulate her before leaving.

He glanced at his watch. It was only hours until he'd head for the airport with his newly documented team. Even though Natalia was incredibly hard-working, the newly appointed president would probably be leaving the office for the day shortly. It was eight o'clock in the evening, after all.

Serge slipped on his jacket for the impromptu visit with Natalia before sharing some information with the folks seated beyond his briefcase at the long conference table. "Three cars will meet us at about eleven o'clock to shuttle us to the airport." He used the American time preference rather than the 23:00 hours military time he would have used had he still worked for the Royal Canadian Mounted Police.

"We'll use Multima's corporate jet because it has a longer range, but plan to get your rest in two stages. We'll have about eight hours available to sleep on the segment to Alaska. We'll refuel there, and the pilots tell me the flying time to Ho Chi Minh City will be another twelve hours or more. I asked them to have some melatonin on the aircraft, but there won't be any booze. If you need a shot or two before we fly, you'd better slip out and do it now, but be back before eleven." He laughed as he glanced around the room and headed toward the doorway.

It took only a few minutes to cover the distance Serge traveled from the conference room where he'd oriented his new team to the elevator up to the top floor, where Natalia was settling into the executive suite. He used the precious short time in the elevator to assess what he'd accomplished in the three days since Suzanne had dispatched him on his own new assignment.

The eight resources he'd secured from Suzanne and Natalia were all bright technology experts. The four from his own team were more junior, but they were highly skilled technicians. All had passed his security clearance within hours, and Đại Dang, had worked magic to get their tourist visas from Vietnam's government offices in both Ottawa and Washington, shaving days from the usual timeline when using internet applications.

Dang had become an outstanding connection to have. In addition to the government documentation, he'd arranged the rental of an entire top floor at an apartment complex in District 7 of Ho Chi Minh City. They'd have separate apartments for each team member, plus a spacious suite where they could all meet and work together when necessary.

Serge realized the Vietnamese government was probably feverishly installing listening devices in those rooms and suites at that very moment, but was confident the new equipment his team had acquired would block them effectively. Though they were now retired, some old friends from his days with the Mounties might also help. He knew of a couple who lived in the countryside of Vietnam to stretch their retirement dollars as far as possible. If neither of those options worked, Suzanne would need to find a way to make her old university classmate an ally, and she was confident she had the tools to do that, if necessary. First, he needed to build a bridge with Multima Supermarkets' newest leader.

"Knock. Knock," he said as he poked his head into her open office door. "Do you have a minute for a visitor?"

Natalia sprang from the plush leather chair behind her desk and dashed around it, her arms open wide, a most welcoming smile in place. She hugged him rather than shaking hands. Was that a sign of newfound confidence, given her recent promotion? Some other signal he should monitor?

"Come in, Serge. Have a seat. What's up?" Her enthusiasm seemed incredible at such a late hour of the working day, but a psychological high from the promotion might still linger.

"I wanted to thank you in person for parting with those four excellent resources you've loaned me. They all look like they'll be excellent contributors." He leaned in as he spoke to convey genuine appreciation, even if he had them only because Suzanne had cracked the whip. The four appeared to be among the most experienced on his new team, but it was too early to share that with her.

They took turns complimenting each other on their new roles and assignments as he read her body language for any subtle signals. He detected none that should raise an alarm, so he ventured into the real reason for the visit. "I know you screened your resources carefully before you put them into intelligence roles with Financial Services, and they all passed my security reviews with flying colors, but is there anything from your experience working with them I should watch for or treat with more sensitivity than usual?"

Natalia immediately shed her smile and looked off into the distance as if expecting some knowledge or inspiration from the space above Serge's right shoulder. She took a moment before she answered. "Archibald Begat. Archie is the smartest of the bunch. I hired him from the cryptocurrency business about a year ago. There isn't a firewall he can't penetrate, and he has a special nose for danger. He seems to know exactly the right buttons to push to penetrate a system and the right time to get out before detection. He's brought me a lot of valuable intelligence."

Serge tilted his head and nodded, showing interest and hoping she'd offer more. She didn't buy it, waiting instead for him to respond.

"I won't pry into what intelligence he stole for you. That's not my goal here." He chose the stronger language to make a point. "Does he belong to any groups on the dark web, or does he go solo?"

"Yeah, I know he's in Hackforum, but I think he's in others as well. I hired him before you created your technology-clearing policy, so you might want to have your people check him out again, but he passed all our internal tests, and he's discovered outstanding information from Latin America-based IT systems. Saved us a few hundred million in the acquisitions we just completed."

Her smile broadened with satisfaction, so Serge remained silent. Sure enough, only seconds later, she continued. "I'd put Constance Hope on about the same level technically, but she's super careful where she goes. You'll probably need to coax her if she senses anything unethical. She's a good counterbalance to Archie, and you probably won't go wrong teaming them together."

Without further prompting, Natalia continued her overviews for another minute or two, succinctly describing the attributes of the other two specialists she had provided for his team. Serge listened intently, interrupting only to clarify an occasional comment or be sure he'd heard her terminology correctly—the woman understood the world of computers far better than he had imagined.

When it was clear she had nothing further to offer that evening, he thanked her for her information, congratulated her again on the promotion, and took care to note the sacrifice she was making over the following few months.

"Thanks for sharing your jet with Suzanne and James as well. Suzanne told me you agreed to share it with them for a while, so I can use her larger corporate aircraft. I appreciate that."

She nodded wordlessly, then shrugged and showed a grin that suggested no ill will.

Serge left on that note and headed for the elevator to the ground floor. He stepped outside the building, punched two digits of a speed dial number, and held the phone to his ear as he dashed toward his waiting limousine to the airport. The person he called picked up on the first ring, and he was able to finish his instructions outside the earshot of the chauffeur, who had opened the rear door as he approached.

"That's right, all four of them. And not the high-level screen—I want to know elementary school grade averages and every other personal detail you can dig up from then until now. And pronto."

Nine

Multima Supermarkets Headquarters, Atlanta, Georgia,
Wednesday November 16, 2023

The moment Serge closed the door to her office, Natalia keyed in the digits for Archie Begat's phone. He responded on the third ring.

"Are you alone?"

"Yeah. You actually caught me in the men's room." He laughed.

"Turn on a tap to create some background noise, then listen," she instructed brusquely. "I just met with Serge. Gave him a glowing recommendation about you. You haven't shared anything with either him or the others about Docket 25, right?"

"Like you instructed, I've shared nothing with anyone." His voice exuded confidence, albeit with a hint of concern.

"Get rid of anything you've got anywhere in the Multima systems. Park it somewhere safe. Serge is probably going to do an in-depth background check on you first, but I expect he's also going to give you more responsibility with the secret search into the organized crime threat. Do whatever he asks. Do you know where you're going yet?"

"We all had to complete tourist visas for Vietnam and are expected to leave on the corporate jet within a few hours. He's asked us all to meet in front of the offices in just five minutes for the shuttle to the airport."

"Okay. We'll have a twelve-hour time difference, but I want a daily update. Use DuckDuckGo and the Swiss VPN. No one is to know you're communicating with me, either. Got it?" She waited for him to confirm her instructions, then added one last bit. "I think he'll team you up with

Constance, so be careful around her. Know everything she's working on, but share only what you must with her."

Satisfied that her protegee had gotten the message, Natalia hung up with a curt, "Good luck," then keyed in another number. A voicemail message answered her call, so she left the standard code words. "Twelve sixty-nine. Urgent." She hung up immediately after delivering the coded message, confident she'd hear back from that director before calling it a night and retiring to bed.

There was only one more essential task before she could leave for the day, and the guy she needed to speak with would be in his Shanghai office now.

Guāiqiǎo Chen picked up the call on the third ring.

"Good morning, Guāiqiǎo. Have I reached you at a good time?" In an earlier introductory call with Suzanne, they had already agreed she'd call then, but she'd learned the habit of opening telephone conversations with that standard question from James Fitzgerald. He'd always maintained that starting a conversation that way helped relax the person called and helped get to the purpose of the call quicker.

With Chen's affirmation, she asked one more question: "Guāiqiǎo, I find your name really hard to pronounce. Is there a shorter form I might use instead?"

He laughed casually before she'd finished the question. "Sure. Just call me Chen. We Chinese use either the first or last name equally." He laughed again, probably to be sure she was satisfied with his response.

"Okay, Chen, tell me more about your discussions with that Vietnamese Minister of Industry and Commerce, Đại Dang—where are we in those discussions?"

"We're at a very early stage. After Gordon Goodfellow named me the president of Supermarkets in Asia, replacing Amber Chan, Suzanne introduced me to Dang during a

Zoom call. He's an old friend of Suzanne's—from her university days, I think. She told him we'd be interested in exploring an expansion into Vietnam but would like to acquire a company there rather than start from scratch. He promised to ask around about potential opportunities and, a few weeks ago, offered to introduce me to the owner of a large chain in the southern part of the country, QueenMart."

Natalia knew all that, of course, but she exercised patience as he worked his way to the information she really wanted. It took only a few moments longer for him to explain that QueenMart was a subsidiary of another large holding company with other interests like coffee shops and organic stores. Then, he outlined its operating structure, management organization, and geographic coverage across the southern part of Vietnam. Finally, he got to the point that captured her interest.

"I met with the senior management team last week in Hong Kong so we could both keep it tight to our vests, as the bankers like to say. They have some interest in talking with us and shared their company's financial information with me. They carry a lot of corporate debt. Apparently, Đại Dang has been exerting some pressure on them to reduce their total debt load. Selling to us might solve that problem, but they don't appear to be in a hurry."

"Have we analyzed the financial statements yet?" Natalia asked.

"Our acquisition team has done a preliminary review. The first pass looks promising, but there are tons of questions. The QueenMart operations appear profitable and are growing rapidly, but the holding company charges huge amounts for overhead and support. The team guesses they designed the structure to minimize corporate taxes for the operating company, but we'd need to understand the actual situation better."

"What gives you the impression they don't appear to be in a hurry to discuss a sale?" Natalia asked.

"When I suggested we organize a meeting to review our findings from the financial statements, they agreed but suggested we schedule it for a few weeks after the Tet Festival, their lunar year celebration. That means probably sometime in March next year!"

"Let me circle back with Suzanne. I'll see if she wants to have Đại Dang exert a little pressure on QueenMart to move the discussions forward more quickly. Now, tell me: what do you expect your Asia quarter-end results to look like in a few weeks?"

Ten

Multima Corporation Headquarters, Montreal, Quebec,
Thursday November 17, 2023

Suzanne started most days with a thorough review of her overnight accumulation of emails, and she'd completed about half of the recent messages that morning when Eileen interrupted. "May I take a few minutes to review your pre- and post-U.S. Thanksgiving travel arrangements? We should let the stores know today or tomorrow to give them notice to prepare."

Suzanne blitzed as many U.S. Multima supermarket locations as possible just before and just after that most important of American holidays. Those visits served multiple purposes. From an employee relations perspective, she'd grasped how much staff in each of the stores valued her words of thanks and appreciation. It was a lesson learned early in her career, and she vowed never to forget the critical role customer-facing employees played in the company's success.

But there was an added benefit. Once local management became aware of her planned visit, stores underwent a massive transformation. She'd seen the photos area supervisors had taken of store appearances before and after news of her visits reached them. It was remarkable: End displays became massive works of art. Shelves brimmed with selection. Store floors were scrubbed and polished. And on the days of the actual visits, employees groomed themselves with meticulous attention to hairstyles, make-up, and clean uniforms.

This combination of events made Multima stores an extraordinary place to shop before and after the holidays, adding untold millions to the company's coffers. So, if Eileen said it was time to notify the stores, Suzanne had a new priority added to this morning's issues.

"You remembered I won't take any personal time around Thanksgiving itself, right? With Serge just getting settled in Vietnam, it's too early for us to meet up somewhere, so I'm good to work right through, including the holiday itself."

"I remember, Suzanne. For the next ten days, starting tomorrow, I have visits to over fifty stores booked. I've commandeered the Multima Financial Services aircraft for you and Natalia to use. As requested, she'll accompany you to all the stores. On the ground, we have limos booked to chauffeur you from the aircraft to the stores and back."

For the next hour, Eileen walked Suzanne through the schedule for each of the cities and reconfirmed specific details like hotels, breaks for meals, and the maximum time allowed for each location. As usual, there was little for her to question and nothing to change. Her administrative assistant had been organizing these visits for long enough that she had the routine down pat. Their review served only to remind Suzanne what she had to do to prepare, starting that night.

At least she no longer had to worry about keeping track of fifty books. When they'd first started this annual routine, Eileen had prepared paper files for each store. Each file provided crucial details about all members of the management team, including backgrounds and yearly performance review highlights. There was always a summary of the store's annual financial performance, with both strengths and weaknesses highlighted by the experts. This year, electronic tablets were used to store all the data files Suzanne and Natalia would use.

Elaine showed her how she had organized files according to the order of visits, so Suzanne and Natalia could each study the data the night prior to the day's scheduled visits, as well as in the car as they traveled between stores. It was an elaborate preparation, but it was crucial for providing the information both leaders needed to communicate effectively with the management teams in each store, highlight positive achievements, and address any deficiencies needing attention.

If she and Natalia performed as expected, the store management and teams would be amazed at the executives' knowledge about their stores, the successes they recognized, and the words of encouragement they offered to achieve even better results in each of their locations.

The key was to make it seem like management truly understood who the key players were, what the store was doing well, and that the company's leadership appreciated their efforts, all while leaving behind a hunger for the staff to do even more to make their stores even greater.

Eleven

Ho Chi Minh City, Vietnam, Saturday November 18, 2023

He awoke with the pilot's broadcasted message that they'd touch ground at Tan Son Nhat International Airport in about ten minutes, subtly signaling to the passengers that they had limited time if they wanted to use the sole restroom on the aircraft. Serge unbuckled his seat belt and bounced up to be among the first to heed the warning.

Someone had beaten him to the toilet door, so he lifted a window shade and peeked outside. They were still over open water, as far as he could see, but the sun shone brightly, without a cloud in sight. A quick glance at his watch confirmed they'd land close to the forecasted nine o'clock hour the pilots had predicted, grateful they had scheduled the departure times from Atlanta and then Anchorage so they'd arrive first thing that morning.

They'd chosen that counterintuitive route to benefit from both the curvature of the earth and its rotation. By flying in a northwesterly direction first, then southwesterly from Alaska, they were actually flying the shortest distance. If relations with Russia were better, they might have shaved even more time and distance by flying up to Toronto, then directly northward and over the North Pole before heading south again. Regardless, the morning arrival would give everyone time to settle into the new environment they'd experience over the next few months.

For a short while, everything unfolded according to plan. Serge's wait for the aircraft restroom was short, the remaining descent into Vietnam was smooth and uneventful, their jaunt along the tarmac to the private aircraft section was quick, and the passport review and stamping appeared no more than perfunctory. Within minutes, four black, polished Nissan limousines, arranged as a courtesy by Đại Dang, formed an entourage and joined the clogged roadways of the city, numbering almost ten million residents.

Serge watched the expressions of the three members of his new team who rode in his car.

First, their shock as the limousines exited the airport facilities to merge onto a three-lane highway with traffic virtually stopped due to congestion. Motor scooters seemed to be everywhere and headed in multiple directions, weaving among the slower-moving cars, trucks, and buses that appeared to beg for space to crawl forward.

Serge had seen it all before when he'd visited the country a couple years earlier while researching another bewildering Multima Corporation mystery. So he wasn't surprised to see his colleagues' expressions shift quickly from amazement to humor as they experienced a culture shock unique to visitors to Vietnam.

His companions first smiled at the chaos around them, then broke into laughter as they compared their observations. Constance Hope noted there were as many women on the deluge of scooters as men. Some wore shoes with high heels, others displayed layers of clothes. And almost all wore both helmets for safety and face masks to protect against the dust and pollution apparent even from inside the limousine.

Archie Begat joyfully pointed out one scooter momentarily stopped beside them. It had a dog in a basket mounted to the handlebars, a young child perched on the gas tank between his father's arms, and another larger child squeezed in between the father and the mother. Mom tightly gripped the safety bar behind the single, black leather seat they were all perched upon.

Few scooter riders showed deference to the limos, even

if the license plates did identify them as federal government cars. Instead, the operators whisked in front of those vehicles, leaving the tiniest of openings, often braking to avoid another scooter trying to fill the same precious space.

As the limousines inched toward their destination, the Multima crew's limousine convoy separated from each other, with dozens of vehicles of all sizes squeezed between them, even when the speed eventually increased for a few moments before the subsequent, inevitable slowdown again. These occurred at almost every intersection, any narrowing of the highway, or on one of several bridges crossing the Sang Sai Gon River that leisurely ambled its way across the metropolis.

After about thirty-five minutes, from the peak of a bridge, Serge noticed the collection of tall, modern, gray buildings clustered together behind another highway. A large rooftop sign on the nearest building read "Eco Green" in English.

From the top of the bridge, the limousines, now closer together, still needed another ten minutes to complete the crossing. They each exited onto what appeared to be a newer and more spacious three-lane highway, and then navigated a couple twists and turns before pulling up to a sleek skyscraper. An illuminated, eight-foot-tall "B" stood at its entrance, their home for the next few weeks or months.

The charming young Vietnamese woman who'd met them at the airport and shepherded them into the cars now jumped from the second limousine to arrive. She rushed first to open the Nissan's door on Serge's side. Then, she flashed her brilliant smile, bowed with her hands pressed together as in prayer, and asked Serge and his companions to follow her.

She led them past a uniformed security guard wearing a military officer's cap and holding a door open for them. As Serge arrived, the fellow clicked his heels together, stood at attention, and saluted the arriving guests. Đại Dang's assigned hostess quickly ushered her entourage through the small lobby, flashed a card at a wall-mounted reader, then led them to an open elevator inside the secure area.

She made small talk as they rode the elevator to the thirty-fifth floor, the top floor of the building. There, she pulled out a sheet of paper and asked each of the elevator passengers for their names. As each of them responded in turn, she pointed to a woman in a team of similarly dressed hostesses and asked the Multima crew member to follow the woman she had pointed to.

A second elevator arrived before she'd finished asking Serge and the others to follow their designated hostess to their assigned rooms. The first group wandered along the corridor as the second arrivals waited for their instructions. Loudly, Serge called out a reminder that they should find their way to the suite where a meeting would take place in fifteen minutes.

The hostess added that it was located right beside Serge's apartment and pointed it out before she keyed a sequence of numbers into an electronic lock on the door. With an inviting wave, she welcomed Serge to his residence, using surprisingly fluent English.

"I hope you like your temporary lodging, Mr. Boisvert." The Vietnamese woman had already checked for his language preference at the airport, where he'd noticed she had a tiny accent in French, but virtually none in English. Where had she learned to speak the language so well?

"Đại Dang asked me to convert one bedroom to an office and another to a meeting room. We left the master suite as a bedroom for you. Is everything to your satisfaction?"

After his assurance that all was fine, the hostess disappeared, and Serge took a moment to survey his surroundings. The apartment was comfortable but not luxurious. The furniture looked functional but not extravagant, with laminated wood on the floors and an off-white color on all the walls and ceiling. Both the kitchen and the bathroom appeared small but adequate, with all the appliances and plumbing a guy should need.

He walked to the living room window and pulled back the sheer white curtains. Floor-to-ceiling windows brightened the interior and allowed a magnificent view. From the towering skyscrapers dotting the horizon to the bridges crossing the river, most of District 7's residential and commercial areas were easy to discern. Looking out the window, he felt the vibrancy of a growing metropolis and it captured all his senses. But full appreciation of the city's beauty had to wait for another day.

The entire team was in the designated suite when he arrived, enthusiastically comparing observations about their new apartments, the fantastic view, and their first impressions. Serge hated to break it up, but they were there on a critical mission.

"Let's all go for a walk," he said, leading them toward the doorway.

Serge's four bodyguards stayed behind. The full group didn't need to know that security intended to scan each of the assigned suites for listening devices with the latest available technologies before their team started any actual work or discussions inside them.

Once again, it took two elevator runs to accommodate the gang. Serge took the first car and waited with his half of the entourage outside the front entrance for only a couple minutes before the others joined. He led them across the street, where they had only a few scooters to avoid, and along that same new, unnamed street for a few hundred yards.

It took only that long for them to leave the modern Eco Green complex and enter a typical Ho Chi Minh neighborhood, with streets about one-quarter the width of those inside the upscale complex. Just beyond the barrier, he spotted a suitable place for them to meet: a coffee shop. It was partially hidden with trees and shrubs that darkened the interior and provided shade from the eighty-degree-plus temperatures they were already experiencing as the hour approached noon.

Cà phê Chất was the name on the sign. During an earlier visit to Vietnam, he'd learned that coffee was an essential in Ho Chi Minh City, and that "chất" signified quality. That morning, the café was completely vacant, which served his purposes well. With Archie's help, he slid two tables together, and everyone pulled a chair in around them.

"I dragged you all out here for more than some humid, polluted air," he said with a broad smile, trying for some levity to start. "You'll notice all the security team stayed behind. Although we're here with the endorsement of the Vietnamese government, I'd be surprised if my folks don't find at least a half-dozen listening devices in the suites."

He scanned each member's eyes as they sat around the table, reinforcing the severity of his accusation. Their eyes portrayed surprise at first. Nods of understanding followed. Still, he gave them a few more seconds to process.

"You can still have a life while you're here. Go out to eat when you're off work. Visit the bars, if you like. Take in the museums and other cultures, if you wish. If asked, say you're here on vacation. But you must not discuss one word of our mission among yourselves outside the suites after we cleanse them. Of course, you also must not share a shred of information with anyone from outside our group. Not a single word."

He surveyed their individual reactions again, a mix of both awareness and acceptance. No one appeared to resist or protest until one of the women from the Supermarkets' team raised her hand, one finger pointing upward to signal a question.

"I get it. Our study of supermarket businesses in Vietnam serves two purposes. First, we want to learn everything we can about QueenMart to determine whether it's a viable acquisition or not, but we're also providing cover for the security research you and the others are doing to see who is behind all the threats to Multima. I get that. But I notice there are half a dozen supermarkets in the complex. Don't we want to visit those stores, talk with the staff, and learn their impressions about the industry in Vietnam?"

"Good question, Joanne." Serge nodded, understanding her concern. "Yes. You and your Supermarkets' team might want to visit and chat with some of the employees in the stores here. Do that, if you wish. You can position yourselves as students, consultants, or market researchers— whatever you choose. Still, maintain that you're on vacation and curious. Don't use the Multima name in any way or in any conversation. And don't share a word about our interest in QueenMart. Be creative, but smart."

Joanne seemed satisfied with his answer. She glanced toward her teammates, who also nodded in agreement.

"We want you to use the dark net and the internet for your research as much as possible, though. You can also be alert there, helping us solve the dilemma of who's trying to harm Multima. Clerks in a grocery store in Vietnam won't be much help with that part of the mission, I suspect."

Serge continued to welcome questions and concerns for the better part of an hour, hoping to build team spirit, a sense of mission, and clear expectations.

The team responded well, enjoyed a couple cups of coffee, and was ready to go when one of Serge's guys called. "Ten well-hidden microphones, and two tiny video cameras in the overhead lighting. Both of them recording. We think we've found everything. What do you want us to do?"

"Yank 'em all. Suzanne will have to find a way to mollify Đại Dang."

Twelve

Chicago, Illinois, Thursday November 30, 2023

Natalia picked up the piece of luggage in the bedroom and headed toward the door of her apartment in Hoffman Estates for probably the last time. A crew would arrive tomorrow to finish packing the rest of her clothes, furniture and personal belongings and ship them to Atlanta over the following few days.

She wiped away a tear that suddenly appeared from nowhere as a final realization registered: the real estate agent she'd met for the first time yesterday would soon sell the single-bedroom apartment she'd owned and occupied for the past dozen years. The good times she'd enjoyed in Chicago, and here in her first condo, would soon be nothing more than distant memories.

It was satisfying to realize some of the career goals she'd established as a young graduate of the Booth School of Business at the University of Chicago. When she'd studied there in the mid-2000s, it had all seemed daunting. After all, her parents had arrived from Panama as poor, uneducated immigrants and, throughout her childhood, they had constantly preached to her the benefits of a good education followed by a successful career with some large corporation.

With her Multima salary, Natalia could afford a larger, more spacious apartment, but she'd chosen to live modestly instead and use her spare income to pay off the large mortgage her parents had struggled to pay down since they'd arrived in the country. That she had just paid off the last remaining balance a few months ago kindled a smile of satisfaction. They'd miss having her nearby in Chicago, but they could now afford to travel and visit her new home in Atlanta.

After she clicked the apartment door closed for the final time, she scurried along the hallway, switching focus to her next task for the day. Another unexpected tear appeared as the door to the elevator closed. The formal farewell to her former team in Chicago was minutes away, and she dreaded the thought of saying goodbye.

In her limo ride to the office, she pulled up on her phone a farewell address she'd prepared on the flight over from Montreal. She'd committed those remarks to memory as much as possible because it just wouldn't be right to read a goodbye from a prepared script. But it was equally important to say all the right words. She practiced them now, so she wouldn't be a bundle of nerves or a blubbering idiot as she expressed her thanks and appreciation to the teammates who'd helped her achieve this new rank in her career.

The limo driver tactfully kept his eyes focused on the road with only an occasional discreet glance in the rearview mirror. Within minutes, he stopped in the large circular driveway in front of the Financial Services headquarters, a tall building only a few miles from her old apartment.

When she looked up from her phone, James Fitzgerald was striding toward her limo, wearing a broad smile and reaching out to open her door with an outstretched hand.

"Welcome home! I asked Dave to let me know when you were about to arrive," he said with a nod toward the limo driver. "Let's show the staff the big change is an amicable one and pass through the cafeteria on the way to your old office. It'll be good for us to say a few hellos together before you say goodbye."

James thought of everything. He'd been that way since the day he'd first hired her as a business intelligence analyst and for as long as she'd known him.

Their detour through the cafeteria took almost half an hour as James patiently escorted her from the elevators at the front of the hall to the executive elevators located at the rear of the large facility. It seemed like dozens of her former staff waved, stopped her for a quick hug or handshake of congratulations, or offered her a friendly tap on the shoulder as they passed while she chatted with someone. James stayed silent throughout, letting her be the focus of their attention and affection.

When they finally made it to her old office on the top floor, her immediate direct reports were all waiting. It took another fifteen minutes to get from the elevator to the spacious office first designed for James, the one she'd only used for the past year and a bit. Instinctively, they moved to the large oval table in the corner. Today, during the transition, no one would sit at the massive walnut-finished desk at the back of the room.

"We've got about fifteen minutes before they expect us back in the cafeteria for the formal farewell," James announced with a smile. "Please share with me anything you think I need to know urgently, especially anything you have on the acquisitions."

"I'm sure Murray Powell has already given you a good insight into where he is with Mexico, Chile, Argentina, and Uruguay. They all looked promising the last time I checked, but let me share with you where I see some potential blind spots."

For the following few minutes, she focused their attention on the political situation in Mexico. Andrés Manuel López Obrador, the president of Mexico, was in political trouble, she explained. Mexico's economy was recovering from COVID-19 more slowly than expected. The most influential political leaders there were pressing for Obrador to resign before the next election and let the Mexican people choose a new leader. She talked about how that development might slow progress with their target acquisition and perhaps even cause the deal to abort.

The sobering conversation left her better prepared when James glanced at his watch. "I value that insight, Natalia, and I'll make a trip to Mexico City with Murray as soon as possible. In the meantime, I think a few hundred of your closest friends are waiting to say goodbye in the cafeteria."

For the first time, he pulled her close for a farewell hug, holding her tighter and longer than she had expected.

Thirteen

Chicago, IL, Thursday November 30, 2023

James Fitzgerald waved a final farewell to Natalia as the limo driving her to the private jet section of Chicago's O'Hare Airport pulled away from the curb in front of Multima Financial Services. Minutes later, he was upstairs, seated behind the large walnut-finished desk in his office, facing Murray Powell, his vice president of acquisitions. He recounted the concerns Natalia had expressed and waited for an explanation.

"I know Natalia has worried about the political situation in Mexico for a while. Clearly, Obrador is having some challenges—he's over seventy years old, after all. I think he will probably step aside, but I don't see a problem with any of the candidates to replace him. Our consultants there tell us all six or seven national parties would rubber-stamp approval if we can acquire Bansure."

Grupo Financiero Bansure, S.A.B. was one of Mexico's largest banks, with over a thousand branches across the country. If Multima Financial Services could acquire Bansure, they would instantly become one of the most potent forces in the Mexican financial universe.

"Tell me about the consultants we're using in Mexico," James instructed.

"Natalia recommended I work with KPMM. Apparently, Abduhl Mahinder suggested we contact them when he got wind of our intentions down there." James knew Mahinder well. He was the current chief executive officer of the Bank of the Americas in San Francisco and a member of Multima Corporation's board of directors.

James spent the next few minutes reviewing their

current status with the Bansure offer, the challenges that remained, and Powell's best guess on when they might finalize the deal. As feared, his vice-president's best guess was sometime late in 2024, almost a year down the road.

"Let's organize a trip there. I want to meet the KPMM team and see how we can speed this up. If we're going to do it, we need it done within three months."

Equally important, given Mahinder's recent behavior, he also needed to check out the KPMM folks' credentials.

Fourteen

Montreal, Quebec, Monday December 18, 2023

Precisely one week before Christmas, Suzanne awoke to the ring of her mobile just seconds before five o'clock in the morning. It was Serge, and he wanted to catch her before she stepped on the treadmill to start her daily workout.

"Sorry to bug you so early in the morning, *chérie*," he started, using the term of endearment he preferred. Without waiting for her to say hello back, he carried on, almost breathless. "We've got a tip, and I need to act fast. I'm heading out tonight for Tokyo. We've successfully accessed two separate servers and learned more about the Yakuza's operating structure. The NPA there, the National Police Agency, wants to work with us. I'm taking Constance Hope and one of my guys to liaise with their experts."

She processed it as quickly as she could before her first cup of coffee. "Accessed" really meant "hacked," so it must be something big if Serge was ready to risk the legal implications of sharing that information with a national police force. A better understanding of the Yakuza's structure could surely lead to a solution to their dilemma. And he'd be taking a brilliant young woman along with him during those days in Japan. She felt a short pang of what she supposed was mindless jealousy.

"Christmas isn't a big deal in Japan, so I suppose they're comfortable allocating some resources. What about you? Do you expect to work through the holiday, or might we meet up somewhere for a few days? I've missed you, sweetheart." Her tone emphasized the last four words.

"Our flight is scheduled to arrive about two this morning, Japan time. We'll lose a couple hours traveling to

Tokyo, but the NPA folks have scheduled a meeting with us for nine. I'm hopeful Constance can start working with their team of experts from the end of the meeting onward. If we can integrate the two teams, I'll fly back to Ho Chi Minh City tonight. Another team is making progress accessing that server I mentioned to you in California."

Ever the cautious former police detective and senior officer, Serge avoided specifics, even on their secure lines. But he still hadn't answered her question.

Suzanne pressed gently. "Okay. When you're back in Vietnam, do you see a window of a day or two when you might leave the team and meet up somewhere?"

"Maybe. I sure miss you, too!" His tone changed for the better. "The team working on the U.S. project thinks they're close to cracking the code, but I need to be close to them to avoid dragging in the FBI or some other U.S. agency. Let's see what we can ferret out this week. When might you be able to break away for a day or two?"

"December 25 and 26 are clear, and I can probably keep them that way. Let me know as soon as you can. Maybe we can each fly to Honolulu the afternoon of the twenty-fourth and get a couple days' snuggle time."

The less-than-fulfilling start to her day aside, Suzanne plowed through her workout, had a stimulating shower, and threw on some casual clothes. That day was a planned work-from-home day, so she had time to make and enjoy a delicious vegetable omelet cooked in the microwave oven before opening her laptop to catch up on the latest news.

She had an hour before Eileen would arrive to work from an adjoining office they'd carved out on the third floor of her spacious estate home in the Laurentian Mountains, north of Montreal.

The first story to catch her eye caused her to grimace and shake her head. The past president of the United States was polling only one percent behind his opponent despite his criminal convictions, multiple pending lawsuits, unresolved criminal charges, and the ire of every person the scoundrel had ever done business with. *What are people thinking?*

She clicked from one electronic newspaper to another until she finished with a US site that focused on business news. She had a good sense of the challenges her world would face that day.

Suzanne met Eileen, her executive assistant, at the side door ten minutes before eight. Eileen had first rung the doorbell, then stepped inside after entering the electronic code on the keypad mounted above the door handle.

Inside, she collapsed the umbrella she'd needed to protect against the light rainfall outside and removed her winter boots. It was strange weather for a winter's day in that part of Quebec, famous for downhill skiing. Usually, temperatures were well below freezing, with deep snow covering the ground. However, there was no snow at all on that morning, and the ski resorts were fearful of ruin if the weather continued.

She greeted Eileen with a wave and a quick embrace—they hadn't seen each other for almost two weeks, after all. Then, as they climbed the stairs together, Eileen briefed her.

"I have calls scheduled every thirty minutes today, just as you requested. At nine, Natalia Tenaz will be ready. At nine-thirty, James Fitzgerald will call in. Then, your individual calls with each member of the board of directors will fill the slots until noon. I've scheduled a thirty-minute break for lunch."

As they arrived at the top of the stairs and headed toward their adjoining offices, she outlined the afternoon. "At one o'clock, the president of the European Union will be available for twenty minutes as her last call of the day. Her assistant was emphatic about the time limit. Then, you have the governor of California, followed by the governor of Illinois, and the governor of Florida. Your last three calls will be with the Canadian banks. The Royal at four, TD at four-thirty, and Commerce at five."

Eileen stopped and turned to face Suzanne before she announced, "The helicopter will pick you up at six and whisk you to Ottawa. The prime minister is expecting you at his place at seven-thirty. By the way, you do know he's separated from his wife, right?"

Fifteen

Ho Chi Minh City, Vietnam, Tuesday December 19, 2023

Once they got past the dozen hidden microphones in their assigned suites and meeting rooms at the Eco Green complex in Ho Chi Minh City, Serge grew more comfortable with both the facilities and surroundings. He still had the security specialists scan each room every day, but hadn't found more, nor had he heard anything from Đại Dang at the Vietnamese government about the devices his people had found and destroyed.

The Eco Green layout was a good one: nine tall, light gray buildings clustered together on a modern compound with excellent paved streets and wide brick walkways, each building adorned with tall white signs identifying the buildings from A to I.

His team familiarized themselves with the facilities and atmosphere. Building B, where they were located, had a large outdoor pool attached to the third floor that connected with another tower. Around the inviting pool, shrubs, flowers, and a cluster of small trees created a warm and welcoming environment.

The team enjoyed the gym, which was also on the third floor. It became an essential feature for those wanting to exercise, as the air quality in Ho Chi Minh City discouraged outdoor running and walking. Surprisingly, the Vietnamese city hadn't made the top fifty in global city rankings for pollution, but Serge and every member of the team complained of coughing and throat irritation every time they spent extended time outdoors, so the gym and pool became their go-to recreation spots.

Still, they occasionally wandered around the complex to

run errands and buy supplies. Each of the suites Serge's team used for their mission had a fully equipped apartment, with a refrigerator, microwave oven, cooking surfaces, and laundry appliances. Some of the team popped out each day to buy supplies, food, snacks, and refreshments as needed from the half-dozen mini-marts spread throughout the complex.

Others took the prepared-food route. With a dozen or more takeout or eat-in establishments nearby, team members easily found food choices ranging from pizza to pastries to local Vietnamese dishes, all modestly priced. Multima picked up the tab for the team's individual expenses, and they had no trouble staying within the company's maximum meal allowance of thirty dollars per day.

Serge gazed around the complex as he, Constance, and Antonio—his security specialist—waited for a Grab to meet them at Building B's front entrance. Constance had learned about Grab as an alternative to taxis, with low fares like Uber, in other parts of the world. Although Đại Dang had offered a government limousine for their stay, Serge expected his team would need to search for listening devices every time they took him up on his offer.

Serge hopped into the front seat with the driver and showed him the confirmation number on his phone. They'd be en route to Tokyo once they arrived at Tan Son Nhat International Airport's private jet area. Again, their short journey became more of a task than expected.

The pilots had left about noon, anxious to have something to do after almost a month of inactivity. They texted about a half-hour later to say that traffic was the same as it was on the day of arrival, so Serge and his team could plan accordingly.

Although their departure from the Eco Green complex was four hours later than on the day they had arrived, this trip to the airport proved to be another long story. Although the Grab driver used the GPS Waze for the best route given traffic conditions, and Serge monitored it on his own phone, it was almost six in the evening and the sky completely dark when they arrived at the entrance closest to the private jets.

Within thirty minutes, Vietnamese customs motored over from the main terminal to check their documents and okay departure.

There was a lot of space for everyone and their carry-on bags on Suzanne's corporate jet. Constance and Antonio reclined their seats for a nap on the flight, while Serge followed up with texts, emails, and voicemail messages from his people back in North America. Every day, it seemed he had over one hundred inquiries, requests, or alerts about issues somewhere in the Multima empire. Although his team now numbered over two hundred people in its security operations around the globe, a significant number of problems still required his personal attention due to either sensitivity or a need to know.

Still, he managed to stretch out on his reclining chair for about three hours of sleep before the private jet touched down at the VIP private jet entrance in Tokyo's Haneda International Airport Terminal 3's Business Aviation area. The pilots stayed behind to finish their paperwork and parking arrangements for the jet, while Serge and the others headed toward the Mercure Hotel, located a couple miles from the airport.

Serge had asked Eileen to make their arrangements from Canada rather than working through the Japanese National Police Agency. He had decided to keep their location private and not tip off anyone who might want to plant listening devices. They'd just show up the next day, on time, at the national police offices.

The taxi had them at their hotel in mere minutes, as

there was little traffic on the streets at two o'clock in the morning. The door to the hotel was locked and the entrance was dark when they arrived at the front door, but someone working at the front desk saw them and dashed over to let them in.

Within a few minutes, all three had been assigned rooms on the sixth floor and, moments later, they arrived outside the one assigned to Constance. She knew the drill and let Antonio pass into the room after she'd unlocked the door with her card.

She stood at the bathroom doorway just inside the room while Antonio wandered about with his device detection equipment. Serge rummaged through a drawer with his own scanner. Less than two minutes after they'd started the process, Antonio's scanner blinked red. A few seconds later, he pointed to the device hidden below the bed frame on the right, only a foot or two from the room's telephone.

He picked up the phone, and his scanner activated again. Holding the device high in the air, he motioned to Serge, who dragged his finger across his throat as he mouthed, "Kill 'em."

To his chagrin, they uncovered listening devices in both the other rooms. They found them in the same locations, using the same equipment. If they hadn't informed even the Japanese National Police Agency about their hotel reservations, who had told whom about their arrangements, and who inside the hotel was complicit?

Serge headed toward the elevator and then down to the front desk. When he arrived, there was a different attendant on duty, a woman who claimed to know nothing about their rooms until Serge flashed his keycard. Then, she maintained that she could find nothing about who had assigned their rooms.

Serge made two quick calls. As politely as the circumstances would allow, he announced his intentions to the uncooperative attendant. "We're not staying here tonight. You'll receive a call shortly from our Canadian office. They'll sort out what, if anything, we'll pay for our unused rooms. While you wait, please call us a taxi."

He waved for Constance and Antonio to follow him toward the rear door, where the attendant indicated that a taxi would arrive momentarily. They'd sleep on the jet and shower at the airport before their scheduled meeting with the National Police Agency. It now promised to be an interesting one.

Sixteen

Atlanta, Georgia, Tuesday December 19, 2023

That morning, Natalia Tenaz started out on a treadmill in her new apartment building's elaborate and well-equipped gym. She'd begun the new habit about a month earlier, when she'd traveled with Suzanne Simpson on those blitz visits to a few dozen Multima Supermarkets during the days surrounding the American Thanksgiving. Natalia had never considered herself an exercise advocate before.

Early on, her mother had taught her that she should eat carefully, in modest quantities, and avoid alcohol. She'd followed that advice and was satisfied with the results. Her weight was under control, even if maybe five or ten pounds higher than ideal. Her health was good, and she couldn't recall fighting off anything more serious than a cold or a very occasional bout of the flu. And although she was far from gorgeous, as she progressed through the fourth decade of her life, she still noticed guys taking a second look from time to time.

What had changed her outlook? In a word: Suzanne. It all started a couple days after they'd started traveling together for that blitz. She noticed that Suzanne always came to breakfast with a healthy glow and asked her how she managed it. Natalia learned that her CEO started every morning at five, no matter where she was. By five-thirty, she was on a treadmill in the hotel where they were staying, and she ran for an hour, then stretched for fifteen minutes. By seven, she was in the shower, back in her room.

Her boss didn't press Natalia to join her, but made it clear she'd welcome the company. Natalia immediately embraced the habit and, within a few days, came to realize one of the factors that made Suzanne such an exceptional leader.

From their first day traveling together, Suzanne had left a powerful impression. She seemed to have a photographic memory. Before each store visit, she took fifteen to twenty minutes on the jet or in a car to read the extensive summary of that store's status and performance prepared by Eileen and posted on her Apple Notebook. With that single read, she retained—and worked into her conversations—all the essential details about the store they were visiting.

Suzanne had been gracious. After introducing Natalia to the staff in each store, she'd let her new Supermarkets president ask a few questions and get to know the team better before raising any issues of her own concern or applauding recent store achievements. Consequently, Natalia felt a strong bond with the teams in each store after only an hour or so, something she had never imagined possible.

But the factor Natalia found most impressive was Suzanne's extraordinary energy. They started those visits every day no later than nine o'clock and never finished before six in the evening. After a quick dinner together, Suzanne retired to her hotel suite for telephone calls, Zoom meetings, and other tasks until eleven or later every night.

Their first week together, Natalia usually crashed into bed at about nine and still awoke tired in the morning. By the end of their second week, she noticed her energy level had increased to almost equal Suzanne's, a woman more than fifteen years older!

Since that blitz experience, Natalia had embraced the exercise regimen and was only a few minutes from completing her run that morning when she noticed an alert on her phone.

She stepped to the rolling treadmill's side rails to check it out.

It was from Gaston Dupont, president of Multima Supermarkets for Europe. She had only met the guy once, during a meeting of the board of directors they'd both attended—but she knew that both her Supermarkets' predecessors, Gordon Goodfellow and Suzanne, thought highly of him.

She checked the text message.

> *Sorry to start your day with some concerning news. I've copied Serge Boisvert because I think we have a serious issue developing. Earlier today, Multima transport trucks were involved in highway accidents in seven different countries. This has never happened. Damages to all vehicles were severe. Five drivers died from their injuries, and there are at least a dozen fatalities reported from other vehicles involved in the collisions.*

Her mind froze in utter shock. Visibly trembling, she reached to slap the emergency stop button on the treadmill. When the belt finally stopped, she stepped down and pressed the phone number displayed on the screen.

Serge responded on the first ring. He'd already read the message from Multima Supermarkets' European president and added more bad news to start an already horrible day. "Moments before I got the text from Gaston Dupont, my people in Singapore reported a similar accident involving either Multima-owned transport trucks or carriers under contract to us in South China, Singapore, and Hong Kong. All involved fatalities."

"What do you think is going on?" Natalia could barely form the words to ask her question. Her hands trembled, and her brain seemed reluctant to process it all.

"It's only a guess at this stage. Clearly, we're under some sort of coordinated attack, but it's too early to say from whom. It's devastating. I'll get my people working on it in all those markets. Email all our U.S. and Canadian warehouses as soon as we finish. Let them know every truck in our fleet, everywhere in the country, must be inspected by trained technicians before leaving our properties. Be sure they focus on brakes and steering."

"Any other measures you think I should take?"

"Let the stores know the news. You'll probably want to run your message past Suzanne before you send it, but the stores need to know there'll be delays and disruptions for a few days. I'll call Suzanne now to brief her on what we know and tell her to expect your draft message to the stores."

He hung up before she could ask her last question. Were the Supermarkets' headquarters offices in danger, too?

Seventeen

Mexico City, Mexico, Tuesday December 19, 2023

They couldn't meet with the Mexican financial consultants at KPMM for almost three weeks, and that caused James Fitzgerald considerable concern. The prestigious financial consulting firm was one of the most prominent and most respected in Mexico, but they didn't seem overly anxious to earn their commission from the major acquisition Multima Financial Services proposed.

From previous experiences with consultants, he expected they'd be almost tripping over themselves in their haste to complete a transaction and pocket the millions of dollars in commission Multima was prepared to pay them for a successful win.

Regardless, Murray Powell finally secured a meeting date, and they touched down after an almost four-hour flight due south of the Multima Financial Services office in Chicago. Their flight had been uneventful despite the winter weather over much of the US, and the pair were now en route to the KPMM headquarters tower in the Reforma district in the heart of Mexico City.

It turned out that the building was close to the St. Regis Hotel, where they'd booked rooms for that evening. James was determined to stay, but only if he learned enough and saw sufficient progress to warrant the investment of another day of his time. His preliminary research on the deal, KPMM, and rumors circulating about both the acquisition target and their financial consultant had alerted his sense of caution. If he didn't hear the right words today, Murray Powell might just need to start over again in Mexico.

James and Murray chatted about their flight, the drive in from the airport, and their impression of the building's unique architecture as their elevator climbed toward the top of Torre Reforma. They had a few minutes to chat because the tower was over eight hundred feet high and one of the tallest buildings in the bustling capital of Mexico.

Gonzalo Garcia, KPMM's managing partner in Mexico City, greeted them, his arms wide and a smile brimming, as the elevator opened to display the highly successful firm's luxurious marble walls and polished floor.

Murray introduced James, and the three exchanged well wishes and flattery, as expected in their elite corner of the business world.

When they entered an opulent conference room that could easily accommodate fifty people, Garcia gestured toward the other side of the room and the magnificent view. There, he took another few moments to give his guests a visual tour of the city from on high before finally getting around to introducing the remaining half-dozen people seated around the table, waiting.

It was Leonardo Alvarez, one of those associates, who started the dialogue. "Grupo Financiero Bansure's enthusiasm for a buyout has cooled," he said with a grimace. "They're not satisfied with the premium we've offered."

For the next few minutes, James and Murray listened to his rationale for the company's hesitation, his perspective on the change of heart, and the reasons for it.

He let Murray respond first. "Whoa! You've just unloaded a plateful there, Leonardo. The last time we spoke, you were confident. Just needed a little more time, I recall you saying. When did you get this new insight?"

"I've been talking with them almost every day since we agreed on meeting today, but it was only this morning that they confessed to their hesitation. They finally divulged that they had another suitor only a few minutes before you arrived. I'm sorry to share the news with you, but it seems they have received a competing offer from Bank of the Americas."

The room became absolutely still. No one spoke. Eyes darted about uncertainly.

James processed the implications for some time before he spoke.

"Let me get this straight: Abduhl Mahinder, the CEO of the Bank of the Americas, recommended your financial consultancy to Murray Powell to represent the interests of Multima Financial Services. We entered into a contract with you to complete an acquisition of Bansure as quickly as possible, and you agreed to the terms and conditions of that agreement. Now, Bank of the Americas has made an offer to Bansure. May I ask who represented Bank of the Americas in that proposed transaction?"

The silence was so profound the old expression "could hear a pin drop" popped into his mind as he waited for a response. For more than a few seconds, Alvarez and Garcia exchanged furtive glances at each other and around the table as their faces became red with embarrassment.

Finally, the managing partner spoke.

"Another team from KPMM handled negotiations with Bank of the Americas and Grupo Financiero Bansure. We created all the necessary firewalls to ensure there was no communication between our two teams, but both are under my direct responsibility."

James stood up and slid his chair back from the table. "What you have done might comply with your apparently relaxed standards and ethics, but they don't match mine. I'm appalled. You also know, of course, that Abduhl Mahinder serves on the board of directors of Multima Corporation, our parent. I am sickened by this entire conversation. Our lawyers will be in touch."

He stepped away from the table and headed toward the door, Murray hastily collecting his files, trying to catch up.

Before they reached the doorway, he heard Gonzalo Garcia call out, "I'm afraid I can't let you leave, James."

Eighteen

Paris, France, Wednesday December 20, 2023

"Send Constance back to Vietnam on a commercial carrier with whichever security guy you have with you," Suzanne had instructed. "Whatever you discovered in your Japan meeting will have to wait unless you see a direct connection to these road accidents. I need you to meet me in Paris as quickly as you can get there."

There hadn't been time for a moment's hesitation. Serge apparently hadn't seen any immediate connection to his meeting that day in Tokyo with the National Police Agency, so he'd agreed to fly to Paris.

Naturally, Suzanne arrived first, but only by a few minutes.

With Serge using her long-range jet and James in Mexico with the second-largest plane in Multima's fleet, Suzanne had to wait for Natalia's jet to travel from Atlanta up to Montreal. Then, after departing from Mirabel International Airport near her home in the Laurentians, the pilots preferred to stop again in Gander, Newfoundland, for refueling before crossing the Atlantic to Paris.

She had decided to wait for Serge to arrive at Paris Orly Airport, located a few minutes from their European headquarters. Gaston Dupont rode out with the limousine and briefed her on the latest developments while they waited for Serge's jet to land. Edouard Deschamps from Interpol joined them.

"It looks like two different methods of sabotage were used," the director of Lyon's Command and Coordination Centre explained. "From Belgium and the Netherlands, our experts confirmed the airbrake lines were partially severed, then came apart upon acceleration. In the UK and Italy, wheel lug nuts were partially loosened, then came apart at highway speeds. Those cases caused deaths in other vehicles on the roadways as the wheels crashed into smaller passenger cars."

"Aren't drivers required to inspect both of those truck parts before they leave their warehouses?" Suzanne asked.

"Yes, and drivers should also inspect them carefully whenever they stop for fuel or coffee breaks. However, the examples we've seen so far occurred after they'd left very busy truck stops, where dozens of vehicles provided camouflage for whoever performed these malicious deeds. Often, drivers only give the trucks a cursory inspection after they've already been on the road for several hours without experiencing any issues."

"Do we have our lawyers involved, Gaston?" Suzanne asked.

"Yes. They're in communication with the police services in each country, getting almost hourly updates on the injuries, deaths, and scope of damages. But it may be weeks before we have a complete picture."

While they waited for Serge to arrive, Suzanne continued to question both men, probing them for more details and information. The situation was terrifying and bewildering. Who would do such a thing, and why?

Their wait was a matter of minutes. Serge joined them at the limousine, reaching for her the moment he settled into the rear. They had an understanding about not showing affection in a business environment, but he disregarded protocol, reached across to wrap his arm around her shoulder, and drew her toward him tightly. She felt her skirt climb up her thighs and made an awkward move to squeeze her knees tightly together as their companions gawked self-consciously.

The probe of his tongue was deep. She had to draw a

breath the moment he released her and pulled back. It was tempting to enjoy more, but Serge got the message.

"Sorry, guys," he said with an awkward grin. "You know we usually don't do that in public, but I haven't seen this gorgeous woman in a month. Now, let's focus on business."

Edouard Deschamps from Interpol spoke first. "We're all French here, so there is no offence taken. I'd encourage you both to take more time to enjoy one another if our crisis weren't so urgent."

For Serge's benefit, he recapped the information he'd shared with the others. He finished with a grim summation. "There's no doubt this sabotage is both organized and coordinated—have you received any messages or demands from those behind this criminal vandalism?"

Serge, Gaston and Suzanne looked at each other with arched brows.

"Nothing yet? From any of our offices?" Suzanne queried.

She received only headshakes and grimaces in return.

Turning to the director of Interpol's Lyon Command and Coordination Centre, she asked, "What do you suggest we do?"

Nineteen

Paris, France, Wednesday December 20, 2023

Serge listened intently to the Interpol director's reply.

Unfortunately, his comments were little more than platitudes, cautions, general warnings, and guarded speculation. About what he'd expected from the circumspect director. Their paths had crossed before, in the days when Serge had ranked high in the Royal Canadian Mounted Police force. Their relations had always been polite and formal. From Serge's perspective, they'd also been unproductive.

That day's input contained no surprises. Serge maintained the dialogue for much of the thirty-minute drive from the airport to the Multima Supermarkets headquarters in Europe, with Suzanne or Gaston occasionally interjecting questions or requests for clarification.

It wasn't yet noon when they arrived at the office. They parted with formal handshakes, assurances they would keep in touch with each other, and pleasant farewells.

Suzanne took control as soon as they reached the conference room on the top floor of the building. "Clearly, Interpol has no idea who's responsible. I feel extremely vulnerable and fearful at the same time—how do we solve this, guys?"

Serge looked at Gaston Dupont and waited for him to respond. After a moment's hesitation to choose his words, the European president spoke. "I sent a message to all our truck drivers across Europe before meeting up today, letting them know about the sabotages, and instructing them to intensify their inspection of tires and hoses before getting into the vehicles every time they stop. Apparently, drivers in

Portugal and Austria discovered their wheel lugs had been loosened before they left some rest stops, so it appears whoever is responsible intended even more damage."

"Have we received any demands? Anywhere?" Suzanne wanted to know.

Once more, Serge waited for Gaston to respond first.

He answered tentatively. "I emailed every employee, urging them to report any telephone calls, emails, letters, or personal visits that might suggest the party had any knowledge whatsoever about the sabotage, and to let my office know immediately. I checked my messages from the car as we drove over, and I have nothing new to report."

Suzanne looked back at Serge before asking her next question. "Did your people in Asia discover any additional events or demands?"

Serge shook his head and met her eyes, allowing her to read the impact of his reaction.

"How about from North America—anything at all reported there?" she asked.

This time, he could elaborate. "I think we avoided damage in North America. On the plane, I received reports that drivers from six separate warehouses had caught planned sabotage before it could occur. Natalia got her memo out early this morning, and I think we dodged the bullet there for now."

"I'll ask again," Suzanne said with a bit of an edge creeping into her tone. "Any demands in North America?"

"I've heard nothing further from Natalia or my security teams in either Canada or the States." Serge looked directly into Suzanne's eyes again as he replied, trying to assure her they were doing everything possible.

Suzanne's phone beeped. She broke eye contact and glanced downward at it. Her face blanched white, and the hand holding her phone trembled. She took a deep breath, wiped something away from her left eye, and held up the phone for Serge to see.

James Fitzgerald and Murray Powell have been unavoidably detained. DO NOT INVOLVE THE POLICE OR ANY OTHER LEGAL AUTHORITIES FROM ANY COUNTRY, AND THEY WILL REMAIN IN GOOD HEALTH. More information to follow.

Twenty

Atlanta, GA, Thursday December 21, 2023

Natalia's phone beeped with the emergency alarm her staff had created and installed on her device for all her direct reports at Multima Financial. It was one of those details she'd overlooked in the transition to becoming Multima Supermarkets' president. It had all happened so quickly that she supposed she should have expected a limited number of dropped balls.

The alert originated from Murray Powell's phone, her guy responsible for acquisitions at Financial Services. It was odd for a couple reasons. First—she checked her watch to be sure—yes, it was before eight in the morning in Atlanta, which meant it was before seven in Chicago. Murray was a good colleague and a successful leader on her former team, but he was also a notoriously late sleeper. Several times, he'd arrived at the office late for morning meetings with the excuse that his alarm had failed. It was improbable he'd be on his phone before seven in the morning, when he might accidentally activate the emergency application.

The second reason she suspected an error was Murray's nature. He carried a fear of personal danger with him. He had been the one to initially request the alarm system. With all his travels to exotic locations in Latin America and other parts of the world, he'd argued that he needed a backup system in the event he was ever accosted or kidnapped. Even if she'd forgotten to delete her name from the notifications list, in the event of trouble, Murray would have almost certainly insisted that Multima Financial's technology system link him to James Fitzgerald from the moment he assumed her former responsibilities.

There was no reason to disturb either Murray or the technology people in Chicago at this juncture. If she heard a repeat of the alarm, she'd react immediately. If there was no repeat, she'd contact the Chicago technology team to make the update when the offices opened.

Natalia returned her attention to the daily sales reports on the wide screen beside her desk. There were four days until Christmas, and the stores were bustling with activity in every part of the country. In the northeast, where snow had fallen a few days earlier, the spirit among buyers was reportedly festive. During those after-Thanksgiving store visits, the staff consistently claimed the weather often determined the success of Christmas sales. The numbers appeared higher than the previous week and higher than the previous year in every category. Good.

In the Southeast, the story was equally enthralling. Sales were up in every department again. This time, she knew the influx in activity came from Canadian snowbirds, Canadians migrating south to escape unpleasant winters for the holidays and longer. Newspapers had recently reported that such travel south was at an all-time high, and the numbers suggested Multima Supermarkets was earning its share of their business.

She scrolled to the Southwest, the area covered by the recent acquisition of Jeffersons Stores. There, Multima was in the middle of a desperate effort to convert all store signage from Jeffersons to Multima, and they were making good headway. But the job wouldn't be completed by Christmas, and it showed in the sales results.

Jeffersons Stores had suffered from lethargic management and, more recently, from negative rumors linking the company to organized crime before Suzanne had engineered the takeover a few months earlier. Profit margins remained surprisingly stable despite the discount sales and advertising that Multima had started earlier that quarter.

Unfortunately, it meant buyers in the Southeast weren't stocking up for the holidays as much. They were only buying the necessities. After the holiday season, she'd need to dig deeper to determine how they might regain their customers' confidence and grow the business.

Suzanne called on her mobile as she was closing the screen to freshen up for her first personal meeting of the morning.

"Have you heard anything from James?" Suzanne blurted before Natalia could even say hello.

"No, why?"

Suzanne read the ominous message, and Natalia cringed. They'd already lost some time because of her failure to act on that earlier emergency alert from Murray.

Twenty-One

Mexico City, Mexico, Thursday December 21, 2023

James awoke feeling groggy, every muscle tight. He was lying on a bed with a mattress, but with no sheets or blanket, as though they'd simply dropped him there unconscious. His throat was parched. Even licking his lips was painful. When he tried to shift positions, he found his hands were bound behind his back with some sort of metal cuffs, and his feet were attached to an aluminum-sounding clamp and chain that rattled with even the slightest movements.

Slowly, the room came into focus. Lying on his right side, a large picture window caught his attention. The drapes were only partially closed, but it was dark outside. It was impossible to see any stars or lights from the city around him. Mexico City was a large metropolis of over twenty-two million, so there should have been streetlights glowing or the sounds of traffic, even late into the night.

James listened more intently. He could discern a slight hum from outside the room where he was confined. It was traffic from the streets below, but there were no horns honking or mufflers roaring, which meant the room was high enough above the street to muffle the sound on the ground.

With his hands bound behind his back, it was impossible to see his watch. However, fumbling with his fingers, he was able to locate it on his left wrist and ran a forefinger over the button used to reset the device and make adjustments. He pressed the button twice and detected no hum, buzz or other sound from the watch. But, he supposed it was still working fine.

He listened carefully again and now detected the hum of an air conditioner, although the room was hot and stuffy. He looked back at the wall again and noticed an air conditioner just below the window, but it wasn't operating. The hum probably came from a unit operating in another room. Had someone painted the appliance in his room the same color as the wall simply so it would blend in? Regardless, whoever had detained him wasn't concerned about his comfort—maybe they were intentionally making him uncomfortable.

He thought about calling out to whoever might be nearby, but paused. How would they react if they knew he was awake? Clearly, someone had drugged him but provided nothing to eat or drink. He couldn't recall the prick of a needle, either.

And where was Murray Powell? The last he could recall, someone had grabbed Murray from the back and spun him into a brutal wrestling hold that allowed only a faint gasp of shock to escape from his companion's lips. That was the last thing James had seen before everything went dark.

James tested to see if he could maneuver onto his back or tilt to his other side. It took two tries, but pressing down, he leveraged enough strength from his feet and ankles to shift to his back. A basic overhead light fixture became visible, mixing with the small amount of light coming into the room from the outside. He detected no switches, chains, or cords to turn it on.

From this position, he made out the form of a large, widescreen television mounted midway up the wall. A small blue light glowed from its bottom. James lifted his head. He discerned some sort of cupboard or other piece of furniture extending beyond the width of the television.

Using the same squirming strategy, James arched his legs again and ended up looking into an empty closet beside the bed, the room's doorway located only a few feet beyond it. He lifted his head more to see light glowing from the bottom of the door, but he couldn't detect any voices, a television working, or music playing. Listening as intently as possible again, he thought he heard a soft sound like someone breathing in their sleep, but he couldn't be sure.

The dryness in his throat demanded attention. His attempts to clear it were fruitless and caused irritation. In fact, his entire mouth was so parched that licking his lips no longer moisturized them. Unfortunately, the extreme dryness didn't extend as far south as his bladder, which pleaded for some relief. James had no idea how much time had elapsed since his last visit to a restroom, but he had no desire to test his limits.

It was that sense of urgency that caused him to call out.

The first time, his voice sounded feeble and hoarse. He cleared his throat again and managed to say hello with slightly greater volume, loud enough to cause the sound of a loud scrape of a chair on a ceramic floor, then what sounded like the movement of another chair, followed by the clacking of shoes or boots on the floor.

James waited.

A few seconds later, the door to his room opened, and someone switched on the overhead light, temporarily blinding him with its brightness and intensity. He closed his eyes, then squinted to see two large bodies fill the doorway and the space behind it. No one spoke. Neither of them moved toward James for a moment.

As his eyes adapted to the intense light and his vision slowly returned, the two dark forms evolved into silent, bearded males with glowering eyes and grim expressions. Both stared at James, threatening with their silence and towering forms. One held a cut-off rifle cocked against his waist, looking like he craved an opportunity to let loose a barrage of bullets.

Both appeared Mexican, but neither spoke. James

shifted his eyes from one to the other. They wore well-worn jeans, baggy shirts, and running shoes. The one with the weapon had an unlit cigarette dangling from the side of his mouth and a chain running from his belt, probably to a wallet in his rear pocket.

"Can I get some water?" James asked politely. Neither responded. "Can you give me some water? *Agua*?" he repeated.

The guy just inside the doorway turned to his companion and nodded wordlessly. Then, he stepped further inside the room as his partner walked away, the faint outline of a malicious smile forming. Silently, he assessed James, his eyes looking up and down his prone body as though inviting some movement or protest. He continued to point the rifle directly at James's face and blinked only once or twice in the time it took the other guy to bring the water.

The fellow set a water glass on the bureau below the television and slowly pulled a key chain from his front pocket, his eyes studying James like a hunter waiting for a reaction from an animal captured in a trap. He stepped around the side of the bed, where he could reach James's arms, secured behind his back.

Before the guy inserted the key, and without warning, the one with the rifle grabbed the glass of water from the bureau and flung the contents directly into James's eyes as he hissed the word, "Puto Gringo!"

As the cold water struck him in the face, James lurched upward in shock. The guy with the key reacted violently as he yelled some other curse in Spanish, before he struck James's wrist just above the handcuffs with a hard object. James heard the bones in his wrist crack, and he howled in pain.

The bastard grabbed him forcibly by his injured wrist, yanked it upward to a more comfortable height, and inserted the key in the slot to unlock one side of the handcuff.

James cried out with each act as intense pain shot up his arms.

A few seconds later, the guy grabbed James's shoulder just as roughly and angrily shouted something to the one with the gun, who wordlessly took the empty glass somewhere to refill and returned a moment or two later with a glare of annoyance, the glass full.

Water splashed over the rim of the glass as he passed it to James, the hoodlum's malicious grin slowly forming once again. James took a couple deep gulps from the glass, downing almost the entire amount. "I need a bathroom, too. *Baño*. Please. *Por favor*."

Disgusted, the goon with the gun first grabbed James's injured wrist and jerked it, causing another scream of pain. Next, he yanked him up from the bed. Then, he pointed toward the doorway. It was then that James realized the contraption on his feet permitted him to walk on his own, but only if he took tiny steps.

Still, his tormentor was determined to make it difficult. He shoved James forcefully toward the door, causing him to lose his balance, crash into the doorway frame and bang his head against it hard enough to lose consciousness as he collapsed in a bundle on the hardwood floor.

Twenty-Two

Paris, France, Friday December 22, 2023

Suzanne called for Serge the moment Natalia divulged that she'd received an emergency alert on her phone. Within seconds, he'd notified his team's technology experts housed at the headquarters office in Montreal, Financial Services in Chicago, and Multima Supermarkets in Atlanta.

Using sophisticated tracking devices, his team eventually located James Fitzgerald and Murray Powell. Murray had earlier insisted that Multima provide those plain looking but custom-made electronic watches to include a feature he could use to activate an alarm if ever he found himself in a dangerous situation in Mexico or South America. Suzanne had approved the exorbitant cost to appease the fellow, but refused to wear one herself. She might need to reconsider that position with the new developments.

James seemed to be in the center of Mexico City, and Murray Powell appeared to be in a warehouse district a few miles farther out of the heart of the city, near the airport. Neither responded to repeated call attempts. Both watches still showed battery life, but it appeared someone had stolen their phones or blocked access to the network, so they couldn't make calls to them to verify their condition. Serge assumed that since both alarms had activated, and they were now in separate locations, they should treat the alarms as legitimate.

It might have been a shade premature, but her instinct assumed the worst about circumstances in Mexico, faced with the limited information they had. They should take action rather than wait to see what might sort out in the coming hours.

"If we know where they are, we need to get the local authorities involved to yank them away from whoever is holding them," Suzanne urged. "We can't sit idly by while James and Murray are captives of who knows what kind of narco or mafia outfit."

"I have connections there," Serge replied. "There are people in the Policia Federal I can call, but they'll involve the local constabulary. They must. Corruption runs rampant at the local level in Mexico, even in a metropolis the size of Mexico City. Responsibility for enforcement is often allocated by street blocks, and the local police officers might easily be on the payroll of whoever is holding them. If we play our hand too early, we might tip off the criminals and give them time to destroy the watches or remove James and Murray."

"What's the alternative?"

"We need to rent a private jet in Atlanta and dispatch a half-dozen of my security team there to Mexico City. It will take my people about three and a half hours to get there. A lot might happen before they arrive, but I think the odds of survival for both are better with our folks than with the locals."

Suzanne didn't reply immediately. Instead she took time to process the relative dangers and "the odds" Serge had argued—she was not, by nature, a gambler.

"It's about eight in the morning here in France. That means about one in the morning in Mexico City, right? If we can get a jet immediately, about what time would your people arrive at the locations?" Suzanne asked.

"Assuming they could take off within the hour and allow another hour to get from the airport to each of the specific locations, they should be at the identified spots by about six in the morning. It will still be dark."

"And can your people go right to the specific spot where

they're holding James?"

"Right now, we have only the address where they're holding him. It's a twenty-five-story apartment tower. Once my people arrive, we can use a more sophisticated digital tracker that should lead us right to the apartment where they're holding him. No guarantees, but I've used the equipment before with the Mounties, and it worked well."

Suzanne weighed the alternatives. None seemed comfortable. Police corruption in Mexico was notorious, so Serge's unease with involving them was understandable. Still, technology wasn't infallible. If the tracking devices Serge planned to use proved unable to identify precisely which apartment James was being held in, locating him in a twenty-five-story apartment building could be problematic. And they were considering the well-being of not only a senior executive in her company but also a long-time confidant and friend. It weighed heavily.

Serge gave her time to process it all. He looked off into the ceiling space above her shoulder as though looking either for divine intervention or an alternative. When his gaze returned to her, she nodded.

"I'll roust Eileen from bed to arrange the jet. Choose your best people. Tell them to keep us posted throughout, day and night if necessary. Once we finish those arrangements, let's get Gaston and his team back in here. We've got to manage all the negative publicity from those truck crashes across Europe."

Twenty-Three

Serge followed her instructions and then popped into the top-floor executive conference room, where the meeting Suzanne had convened was already underway. Seated at one end of the long table, Gaston Dupont, Multima Supermarkets' European president, was speaking.

"So far, our public relations experts in each country have kept a damper on the news. Edward Hadley asked me to get them all together for a Zoom conference before I drove out to meet you at the airport. He asked them all to proactively call their primary media contacts in each country, let them know about the reports we received, and ask them to keep the news under wraps for a few hours to give the police in each country a bit of time to investigate."

"And the media people respected that request?" Suzanne's tone suggested either skepticism or sarcasm; Serge couldn't be sure.

"For the most part, yes," Gaston replied. "Hadley encouraged the PR folks to discreetly remind their contacts about the large advertising budgets we spend with them and our need to keep our sales buoyant to continue paying our bills. Unlike in North America, where every outlet seems driven to be the first with any story, newspapers, radio, and TV here in Europe take a more measured approach. They tend to be more pragmatic and understand the delicate synergies between their outlets and our promotional budgets."

Suzanne nodded and turned toward Serge, her eyes seeking information.

"The teams have been dispatched to Mexico. They'll be

airborne in minutes," he said, looking around the table. "I won't go into details here, but I put together two crack squads of a half-dozen specialists each. I briefed them via Zoom, and they understand the mission."

Suzanne nodded her understanding. She seemed to grasp both the sensitivity and confidence underlying his message. He switched the discussion back to Europe.

"Do we have any more information from that lead out of the Netherlands?"

"Police there have taken into custody a guy seen in the truck parking area at our facility in Den Hague the night before the crashes," Gaston volunteered. "They describe him as a homeless lowlife who's been involved in mischief before. He stays at an encampment outside the city, a kilometer or two from our warehouse. The Dutch police believe he also has connections to folks involved in organized crime, the illicit drug trade, specifically."

"Any indication which organized crime outfit he may be working for?" Serge wanted to know.

"Penoze. They work out of Amsterdam, but they also have a connection to the Mocro Mafia outfit operating out of Morocco. The fellow they arrested speaks Dutch but appears to be of Moroccan ancestry," Gaston explained.

"Are either of those gangs related to the Yakuza out of Japan?" Suzanne asked.

"Perhaps," one of Serge's security people replied. "In fact, I recall a story out of Morocco earlier this year. The son of a prominent judge there was murdered, and a witness claimed the killers appeared to be Asian. The murder took place at night, and the witness was never able to identify the assailants from any of the Asians that Moroccan police arrested for questioning. But I remember reading that at least some Moroccan investigators were working to establish a connection to the Japanese Yakuza."

Serge looked at the young recruit, who'd recently joined

his French security team. "I know you've spent some time in North Africa, Francois. Please work your contacts there. If you find a lead, let me know, and we'll fly you down with one of the company's aircraft. We can have you there in about three hours, right? And if you need someone with you, let me know."

With that dismissal, Serge turned his attention to another member of his security team, seated on the opposite side of the table. "Alain, have we heard anything yet from Edouard Deschamps over at Interpol?"

"I received a text while we've been talking. Let me read it to you." He paused to bring up, then read, the message on his screen. "Found evidence where the vehicle involved in the A-6 mishap had parked the night before. Suggests foreign involvement. Tracks analyzed from mud prints near the truck's parking spot suggest footwear rarely worn in France, used mainly in Northern Africa. Does Multima have any employees from Morocco on the payroll in France or do any business there?"

Serge pounced immediately. "Gaston, do our human resources records in Europe record each employee's nationality?"

The European president nodded, and Serge sent him off on a mission. "Let's run a printout of every Moroccan working for Multima in Europe and share it with Interpol right away."

"I'm afraid we can't do that, Serge." The European president cringed apologetically. "European laws prevent us from using employee records for any purpose not related to their employment with the company. Regulators could shut us down for a violation."

Serge looked to Suzanne for help.

"We're not going to break any laws," she said as she looked sternly in his direction. "Would it help if Gaston asked the human resources people to run a report and share it only with your security team for analysis? And you agree to draw in the police only if there is a specific employee or two who might fit the profile you're looking for?"

He nodded in resignation. This wasn't a battle he could win.

"Alain, it looks like you get that assignment. Please go with Gaston now and get started. Talk with Interpol as well to get a better description of that shoeprint so you know their best guess on the shoe size and body weight of the suspect they're looking for. And let them know our plan."

Serge stood up to signify that the meeting was over. He waved for Suzanne to follow him. "We need to talk with Natalia again."

Twenty-Four

Atlanta, Georgia, Friday December 22, 2023

Since Natalia's brief telephone conversation with Suzanne and Serge earlier, she hadn't slept. A few hours later, she took time to shower in the bathroom off the entrance to her office and changed her clothes to the garments she stored in a locker there for just such an emergency.

Otherwise, for hours on end, she explored the dark net in a desperate search for information or hints about what might be going on with James and Murray down in Mexico.

Serge and his security people had spent hours tracking signals, and the last she'd heard, they were getting some optimistic hints about the missing pair's whereabouts. But she felt horrible about her delay in reporting the emergency alert from Murray's watch. She also felt a responsibility to contribute to their rescue in some way. Although it had been late in the day when she'd last spoken with Suzanne, Natalia wanted to call upon a couple researchers in Chicago. The pair had reported to her back in the days when she led a small group within Financial Services dedicated to ferreting out information from unconventional sources.

Unfortunately, both former colleagues were now working in Vietnam on Serge's secret project. Despite the twelve-hour time difference, Archie Begat and Constance Hope bought into her odd request, although it was the wee hours of the morning there.

Briefed on the mission and its urgency, Natalia's former colleagues had delved as deeply into the dark net as they dared. For hours, their efforts were fruitless, reporting back only dead ends to once-promising signals. Now, as dawn approached in Atlanta and they prepared for darkness in

Japan and Vietnam, Constance requested a secure Zoom call.

"During the few hours we were parked on the tarmac in Tokyo before Serge sent me back to Ho Chi Minh City on a commercial flight—at two o'clock in the morning—I spent some time sniffing around the dark net in Japan." Her opening sounded a little dramatic, resentful, or both, but Natalia remained silent while Constance got to her point.

"I didn't explore it much while I was in Tokyo, but when you called earlier, I decided to try the new location. I was able to access it from Ho Chi Minh City but, for some reason, was routed through Thailand to a Tokyo address. All the correspondence was in Japanese, which my computer's software translated.

"Here's the strange thing: every sequence of messages on the site was either to, from, or about someone identified only by the English letter 'A' instead of the Japanese character 'あ.' In one entry from 'A,' they said they were in Thailand, but the very last entry referred to 'A' being in Seattle."

She paused again for a deep breath before she continued. "I remembered reading sometime last year about a senior leader in the Yakuza crime outfit being arrested in Thailand and transported to Seattle to face American charges for drug trafficking. When I did some research, I discovered that the person's name started with an 'A' in English. And when I re-read the entry on the dark web, I noticed the reference to 'A' used the Japanese equivalent of the term 'currently indisposed in Seattle.' Do you think there's any chance he might be the connection Serge is looking for?"

Within moments, Natalia had tracked down both Serge and Suzanne in the Paris office, and both joined the Zoom call. Constance repeated her story.

When she finished, Serge looked intrigued with the idea

but gazed off into space as he processed the information.

Suzanne asked the first question. "Great research. While Serge figures out where we might want to go with this new information, I'd like to better understand the Thai connection. Were you able to glean any insight about who in Thailand or what organization was involved with the Yakuza?"

"I got the impression two illegal activities were under discussion. Lots of the dialogue related to the drug trade, particularly heroin. But almost as many exchanges were related to weapons—everything from handguns to powerful, military-style rifles. To be honest, I didn't understand much of the technical details because I know little about weapons. But I can show you how to get into the site if you have someone who speaks Japanese or has good translation software and knows more about both."

Serge had finished his processing. He nodded as Constance summed up her thoughts. "Yeah, I want to add my congratulations on this discovery, too. I think you're onto something, and I have a Japanese-speaking resource at the Montreal headquarters. As soon as we finish this call, I'll ask her to connect with you. She's cleared all security levels, and I'd like you to guide her into and around the site if she needs any technical assistance. Are you okay to do that from Ho Chi Minh City?"

Constance's response was immediate and affirmative, and the call ended in a matter of seconds. Natalia was about to sign off when a loud alarm blasted from Serge's phone. Everyone froze for a second as he picked it up, tapped the screen, and held it tightly to his ear.

He listened for a few seconds, then interrupted the caller. "Bernie, I want you to call me back. I'm sending you a secure Zoom link to use. I'm here with Suzanne and Natalia and want them to join the conversation. Connect with us back here as quickly as you can. Constance, you can leave the call now. I'll have Asuka Sato contact you as soon as possible, but this may take a few minutes."

Natalia watched as Constance's image disappeared and Serge turned to Suzanne. "It's Bernie Perez. His team is at the apartment where we think they're holding James."

Within a few seconds, the face of what appeared to be a lean Mexican American appeared on the screen, but one couldn't be sure because his face was painted black, and every item of clothing he wore was also black, including gloves that covered his hands.

"Tell us what you found," Serge instructed without any pleasantries.

Bernie launched his message without hesitation. "We have thirty-seven minutes until sunrise. If you give me the go-ahead, we'll have time to do it before light, but if we can't be operational in about five minutes, I'd prefer to delay until tomorrow."

"Fire away, Bernie. We'll decide quickly," Serge pressed.

"We're sure he's in apartment 1901 in a twenty-five-story high-rise tower that's commercial for the first four floors, then residential to the top. Light security at the front desk. Cameras on the floor were disabled without attracting attention. We've already entered the building once and used the elevator to get to the apartment. We got a match on James's watch, so we're confident he's there. We did a body scan from outside the door and learned there were two guys—both armed—and James. He's in a separate bedroom. The guys are in the living room, about ten to twenty feet from the doorway. We're confident the three of us can take out the guards and get James to our vehicle in the basement, even if he's injured. We'll leave our fourth man at the vehicle with its engine idling for a quick departure if there are any surprises."

When Bernie paused for a breath, Serge jumped in with a quick question. "What else is in the area? Any people around?"

"Yeah. There's a hotel next door, about the same number of stories. Attached to the hotel is a shopping center, with about thirty stores on three levels. We haven't spotted a pedestrian on either the street in front or behind the building since we got here, but I'll say it again: we'll have to be quick if you want us to do it today. This place will be humming before long."

"One last question before we decide," Serge said. "Is there an escape besides the elevators?"

"Yeah. The apartment is at the end of the hallway. Strangely enough, the building is designed with the end of the hallway open to the outdoors. With the warmer weather here, they can get away with that. At the opening, there's a stairway escape to the ground floor."

Natalia looked on as Serge turned toward Suzanne seeking concurrence. She nodded, and he gave the okay to Bernie, with some new instructions.

"Once you've got him, take him directly to the airport and onto the jet. If he's injured, try to find a doctor to travel with him. I'll wait for Willie's call from the warehouse. If it's a go, I'll let you know by text, and you can meet up at the jet."

Bernie nodded his understanding and agreement. Then Serge added one final detail. "Don't say anything to James until you're in the air from Mexico. Then, check with the pilots when you're a few minutes away from the city at cruising altitude. They'll tell you the new destination, and you can let James know at that stage. He'll probably protest, but disregard any alternative instructions he gives you. He'll be away a few days longer for his own good."

On that note, Natalia's screen went dark.

Twenty-Five

From his bed, James heard only a large swoosh followed by a boom that shook the floor of his room, then four pops, each of them sounding like corks from a champagne bottle shooting upward and hitting the ceiling.

He jolted in the bed, straining to see the doorway and what might be happening.

Before he was fully seated upright on the bed, a massive impact hit the door to his bedroom, shattering the door open, and leaving it dangling from a single lower hinge. A black face peeked around the corner with a device that resembled a sledge hammer in one hand, and pointing a semi-automatic rifle at James's face with the other. "Can you walk?" the man asked.

Stunned, James tried to nod. He pointed toward the metal clamp on his feet, exposing the handcuffs on his wrists. Another black-faced man appeared. Holding a tool, he stepped around the one with the gun and, with one expert motion, cut through the leather strap that connected the feet clamps. Then, he freed James's hands from the handcuffs with another expert jab of another tool that sprang open the lock.

The one with the tools jammed them into his backpack as the fellow with the gun stepped forward to yank James upward and onto the floor in one fluid motion. One guy dragged James by his good arm, with the other pushing him from the rear as he tried to find his balance. They were in the hallway before James had a chance to speak.

"Don't say anything, James," the guy from behind him whispered clearly into his ear. "Serge sent us. Just follow us.

We'll have you safe in just a few minutes."

At the doorway, the man leading James veered abruptly to the right and dashed toward an open wall just a few feet farther ahead, where there was an opening to the outside of the building. Soon, they were all dashing down a metal staircase, one fellow semi-dragging James and the other providing some balance from the rear.

On the next floor, the leader suddenly headed inside the building again and down the long corridor. Halfway along, another man was waiting outside the open doors of an elevator he had commandeered with one of the buttons on the wall. They dragged James inside, and the others joined as the door closed. The movement jolted James's mental alertness up a notch.

"Where's Murray? My colleague, Murray," he stammered, guilty he hadn't thought about him earlier.

The leader raised a finger to his lips, requesting silence, then whispered, "He's in another location. A team is there now, getting him out."

Within seconds, the elevator stopped in the basement, where a large SUV parked a few feet from the elevator door, three of its doors opened wide, waiting for them. Quickly and smoothly, the men shoved James into the middle of the rear seat.

The driver accelerated before the doors were completely closed and climbed a short driveway up to the street. It was still dark, but multiple headlamps were evident on the thoroughfare, and a lone walker took little note of their passing.

As they headed toward the intersection, James asked again, "Where are they holding Murray? Are we headed there now? Is he all right?"

"His accommodations weren't as luxurious as yours. We traced his watch to a warehouse nearby. We'll pass it on the way to the airport. We have another team there pulling him out now. I expect to get a report from them any minute."

"Who are the guys who grabbed us? Who are you, for that matter?"

"We're all Multima security employees. We report to Serge. Here's a card with my details. We don't know who was holding you or why. We had no time for conversation or interrogation. Our job was just to get you out of there and to the airport. We'll deliver you to the corporate jet you used to travel here. You'll have a different crew, though. We're still trying to track down the other pilots."

It took a few minutes to fully process these comments. The pilots from the flight that had brought them to Mexico City were missing. Had they been captured and spirited away somewhere by the same gang that seized him and Murray? Might the pilots have been involved in some other way?

Their SUV weaved through the increasing traffic congestion as they approached the airport, and James tried to make sense of it all.

About fifteen minutes after they'd left the apartment building, a phone from the front seat beeped a text message alert. The leader looked down. From his position in the middle of the rear seat, James could see the image of the guy in front through the driver's mirror. He noticed that the leader had drawn a big breath before reaching for his phone.

"Are you at the airport now?" he barked. "We're about fifteen minutes away, maybe less. Get loaded. Have the pilots get departure clearance and be ready to leave the moment we arrive. Stay on the lookout in all directions until we get there."

The leader in the front seat shifted toward the center of the vehicle, turned his head, and looked back directly into James's eyes. He drew another deep breath before he spoke. "There was gunfire at the warehouse. Murray was hit multiple times. He died on the way to the airport. They'll load his corpse onto the aircraft. I'm sorry about your colleague. There was nothing my team could do."

James drew a long breath. His broken wrist ached. He was hungry and thirsty. But he was alive. The shock of the news caused him to tremble slightly. He became cold and numb and stiffened his back to control a tempest of conflicting emotions.

At the airport, the driver stopped at the entrance for private aircraft and showed an identification card. There was no conversation while the guard bent to survey each of the occupants before waving the driver through.

The jet was only a few hundred feet from the entrance, with guards positioned on all four corners. Murray's body was out of sight, probably already loaded into the small cargo area at the bottom of the aircraft.

The instant their SUV stopped beside the staircase to the jet, all its doors opened, and the security team spilled onto the tarmac. Again, the leader grabbed James's good wrist and dragged him toward the plane, urging him to step up as quickly as possible.

Inside, James worked his way to a seat with a window view and buckled himself in as the engines roared. By the time James had completed that simple process, the leader had locked the door, and the plane was moving away from the parking tarmac even before the guy had found a seat. He opened the door to the pilot's compartment up front, leaned in, and said something before working his way back to the seat next to James.

More questions flooded James's mind: Why did the members of both security teams stay behind on the ground except for the leader? Was Murray's body really on the jet? Why were they all in such a rush to leave the airport? Where were they headed now? Even if he had the chance to ask those questions, he wouldn't have been heard over the roar of the engine as it prepared for departure.

He leaned back in the seat, drew long, deep breaths, and tried to put it all together. Seated beside James, the leader of the security team closed his eyes as they roared down the runway for takeoff and kept them shut even after they'd climbed well into the sky. The fellow kept them closed for several minutes until there was a loud ring, and a flashing light illuminated above the cockpit doorway, a signal requesting that someone visit the cockpit for information.

James started to unbuckle his belt, but the leader suddenly opened his eyes and grabbed his wrist—the injured one.

"I'll handle it," he insisted as he detached his seatbelt and rose from his seat.

He stepped completely inside the cockpit and closed the door behind him. It was a couple minutes before he came out again and returned to his seat, watching James every step of the way. Once seated, he broke the news.

"The pilots have been instructed to deliver us to a small airfield in Quepos, Costa Rica. Serge has arranged accommodations for both of us in a nearby apartment complex for the next few days."

"I need to talk to Suzanne immediately," James insisted. "Let me use your phone."

The leader shook his head slowly and looked James directly in the eye again. "I'm sorry. That's not possible. We left your disabled phone behind in the apartment so they couldn't track us with it. I left my phone with the rest of the crew for the same reason. Only the pilots have communication with the air traffic control folks until we're on the ground in Costa Rica. We can call Suzanne or Serge then, if we can find a secure line."

James started to protest, but he realized the futility of it.

The leader nodded appreciatively, then added a few

tidbits of information. "We don't know who is responsible for all this, but Serge is worried that you're the victim of a coordinated attack against Multima that's taking place in multiple locations around the world. We've had several truck accidents in Europe from deliberate sabotage, and attempts to sabotage trucks in America were discovered the same day they kidnapped you. We have our hands full right now."

The leader paused and shook his head in either disgust or exasperation. It was hard to determine which. "I'm Bernie Perez, by the way," he said when he spoke again. He reached out to shake hands in a formal introduction. His grip was solid and reassuring. His eyes portrayed a degree of sympathy. "I realize this is all too much to process with what you've been through over the past few days, but things will get better. I promise."

"They can't get much worse." James smiled to break the tension.

"Suzanne and Serge want you to stay in Costa Rica for at least a week and probably longer. They want to identify and stabilize the risks before you try to return to everyday life. This jet will drop us off at the airport there, then take off again immediately. It will return to Canada and pick up a new crew to assist me in keeping you out of harm's way. Serge rented the entire complex where we'll stay, and we'll use a team of six, including me, to guard it.

"Now, they realize it's only three days to Christmas, and they don't want you and your lady separated over the holidays. When we arrive in Quepos, we'll arrange for a secure phone. You can call her to let her know you can't divulge where she's going, but you'll have a jet pick her up and bring her to you. I know you'll be very careful to keep our location secret when you speak. She'll just have to trust you." Things seemed to have become increasingly odd, maybe even weird. For the moment, James just nodded.

Twenty-Six

Paris, France, Friday December 22, 2023

It was evening in Paris when Serge told Suzanne that James was safe. But when he interrupted her discussion with Gaston Dupont, summoning her with his index finger, she sensed something was wrong. It was his way of letting her know he needed to speak with her privately.

Her president of European operations also caught the signal, and he rose from his chair without a second's hesitation. He offered a sheepish smile. "I need to take a quick comfort break. You two go ahead with whatever you need to discuss. I'll be back in a few moments."

She gave him a grateful nod and waited for Serge to move closer. When Gaston had closed the door behind him, she asked, "Is everything okay?"

"James is well and in the air on the corporate jet. We should be able to speak with him directly in an hour or two. The pilot wants to get clear of Mexico City, and my guy, Bernie, wants to run a test on the secure devices to be sure they're operating as planned."

"Murray Powell is all right, too?" Suzanne detected the quick downward shift of Serge's eyes as she posed the question, and she braced herself.

He shook his head slowly as if seeking the right words to convey his message. He first looked downward, then shook his head slowly, as if in disbelief, before he spoke.

"No. Murray didn't make it. I'll spare you all the gory details, but the criminals holding him riddled him with bullets. As soon as my people broke through the doorway, they heard a rapid succession of shots, probably from a semi-automatic weapon. Before they could aim at the perpetrators, Murray had slumped to the ground, bleeding profusely. My guys took out the three men guarding him in about two minutes, but Murray had stopped breathing by the time they got to him, and he was beyond resuscitation."

Suzanne wiped away an unexpected tear from her right eye and drew a deep breath. "Did you get someone from Chicago to visit his family? He lived alone, right?"

He nodded. "I called Hoffman Estates when we first heard the news. I spoke with one of my security people there before I came in here. She checked the human resources records and identified a family contact. A sister lives about fifteen minutes away from Murray's mother's home in downtown Chicago, in a seniors residence. My gal will break the news to her and be sure she has all the necessary support for the next few days."

"Good. Give your gal's contact details to Eileen. I'll ask her to keep in touch and arrange a call from me as soon as she thinks it appropriate." Her voice broke slightly. "What terrible news to get days before Christmas!"

When Gaston returned to his office, they broke the news about both victims. Of course, he was shocked and alarmed. Company presidents didn't usually receive that kind of news about colleagues. Most would never have to deal with such a tragedy over their entire careers. It was clear he didn't know what to say or do next.

Suzanne took the lead. "Serge, you have your hands full. I'll let you get back to managing the crisis from a security perspective. I'll take care of employee communication. Gaston, let's get back to our discussion on European operations. We still have a business to run."

Sales in Europe had taken a hit the previous day in the areas serviced by the trucks involved in the accidents. Because European stores are generally smaller in floor area and display spaces than American supermarkets, Multima shipped products from central warehouses to individual stores almost daily.

Whenever an accident occurred, like the ones that week, the disruption was severe. Not only was there the cleanup and disposal of the goods damaged by the collision, but buyers also needed to accelerate warehouse shipments to fill the urgent gaps.

They would need at least a week to get store operations back to normal. With Christmas only a few days away, Multima was poised to lose significant sales and profits during the critical holiday season, while customers bought heavily elsewhere for their holiday festivities.

Suzanne participated actively in the discussion with the management teams responsible for buying, warehousing, and shipping goods to the stores. It occurred to her more than once that speaking French was an asset most North American leaders didn't have, and she was determined to use that advantage to minimize any inconveniences to Multima's customers, relieve stress on its employees at all levels, and make the best of a deplorable circumstance. As a result, meetings hummed with her challenges, encouragement, and appreciation in equal measure.

For technical reasons, Serge's guy, Bernie, wasn't able to connect with Suzanne in the Paris office for a few hours after they were in the air. In fact, they had already entered the airspace controlled by Costa Rica when Serge interrupted her meeting with the operations team to take the call.

"James, are you all right?"

"It looks like I have a broken wrist, but nothing serious. Unlike Murray Powell." He used a subdued tone. "You heard the news about him, I assume."

Their reception was so clear she felt the pain in his voice as he spoke.

"Yes, I heard. I'm shocked and feel so bad for his mother and other surviving members of his family. Serge's team is notifying his next of kin, and we'll provide support for them.

"How about you? Were you able to speak with Marie?" Marie Bruning was the most recent love in James's life. Since the premature death of his wife a few years earlier, there had been hardly any women in his life and this one seemed important to him.

"Yeah, Bernie got us connected just before we called you. She's relieved and has agreed to come down to Costa Rica for a few days. But I'll tell you frankly, Suzanne, I'm not happy that Serge has shoved me off the playing field into a Caribbean hideaway. I assume it's with your approval—what's up?"

James had long been a trusted confidant. Suzanne couldn't think of a thing she wouldn't share with him, knowing he'd use the information discreetly, wisely, and with complete confidence. The problem? There just wasn't much concrete to share.

"I assume Bernie briefed you on the truck collisions across Europe yesterday. There were also accidents in Asia, and we thwarted attempts to sabotage more trucks in the U.S. and Canada. Frankly, we've got chaos in Supermarkets' business around the world, and Serge believes these incidents are all related and instigated by the same folks. He believes they planned to attack us further by kidnapping you, perhaps for ransom, perhaps for something else. I agree with Serge: we need to keep you out of their reach until we get a better grip on who we're dealing with."

James didn't reply immediately, apparently still processing the data. When he spoke, his voice seemed stronger, perhaps even combative, although it was clear he'd chosen his words politely. "Fair enough, Suzanne. I get it and won't cause you unnecessary grief. But if I'm to run Financial Services, I can't do it from Costa Rica. The next few days aren't crucial. We can treat it like I'm on vacation, and the organization will hum along smoothly—I'm confident of that. But if Serge still doesn't have a solution by the New Year, I want the jet to take Marie and me on a flight to Chicago."

"I hear you, James, and we'll do what we're able to do. Serge plans to head back to Vietnam in a few hours to learn as much as he can. He's still getting signals that our adversary is somewhere in Asia, probably Japan, but he needs more time. I must ask for your patience and understanding in the meantime. He's also asked Bernie to get you fully secured in Quepos in every respect, including communication. You should be able to work with your people in Chicago as if you were right next door after tomorrow."

She returned to the European operations meetings until well past sunset. She glanced at her watch; the hour neared nine. She tracked down Serge to join her for dinner at the hotel in the heart of Paris, arranged by Eileen. Their assigned driver had them at the luxurious Hôtel San Régis's entrance within minutes.

"Let's order dinner and a bottle of wine," Suzanne suggested as she closed the door to their suite. She turned up the wattage of her smile and teased him invitingly with the tip of her tongue.

Twenty-Seven

Paris, France, Friday December 22, 2023

The way she controlled her body language always amazed Serge. Suzanne seemed able to adapt to any situation instantly and appropriately.

Back in his days with the Canadian Mounties, he'd learned the importance of body language: Crossing the arms at an appropriate moment to shut down discussion. Creasing the forehead to learn more. Smiling to put someone at ease. All these body language traits were ingrained in new officers' mindsets, and senior leaders always pressed their subordinates to master these skills to defuse situations or calm tempers during interactions.

But Suzanne performed at a level he'd never witnessed before. Of course, in the boardroom, she did all the right things. Her posture was always erect, her shoulders back, her confidence displayed. Seated or standing, she used her sparkling blue eyes to penetrate or relax observers as the situation demanded, and she'd learned to use them to flash displeasure without intimidation.

When she'd suggested dinner and wine, the way she'd shown just the tiny tip of her tongue as she swept her hair back from her eyes left no doubt that the meal would be a prelude to something else. Yet she managed to convey that message so subtly that it was impossible to blame her for thinking about sex so soon after dealing with issues related to James's capture and Murray's murder.

That was another fundamental aspect of her character he admired: her ability to compartmentalize the multitude of issues she dealt with during an average day. Like a librarian methodically puts books on precisely the right shelves in the right sections, Suzanne adapted her outlook, her focus, and her body language to deal with each new circumstance.

And her subtle tease had precisely the effect he was sure she'd intended. He had entered the hotel still consumed with Murray's death, second-guessing what he and his team might have done differently to achieve a better outcome. His mood wasn't morose—that would be too dramatic—but he had no doubt his own body language appeared more sullen than desired.

With Suzanne's tiny shift in demeanor, he instantly recalled that it had been over a month since they'd last seen each other in Montreal, and his body reminded him that a man has needs. Those needs grew as he processed how masterfully she shifted their focus while showing no disrespect to Murray's memory or callowness toward James's current plight in Latin America.

By the time she'd removed her suit jacket and hung it up in the closet, he was ready to leave those challenges behind and rekindle his love for her. He stepped silently behind her and wrapped his arms gently around her waist. With his nose, he swept back enough of her long hair to clear a spot on her neck behind her right ear. He kissed her there as gently as he could manage, then delivered another kiss with a bit more pressure. The third time, rather than finishing the kiss, he explored her neck with his tongue for a few seconds before twirling her around to face him. She leaned toward him, apparently seeking the same intimacy he suddenly craved.

Their lips parted as their mouths made contact, and he tugged her as tightly to him as he dared. Their embrace should last forever, but squeezing her too tightly might inhibit her breathing and perhaps cause her to push him away involuntarily. They explored each other with their tongues. Serge withdrew his slightly before re-entering her mouth suggestively. He repeated the motion, each time with greater passion and urgency.

When they suddenly stopped long enough to gasp for air, Suzanne shrugged off their embrace, reached out to remove his jacket, and let it fall aimlessly to the carpeted floor. She raised her head and moved to his mouth, her tongue already teasing him, unfastened the top three buttons of his shirt, and tickled his chest with a gentle finger as he probed deeper into her mouth.

Both breathed more deeply and quickly. They'd always expressed their love for each other on both emotional and physical levels, and that evening in Paris, each displayed an urgent passion they'd been unable to satisfy for over a month.

Almost without realizing it, they had shed all their clothing and thrown back both the decorative bed cover and one of the brilliant white sheets. With a single motion, Serge wrapped her in his arms, lifted her gently onto the bed, and planted his own body as close to her as possible.

They explored each other's bodies, from foreheads to toes, with their tongues and fingers. Alternatively, they wrapped themselves closely together, lying on their sides, with him penetrating her or with her on top, welcoming him inside her, spread thighs wrapped around his aroused body.

He had no idea how long they made love. When they finished, their sexual appetites temporarily satisfied, his stomach growled—a reminder that they'd forgotten the meal and wine.

Suzanne giggled. "We'd better place that order for some food before you run out of energy!"

They laughed and slowly worked their way from the bed to the bathroom to properly clean up from their sexual adventure.

Suzanne glanced at her watch before saying, "Wow—it's after midnight; I hope the hotel kitchen is still open."

It wasn't. The chef had left at eleven, the voice informed Serge, but there was a concierge on duty, and he might be able to help. Within a couple minutes, the concierge briefly described three nearby restaurants still open. Serge chose the Italian one, and the concierge offered to run down the street and bring their orders to their suite. While they waited, Suzanne shifted personas, bringing them back to reality.

"Did I perform well enough to tempt you not to leave in the morning?" she asked as she smiled, tilting her head enough to portray innocence, although she knew damn well how magically she had performed. Her tone implied that she had already guessed the answer.

"You know how magnificently you performed. There's nothing in this world I'd like more than to stay here with you, but I don't think it's going to happen unless you make it a direct order. I need to go back to Japan. The gang in Ho Chi Minh City picked up a new lead."

He described the information Constance Hope had discovered in her cyber visits to the dark net and why he felt compelled to leave for Japan within the next few hours. It took several minutes as she listened, spellbound, nodding her understanding with each new bit of information he shared with her. He summed up his perceptions that there were no alternatives only moments before he expected their suite doorbell to ring.

"Everything we glean from those intercepted messages suggests that major players in The Organization will be meeting in the small Japanese city of Hamamatsu, while the Western world celebrates the Christmas holidays. We're sure they have the goal of reaching a consensus on how they will attack Multima Corporation next and try to overpower it. We can't rely on either the Japanese authorities or Interpol to subvert their plans. I'm getting together a team of my best resources. Tomorrow morning, I'll fly to

Montreal to meet with both Canadian and American specialists. We'll all arrive in Japan on the morning of Christmas Eve."

Once the concierge had rung the bell to their suite, handed over a piping hot pizza, and pocketed the fifty Euro tip Serge had pressed into his palm, they enjoyed their meal.

Neither had an appetite for the wine Suzanne had suggested earlier. Their stomachs sated, they returned to the bedroom, intent on satisfying their other appetite before their unwanted farewell the next morning.

Twenty-Eight

Atlanta, Georgia, Saturday December 23, 2023

The beep of an alert awakened Natalia from a deep and much-needed sleep. She twisted her head and shoulders toward the nightstand, where she'd laid her phone before turning out the lights, and reached out, fumbling for either the device or the lamp switch, whichever she came upon first.

Archie Begat. At three-thirty in the morning. Why on Earth would a smart guy like Archie disturb her sleep at that ungodly hour? He knew there was a twelve-hour difference, so it must be important.

Yanking down the blanket, the sheets, and the nightgown that had crept up around her hips as she tossed and turned during the night, she swung around, turned on the light, and touched the screen of her phone.

At first, the message seemed bizarre:

> *Constance is flying to Japan today to meet Serge. Checking out rumor from dark net that eel monopoly in Hamamatsu is behind latest Multima attacks in Asia and Europe. Something about a meeting of powerhouses in crime there on Christmas Day. She wouldn't share other details.—A*

Natalia bolted upright and tried to remember how she'd heard about Hamamatsu before and why it had come to her attention. She drew a blank, so she did what everyone else did when they wanted instant information and googled the name. But rather than ask what the place was known for, she asked which companies originated there.

Names like Suzuki, Yamaha, Kawai, Roland, and Hamamatsu Photonics all popped up, clarifying that the city was famous for cars, motorcycles, musical instruments, marine products, and technology. A headline lower on the page pointed out that Hamamatsu was once known as the city of music.

She got out of bed and headed toward her kitchen for a glass of water. On the way, she mulled over the possibilities. In the US, law enforcement identified motorcycle gangs with links to organized crime, but it was unlikely that large, publicly traded companies like Honda, Suzuki, and Yamaha would be involved with an outfit like The Organization.

Her thirst satisfied, wide awake despite the hour, Natalia plunked herself onto a sofa in the living room instead of trying to go back to sleep again. Armed with her phone, she typed in a series of Google requests and read the replies.

It turned out that the musical instrument companies were also big, broadly owned companies, and the technology company she'd never heard of was a leader in research, development, and production of products that capture, measure, and generate various types of light. She chose another prompt to gain some insight into its financial strength and was impressed: sales were greater than a billion dollars per year. The company was capitalized at over two billion dollars, and its profit the previous year was almost three hundred million.

None of the companies highlighted there sounded like possible conduits for organized crime. Still, she made a note of the technology company for two reasons: While the company might not be involved in crime, perhaps current or former technology whizzes might provide the Yakuza with expertise for one of its operations in Japan. Further, when she had more time, it might be worth exploring as an investment opportunity with the nice bonus she expected to earn in a few months.

She shifted her prompts to eels. Archie's message implied there was some connection between the Japanese eel industry and the Yakuza. Natalia dove down the black hole of the internet to explore the world of eels. Although she'd eaten and enjoyed the Japanese dish called *unadon*, she'd forgotten that eels were its primary ingredient.

She also learned that every year, the eel industry harvested over 130,000 tons of the delicacy, generating over four billion dollars in revenue, with seventy percent of it consumed in Japan. Several articles mentioned problems with overfishing, declining stocks, and rising prices.

All these factors made the Yakuza's involvement more likely there than with any involvement in the mainstream manufacturing companies she'd explored earlier. Harvesting eels involved hundreds of small companies and contractors, some probably ripe for exploitation by organized crime. And there was a connection between Hamamatsu and a neighboring town called Isshiki. Both were considered among the most vital areas in Japan for the eel industry.

So, she could reasonably assume Serge would meet up with her former staffer, Constance, in Tokyo, and they'd probably travel together to Hamamatsu. Still, since it was Natalia who'd served up her colleague to Serge for the Asia assignment, she felt some responsibility for the girl's safety.

She sent off a secure text to Archie, inquiring about the safety arrangements in place for her travel.

Within seconds, he replied:

> *I asked the same. She told me Serge left it up to her to decide if she wanted a guard to travel with her, but she wasn't to leave Haneda Airport until he arrived, about three hours after her. He'd have a large contingent with him for their expedition.*

Constance thought she'd be fine for three hours in the airport.—A

It sounded all right. Still, it might depend on where Constance waited at the airport. In the main passenger terminal, there would probably be people around at all hours of the day. In the private terminal, there would likely only be a skeleton staff of one or two, without a lot of cameras. Dangerous people might easily dispose of the staff and turn off those cameras.

She sent another message to Archie, asking him to caution Constance about staying in the main terminals. Since she really shouldn't communicate directly with her former staff, she also cautioned Archie not to use her name in his warning.

It was now close to her habitual waking time, so after a shower, getting dressed, and breakfast rituals, she headed out to Supermarkets' downtown headquarters. It was a short walk from the luxurious Airbnb suite Eileen had organized for her temporary accommodations in Atlanta. However, Natalia had no intention of living in the downtown area for the long term. It didn't fit well with her lifestyle and was considered dangerous by some.

Before she stepped out of her temporary home's lobby door, she looked carefully in both directions, trying to observe as many details as possible in her field of vision. All seemed quiet.

A bus approached from a distance, and half a dozen cars and taxis passed. One other pedestrian, a woman, walked in the opposite direction.

Only a few hundred yards separated her building from her division's headquarters, and she'd survived downtown Chicago, after all. She stepped outside, slipping her bare hands into her coat pockets as the wind was stronger than expected and the outside temperature colder.

With an erect posture, long strides, and constant focus on her surroundings, she crossed the street on the green light signal. There were no cars to either slow or stop her. Still, she was the only pedestrian in the area. Far on the horizon, probably a block or more away, she detected the outline of someone walking in her direction on the opposite sidewalk.

She was surprised at the tension she felt and took a deep breath to calm her nerves. It helped, but she quickened her pace slightly as the front doors of Multima Supermarkets' headquarters lobby came into view. She took another quick look over her shoulder, and all was clear behind.

Natalia hopped up the cement steps from the sidewalk to the door of the office tower. As she took her second step, she felt something cut into her ear and also heard something whizzing past. She pulled her right hand out of her jacket pocket and clutched her ear. Her knees collapsed, and she fell awkwardly to the ground before she could get her left hand out of the other pocket. Her head banged hard against the cement surface, and she cried out in pain.

The last thing she saw was the form of a large person in a beige trench coat reaching down toward her.

Twenty-Nine

Quepos, Costa Rica, Saturday December 23, 2023

Multima's security team delivered Marie to the complex where they were protecting James. He had to spend several long minutes calming her. She'd broken into desperate tears after running from the parked rental car to where he stood inside the large metal gate that had been locked for his protection. Bernie opened it when she approached, but only long enough for her to dash through and collapse into James's outstretched arms.

She clutched his shoulders tightly as she buried her head in his chest. It was impossible to even welcome her with a kiss. Her shoulders heaved with her tearful gasps, and he felt the warm flow of those tears trickle onto his chest, bare where he'd left the top three buttons undone to enjoy the tropical air.

When she'd calmed, she stood suddenly on the tips of her toes and smothered him with kisses, giving him the impression she'd just discovered some long-lost treasure. It made him smile, then laugh a little, uncomfortable with her odd display of emotion. It was enough to prompt Marie to start laughing, too. With his uninjured hand, James wiped away the tears dripping from her face, then planted another long, resolute kiss on her lips.

When they broke apart again, Marie noticed the cast on his wrist. She gasped. "What happened?" Her damp red eyes appeared ready to let go of yet another torrent of tears.

"A fracture. Nothing major. A doctor here x-rayed it and found two bones in my wrist broken and displaced. He cleaned them up and put on this clumsy cast. I'll need to keep it for a few weeks, then I'll manage with a tensor bandage or something like that."

"They told me a gang held you captive for almost two days. What the hell is going on?"

James smirked at the question—not because it was funny. Rather, it was because he hadn't often heard Marie use such strong language in the short time they'd been together. She'd been an enthusiastic Evangelical Christian before they'd met and started living together "in sin," as she so aptly described their relationship. Stronger language was another sign of her "backsliding" behavior, she often said.

"We're not sure. Someone or some organization is attacking the Multima Corporation. In addition to temporarily kidnapping me, they killed a colleague from Chicago and are suspected of causing Multima transport truck crashes in both Europe and Asia. Do you remember meeting Serge Boisvert? Suzanne's guy in charge of the firm's security? Well, he wants us to stay here for awhile. I told him we'd stay until the New Year, so let's enjoy our little holiday."

Bernie had respectfully disappeared while they reacquainted, and James calmed Marie from her distress. Now, the security specialist reappeared with a backpack on his shoulder and a cap on his head.

"I must dash away now. Serge called me back to Montreal, and we have only a few minutes' cushion in our flying time there." He pointed to the man standing beside him, the one who had arrived with two other security guys in the car behind Marie. "This is Jacques Legault. He'll oversee your security. I've asked him to give you a full briefing with the other two fellows so everyone is on the same page and keeping you safe."

He shifted his eyes from James as he spoke and held them on Marie as he finished. Then, he gave them each a firm handshake as he stepped backward. With a sheepish grin he gave a parting wave that almost resembled a casual salute. Within seconds, he had disappeared out the gate held open by one of his security colleagues, and entered the waiting car.

"Shall we all take chairs around the poolside and review the protocols Serge instructed us to follow?" Jacques asked before the car had left its parking spot.

He didn't take much time to review the basic rules. None of them—neither James nor Marie nor the other guards—would leave the compound for any reason, and the gates would be locked all day and night. Jacques would order anything they needed—food, refreshments, clothing, suntan lotion—anything else they might want, and a taxi would deliver it. James and Marie had to remain inside from the time of the order until the deliveries were finished so the drivers couldn't identify them.

Jacques didn't, however, share one rather vital bit of information: the electronic code for that locked gate to the compound.

Thirty

The alarm on her phone rang at five that morning, before each had prepared for their coming day, using the luxurious separate bathrooms their suite included. Suzanne finished first and ordered breakfast to their room. It arrived just as Serge finished not only dressing but packing up for his departure that morning.

He had suggested she return to Montreal with him and stay at their home in the Laurentian Mountains for Christmas while he flew on to Japan. She considered that idea for a few moments, partially buying into his argument that he had more resources in the Montreal area than in Paris and could better assure her safety. After a reasonable amount of consideration, she turned him down gently.

"I know you've got my best interests at heart, and I'd love to have a few more hours with you during the flight, but we must work together to resolve these issues. I feel as if the very existence of Multima is at stake here. Kidnappings, truck crashes, and the like aren't just bad publicity—we'll lose customers this weekend in both Europe and North America. Some people will stay away from our stores in the future because they're angry with the inconveniences our dilemma has caused them. Others might fear that the violence will extend into the stores where they shop. It's Christmas tomorrow. The celebrations start today in Europe and last for at least a couple days. I'll stay here and make certain there's no holiday at Interpol."

With a resigned smile and his typical bear hug plus a peck on her cheek, Serge set off for Orly Airport. Before she guessed that his elevator had reached the ground floor,

Suzanne had already dialed the number for Edouard Deschamps.

The Interpol leader answered on the second ring.

"I'm sorry," he started the conversation, his tone subdued. "My people have only been able to interview three or four witnesses. We can appreciate that families are shaken at this stage and refuse to meet, so it may be a number of days before we get interviews scheduled. I checked with each field office this morning, and there are no new developments. The labs are also closing early today for Christmas Eve, and they won't open again until Tuesday. Even then, there'll be only a skeleton staff because a lot of people have booked off for the holidays."

"I understand, Edouard. It's a difficult time of the year. We have the same challenges with staffing in our business operations around the world. But I'm calling to see if you'd like to join me for the day. Gaston and I are planning visits to both injured drivers. They'll be brief courtesy visits, but you're welcome to join us and personally invite the drivers to meet with your people. If you can have resources on standby, perhaps we can accelerate things by a few days."

She waited while he mulled over the suggestion. Of course, her idea impacted Edouard more than his colleagues. They might be called away from whatever they had planned for that day for an hour or two, but he would lose the entire day and maybe his evening.

It took longer than expected for him to respond, so she prepared for the worst.

"I can rearrange my plans for the day, even with the short notice." No doubt he added that qualifier to signal his intentions. "I can join you, meet the drivers with you, and ask for their cooperation. If they are agreeable, the best I can promise you is a call to the local office to see how quickly they can get someone to that driver's bedside for an in-depth interview."

The response was probably the best she could expect, so she sealed the deal. "Great. I truly appreciate your support in moving this investigation along as quickly as possible under difficult circumstances. Can you meet us at Orly Airport at 9:00 this morning?"

The instant he agreed, Suzanne concluded the call and used the speed dial feature on her phone to connect with Gaston. He was eating breakfast at home with his family, but he agreed with Suzanne's proposal to visit the two surviving drivers in Italy and the UK.

"I'll ask my assistant to connect again with both families—she's already spoken with them, and I have no doubt they'll welcome your visit. I'm not entirely sure about welcoming Interpol, so I won't mention that aspect to my assistant. Both drivers are still in hospitals, but they are supposed to be alert and healing. We'll play it by ear and find a way to introduce Edouard while we're there. We'll use your jet?"

"Yes," she replied. "We'll only need your assistant to coordinate with the families. Edouard will meet us at Orly at nine, so let's plan to meet with the driver in Italy at noon, and then with the UK driver about six o'clock in the evening. That should allow us enough time. As soon as we finish, I'll ask my security team to book the ground travel in both locations. If your assistant can deliver some cold food to the aircraft before we leave, that might be helpful."

They all met at Orly Airport on the outskirts of Paris just before nine. The usual pilots for the corporate jet met them at the aircraft, one at the bottom of the steps, the other when they stepped inside the cabin. The five passengers spread out in the comfortable area that resembled a luxurious office space.

Suzanne took her usual seat in the middle of the aircraft. From there, she could swivel in either direction for discussions with her traveling companions. She pointed for

Gaston and Edouard to take the seats on either side of her, but slightly closer to the rear. Those seats were equally comfortable, and both also swiveled so they could form a semicircle for discussion when the jet became airborne. The security guy and gal Serge had left behind to protect her took their usual seats in the rear, where they could survey the entire passenger compartment.

By 9:30 that morning, they were in the air. Suzanne showed her guests how the swivel chairs operated, and they chatted for the entire ninety-minute flight to Linate Airport in Milano, Italy. She used the time to better understand how Interpol organized itself in Europe, and how the investigators communicated with one another to share the optimum amount of information as quickly as possible. Of course, she also learned that they were far from solving the mystery.

A limousine awaited their arrival at the private jet section of the airport and, within moments, was en route to Policlinico di Milano, one of its largest hospitals located in the heart of the bustling city. Google Maps suggested they'd arrive at the hospital more than one hour ahead of the agreed-upon noon hour.

When Suzanne wondered if they should call ahead to modify their appointment time, Gaston held up a hand of caution.

"It might take longer than you expect." He laughed. "I've never made it from the airport to our office here in less than an hour, and it's just a few minutes away from the hospital."

Sure enough, they arrived only minutes ahead of the scheduled time. Traffic was chaotic, with long delays at intersections. Horns blasted almost continually, and cars seemed to switch lanes almost erratically, each jockeying to gain some advantage. It might have been comedic if their mission were less critical.

At precisely the agreed time, after complying with all the hospital requirements for visitors and getting special permission for their armed security guards to wait outside the room, they entered the area where the injured driver lay in bed. Suzanne led the parade.

Enzo Bianchi sat upright in his bed behind a row of refreshments and a paper tray holding pills of various colors. His head was bandaged with white strips that stopped just above his eye. His head had collided with the branch of a tree that had entered his compartment during the collision. His left arm was in a sling, and his chin showed some abrasions covered in a foul-colored ointment.

He smiled as he greeted Suzanne with a wave and a few words in Italian. The smile revealed a couple missing teeth, probably victims of the impact during the collision.

A woman who appeared to be about the same middle age as Enzo stood up from a chair and stepped forward. "I'm his wife, Angelina. I speak a little English," she said. "Enzo says he's honored to meet you."

Suzanne moved close to the bedside and reached out to touch Enzo's uninjured hand as it rested on the tray in front of him. "It's my privilege to meet both of you. I'm so sorry about your misfortune, Enzo, and want to assure you that Multima will do whatever it can to make your recovery as easy as possible. Of course, we'll pay all the expenses you incur to recover from your mishap, and you should feel welcome to take as much time as you need."

Angelina's shoulders appeared to relax as she took in the news and translated it for her husband. His eyes welled up before he smiled again and offered a heartfelt thank you, bending his head toward Suzanne and holding it there for several seconds.

Gaston stepped forward to offer his best wishes and chatted with Enzo in Italian for a few minutes. Suzanne stood off to the side and waited, observing the interaction and the wife's tense neck and shoulders. After a brief chat, Gaston pointed toward Edouard and explained who he was and why he was there that day.

Enzo displayed no visible reaction to the explanation, but his wife blanched, and her eyes darted from Gaston to Edouard and then to Suzanne as she processed Gaston's request.

Within seconds, in an almost angry tone, she said in English, "No. He is injured. His head is injured. His brain might be damaged. No. No interviews today."

Suzanne felt the weight of the woman's desperation as she glared towards her. She took a moment to choose her words carefully and strived for a soft, reasonable tone to deliver a reply. She looked at Angelina first, then moved her eyes to Enzo.

"We understand. If Enzo isn't comfortable speaking with one of Edouard's people today, it can wait for another time. We're here to show our appreciation for the sacrifice he made for the company, not to add to his burden. But the people who did this are still out there. They killed five of Enzo's colleagues and tried to sabotage trucks and drivers in America, too. The sooner Interpol finds out who is attacking Multima, the safer it will be for our colleagues and our customers."

Enzo didn't wait for a translation. He raised his good hand toward his wife and spoke to her softly but firmly in Italian. When he finished, Gaston said a thank you and squeezed his arm in appreciation. Edouard stepped forward and started conversing with Enzo, also in Italian, his tone appreciative and calm. Suzanne stepped away from the bedside and observed their interaction.

Perhaps five minutes later, Gaston stepped back beside her and whispered, "Your appeal worked. He's already shared a detail or two with Edouard and agreed to an interview of no more than thirty minutes at three o'clock this afternoon."

Two hours later, they were airborne again and on their way toward Manchester in the United Kingdom. It was still Christmas Eve, but they'd made some progress. Suzanne listened as Edouard summarized their visit and his findings to a colleague, speaking French. When he finished, he looked directly into Suzanne's eyes. "Thank you. Now, we just need you to perform your magic again with your British truck driver."

Thirty-One

Haneda Airport, Japan, Saturday December 23, 2023

Serge couldn't understand why his people on the ground in Atlanta couldn't connect with him in the air, but they delivered the shocking news about Natalia within minutes of his arrival inside the private jet section of Haneda Airport on the outskirts of Tokyo.

Floyd Demerais, the guy Serge had left behind to monitor Natalia, called from inside the lobby of Supermarkets' Atlanta headquarters. While waiting for her to arrive, he'd spotted a flash from a second-floor window across the street, then saw Natalia crumple to the ground steps from the doorway. He raced outside and dragged her in before she regained consciousness.

"She was groggy for a few minutes. We called in a doctor, and he checked her over, cleaned up the ear, and suggested she might get a hearing test, but other than a tiny bandage, you wouldn't know there had been an incident."

Serge was stunned by the news, but he wanted more. "There was only one shot?"

"Yeah. As a former military guy, I'd say this shooting seemed to be a warning of some sort rather than a genuine attempt on her life. I remember some guys in my old brigade used to joke that the hardest shot was the one that scared the shit out of someone with the least possible damage. We found a single bullet embedded in the front brick facing. It came from an AR-15. That rifle can fire six hundred rounds a minute. If they really wanted to harm or kill her, those bullets could release as fast as the guy could squeeze the trigger."

"And you saw nothing from your vantage point?"

"Nothing. I was looking out the window and saw the flash. I checked the window where I'd seen it and along that level of the building. I no longer saw even a shadow. Again, I'm guessing he wanted to make that shot perfect and then got out of there as quickly as possible. I really think we're dealing with a pro on a mission. He accomplished that mission, then left."

"Did we check the places across the street?" Serge wanted to know.

"Yes. I went over there right after a couple other employees came in, and I realized they could keep an eye on Natalia until the doctor arrived. The ground floor of the building is all retail. The stores were all closed at that time of the morning. The second floor is allocated to offices used by professionals: doctors, dentists, accountants—those kinds of people. I tried all the doors, and they were all locked. I reported the incident and asked the Atlanta police to investigate. They also visited every office, asking if the occupants had noticed anything out of the ordinary. They found nothing."

It was perplexing. It looked as if Floyd had covered all the bases but still came up empty. Serge shifted his approach. "Is Suzanne aware of the incident?"

"No. I reported it to your office in Montreal and left it to their discretion to notify you and the boss. I checked back three times throughout the day, but young Lori insisted everything needed to go through you. She said she was having trouble reaching you on the flight as well. I doubt Suzanne is aware."

"Have we been watching Natalia all day?"

"Yes. She hasn't left the building. I have two other guys watching her office on rotation. Her admin assistant hasn't reported any unusual calls, and she's had no visitors. I think she's spending most of her time scrutinizing sales reports as the numbers come in across the country."

Serge dismissed Floyd, thanking him for both his valor and the information he shared. It was important for the guy to know his efforts were appreciated and his judgment respected.

Just as Serge was about to say goodbye, another thought sprang up. "One last thing, Floyd. Let's be sure we drive her back to her rental condo when she leaves the office. I think all three of you fellows need to spend the night there. You figure it out, but one needs to stay with her inside the apartment, and the two others can rotate outside her door in the hallway. Let me know if you see anything suspicious."

Serge turned his attention to Constance Hope, who'd just arrived from the main terminal to join his contingent before they headed out to Hamamatsu. He told her the story and wanted to know if she'd noticed anything unusual on the dark web or heard any news from the rest of the team in Ho Chi Minh City. She hadn't.

"Okay, we'll leave for the Shinkansen station—the high-speed rail line—in about ten minutes. Get with Archie and see if anyone on the team there saw any mention of a shooting related to an ear or someone shot in the ear or a near-miss hitting an ear, anything like that. And get changed—you'll be spending most of the evening at the Hamamatsu rail station, and it's cold out there. The forecast for tonight is just above freezing."

He disregarded her grimace, which was followed by a defiant shrug of her shoulder, as she spun on her heel and left for another part of the empty private aircraft terminal. Since they'd arrived almost half an hour earlier, Serge hadn't noticed either an employee or another jet coming or going.

He pulled the team together and briefed them on the latest news out of Atlanta, then ran through the instructions one last time. There would be other passengers with them on the Shinkansen and probably little privacy. He'd traveled the system several times before and had never seen it less than half-full in every car. Although the Japanese didn't celebrate Christmas, he still suspected the passenger load might be heavier than on a typical Sunday evening.

His team totaled nine members that night, including Constance. He divided them into three different groups and sent them off, five minutes apart, to find taxis at the main terminal for the almost one-hour ride in Tokyo traffic.

Constance returned from wherever she'd changed from her cool Vietnam attire to clothing more appropriate for a Chicago winter. She looked ready for the mission and smiled coyly as she approached.

"I checked the weather report for Japan before I left Ho Chi Minh City. Thought I should bring these along just in case." She gestured to her outerwear with satisfaction, then changed her expression to deadly serious. "More importantly, when I mentioned the 'ear thing' to Archie, he checked with the others and discovered Melissa had indeed noticed a reference on the dark net in Japanese. The translation program produced the phrase 'successful execution with only slight ear damage 07:04 12-23-23.' Melissa assumed it was a translation error until Archie asked her about it."

"Did they trace the routing?" Serge asked.

"Yes. It was a very odd routing for the message: from Atlanta, Georgia, to Palm Beach, Florida, to Vladivostok, Russia, to Hamamatsu, Japan."

"Copy the number and have Archie text it securely to Floyd. Wait for me here." The private aircraft terminal used cameras. Serge had spotted four of them earlier and kept himself in a conclave across from the restrooms to minimize his exposure to them. But there might also be recordings, so he slipped outdoors into the darkening skies and pulled his secure phone from his outdoor vest.

The call connected on the first try.

"Floyd, use our usual source to find a jet to Palm Beach, Florida. I need you there as quickly as possible. Use whatever plane they have available, and you should be there in about three hours. The team in Vietnam will send you a digital address somewhere in Palm Beach, and I want you to track down its specific physical location. Call me as soon as you figure it out."

He disconnected and dashed back inside to collect Constance and Sheila, the only other women on his security team that night. Within minutes, they were in the third taxi headed for the Shinkansen high-speed rail terminal. Hamamatsu—and whatever waited for them there—was still a few hours away.

Thirty-Two

Atlanta, Georgia, Saturday December 23, 2023

Glancing around her still relatively new surroundings, Natalia decided to stretch out the day in that office for as long as possible. Multima Supermarkets' locations on the west coast of the US would close at eleven o'clock that night in deference to Christmas Eve. It would be two in the morning in her current time zone. Normally, they operated around the clock, but Suzanne had started the tradition of observing a Christmas break when she'd led the division a few years earlier.

The holiday didn't mean much to Natalia, but she knew many of their employees still observed it. For some, it was the most important day of the year, so the tradition continued. If everything worked out as planned, she'd spend about twenty-four continuous hours in the office that day, and it would be Christmas before she returned to her apartment.

Of course, she could still go back to the apartment and dial into the company network from there, but earlier that morning the security guy, Floyd, had inadvertently disrupted that possibility.

Initially, Serge had instructed him to stay overnight with her inside the apartment while his two colleagues rotated oversight from her building's corridor. He'd stayed in the spare bedroom the previous night, and it hadn't bothered her. He was a nice enough guy, older than her by a few years, and he handled himself with respect and consideration during all their interactions. But when she had come out of her bedroom that morning, he was already dressed and preparing to leave the apartment.

"I just got a call from Serge. I need to make an urgent trip to Florida. Guillaume will take my place, but you'll still have a guard outside your office today and at the apartment tonight. He won't be able to rotate with anybody, but I'll be sure he gets lots of sleep today so he can manage a few hours on his own."

Thinking back to that new arrangement left her uneasy on two levels. First, whether the shot grazing her ear had been intended to kill her or just warn her, as Floyd had suggested, it was unsettling. It still left her trembling at times, alternatively feeling cold shivers and hot flashes, and constantly losing her train of thought. She'd slept for only a few minutes the entire night. She couldn't recall feeling such fear before. For some reason, she felt more secure inside her new office, high above the ground, with security guards on the ground level and one or two parked right outside her office door.

Second, Guillaume gave her the creeps. She'd seen him around the office before he was assigned to her detail. He was exceptionally tall—well over six feet—and looked down on others with a certain arrogance or sense of superiority. Like many others on Serge's team, he had a beard. But rather than a neatly trimmed version, like most of the other guys, his facial hair was scruffy, at best, and she wondered how often he even washed it. More unsettling, he ogled her every opportunity he got. She could feel him undressing her with his eyes as she strode along a hallway or exchanged greetings with a colleague outside her office. Lots of guys did that, but Guillaume was so obvious that he'd quickly look away whenever she glanced in his direction or made eye contact.

With the combined fear and unease, she settled in for another stressful day, determined to watch the hourly sales results and daily summaries on the large screen monitor on her office wall with a new passion.

Suzanne's call interrupted her train of thought. "I just heard the news from Serge. I feel terrible about everything. Are you all right?"

Natalia could feel the sincerity in her boss's tone. Before he left, Floyd had explained his difficulty connecting with Serge to break the news about the shooting and the decision not to inform Suzanne until Serge was in the loop. At first, Natalia had seethed at the lack of communication, but after some time spent processing it, she'd accepted the corporate reporting reality.

"I'm feeling better. It's unsettling, and I wish we had a better explanation than someone sending me a warning. What were they warning me about? Why has there been no further communication?" She heard a sound closely resembling a sob slip from her throat and left it there for Suzanne to reply.

"I feel bad that you must deal with all this, Natalia, but you're part of the senior Multima team now. We've been subjected to this harassment for a while—that's why Serge is working with the group in Asia. I also feel bad that you had to experience the turmoil alone, and I've already instructed Serge to put new processes in place to ensure this kind of communication gap never occurs again, regardless of technology failures. He'll make it a priority as soon as we have this mess behind us."

It was of little comfort, but there was also little she could do about it, so Natalia shifted the conversation. "Is Serge making any progress in Japan?"

"Not yet. He texted me a few minutes ago, and the team has embarked on its Japan mission. It's night over there, and I don't expect we'll hear much for a few hours—maybe tomorrow our time. Do you need some time to get away from it all?" Always thoughtful, Suzanne usually asked precisely the right questions using the right tone, an example of one of the skills Natalia should hone.

"No, I think I'll hunker down with the numbers for a few days. I thought about inviting my mother to visit for a bit, but it's too unsettled here for that. We don't really celebrate the holiday anyway. Instead, I'll use the opportunity to learn what all these growing sales numbers mean so I can hold my own with your probing questions at the next meeting of the board."

She laughed to add levity. It was essential to leave Suzanne with the right impression—one that she was adequately coping with it all—even if it wasn't entirely true.

Thirty-Three

Quepos, Costa Rica, Saturday December 23, 2023

The sun shone in through a crack in the curtains and crossed James's bare chest. He shifted to his right to block the light and noticed the bed beside him was empty, with its crumpled sheets rolled back toward his side. He lifted his head and glanced around the room.

The master bathroom off the bedroom was vacant. He eased himself out of the bed, taking care not to press too heavily on the cast on his fractured wrist. He grabbed fresh clothes from a drawer in the cabinet beside him, choosing all the necessary items from the new clothes the security guys had ordered for him yesterday. There was no need to worry about matching colors or highlighting his better features, as few would see him that day. It would be his first full day in Quepos, after the best night's sleep he could remember. It was also his first full day of "captivity" in a delightful complex he wasn't allowed to leave.

So, where was Marie?

The latest woman in his life had struggled after her arrival the day before. Clearly, his kidnapping, injury, and rescue had unsettled her, and she seemed continually on edge. It took several hours and a couple glasses of wine to ease her anxiety. Marie rarely drank any form of alcohol. Her Evangelical Christian sect considered drinking wine a sin, just like having sex outside of marriage.

However, since her passion for him seemed to overrule the teachings of her church, she had recently ventured into other sins as well. After gingerly sipping the red wine while devouring a delicious rice dish the security guards had ordered in, she almost gulped down a second glass.

She didn't become lightheaded or tipsy as James had expected. Instead, she'd fallen asleep on the sofa as they watched a Spanish movie with English subtitles. When he'd heard her gentle snore, he half woke her and partially carried, partially dragged her to their bed. There, fully dressed, she'd rolled onto her side and went immediately back to sleep. At some point, she'd left without disturbing him.

He found a coffeemaker and added one of the pods the team had ordered yesterday to get his day started, as usual. James never considered himself fully awake until he'd drained a second cup each morning. Habitually, he drank as many more during the rest of the day, either at his desk or around the house, as he needed to feel totally alert and for his mind to function at its optimum level.

Cup in hand, James took a first sip, then stepped out of their unit at the rear of the lovely complex. He headed toward the large pool, scanning for Marie in each direction as he made a full circle and ended up where he'd started.

"I'm up here," he heard Marie say.

He took several steps to the left of the doorway, where a large, aged tree spread its umbrella-like crown between the corner of their unit and the apartments next door. He looked up at Marie perched on a sturdy lower branch, her back leaning against the main mast growing upward. One of her legs was stretched out, the other bent at her knee, both of them balancing her lower body as she crossed her arms casually across her chest.

James felt slight arousal when he noticed her breasts peeking out from her low-cut top, apparently unfettered by a bra, showing almost enough to see one nipple. He smiled.

She waited while he took in the picture, then explained. "When I was a young girl, whenever I was fearful or worried about something, my mother always told me to act like a boy. Do the stuff boys do. So, I learned to climb trees quite well, and I thought it would be a good idea to come here this morning."

James held his smile as he processed her message. Clearly, two glasses of wine and a good night's sleep hadn't entirely assuaged her distress. "Did it help? Climbing the tree?"

"As you may notice, I needed to climb straight up this tree, well beyond my height, with no other branches to help me. The bark was very rough. Scraping against it drew blood from a few spots on my knees, so, yes, I got some satisfaction from getting up here. I'll bet you're not willing to try, though, are you?" Her smile broadened knowingly as she held out for a response.

"My tree-climbing days are long past," he said, forming a sheepish grin. "Even if my wrist weren't fractured, I have no desire to replicate your feat. I am, however, impressed."

A few moments of silence followed. The complex was more than tranquil, with none of the security guys in sight and no other guests allowed on the property. Birds chirped cheerfully in the background. A few insects hummed as they dashed past. A dog barked a few times from a place some distance away, and a breeze rustled the leaves on the tree.

James took another sip of the strong, hot coffee.

"I'm not sure I can stay here a week, James," Marie started. "It's a lovely spot. I love being with you, and I know the security guys know how to do their job, but I'm scared. I'm terrified. Someone kidnapped you in Mexico and killed your colleague. I hate that you need to come here and hide out, no matter how beautiful the locale."

James paused long enough to be certain she had finished her thoughts. To bolster that assurance, he took another sip of coffee before he replied.

"I understand. We've known each other for only a few months. During that time, I've performed two completely different roles in the company, and both times, colleagues were viciously murdered. But I'm committed to this company. I've spent my entire career with Multima, and most of that time has been unquestionably satisfying and rewarding. Suzanne, like her father before her, is a wonderful person. Neither deserved the bumps they encountered on the road. I'd love for you to get comfortable with what I do, but if you prefer to leave, I'll understand."

She sniffled and drew a deep breath. "I know how you love your job and your company, and I love the way you love me. I've never had a man so thoughtful, tender, and appreciative. But I have this feeling of dread, a feeling that something bad will happen, and I'll be a part of it."

Again, James allowed a long moment to pass. He looked up at her in the tree and stared into eyes that were clearly watering. She grimaced, as though her tears might erupt at any second. He set his coffee cup on the ledge of a nearby window and spread his arms wide. "Let me help you down from there. Let's go inside and talk some more. If you feel you need to leave, we'll get a flight arranged as soon as possible, and we can get you some extra protection either here or back home."

Wordlessly, still on the bough, Marie worked her way back to a standing position near the main trunk of the tree. Then, with a leap, she jumped back from the tree enough that she was able to grab the big branch as her body dropped toward the ground. Dangling by her arms, she looked down at James, then let go. She landed against his chest, and he swept his arms tightly around her waist before she touched the ground.

When he lowered her to the cement sidewalk, she wrapped her arms around his shoulders and drew him in for a long and passionate kiss, the most passionate he could remember. They held that position for a few seconds, savoring their closeness.

Their embrace broke with the unsettling sound of

breaking branches and violently rustling leaves from the space between the next unit in the complex and a work shed beside it. A male form in a white T-shirt and jeans appeared, running. Someone else dove from the same tight space, tackled the first fellow from behind, shouting, "Intruder! Intruder!"

The guy in the T-shirt landed with a violent thump on the cement sidewalk encircling the pool.

James grabbed Marie and dragged her toward the open door of their unit as two other security people dashed toward the struggling bodies on the ground.

The guy in the T-shirt was much smaller than the security dude who'd brought him down, and his face was bloodied as he struggled to escape his assailant's iron grip. It was to no avail, as the reinforcements arrived seconds after the guy had wrestled the attacker to the ground. After a kick to his legs, followed by a violent grip around his neck, the intruder succumbed.

"Stay inside and away from the windows," one security guy shouted at James and Marie. "He has a gun!"

Thirty-Four

Paris, France, Saturday December 23, 2023

On her flight back from Manchester after another successful visit with an injured company truck driver, Suzanne learned about the attack on Natalia.

Unlike his colleague in Italy, the English driver and his wife had appreciated the visit and interacted warmly after Suzanne introduced the representative from Interpol. Before Suzanne and her team had left, Edouard Deschamps confirmed a meeting with one of his people for an in-depth interview with the driver one hour later.

She heard the news about James and his lady as the plane touched down in Paris after a one-hour flight. Again, there had been a delay informing her of the event in Costa Rica, and Serge's people once again showed reluctance to contact her before clearing it with him.

Suzanne seethed as she processed both the alarming armed intruder at the complex where James was hiding out and the unacceptable delay in getting such vital information to her. But she could do little about it immediately. Serge was on the Shinkansen high-speed rail line, focused on digging deeper into the Japanese Yakuza's suspected involvement in the constant attacks on Multima.

Serge had requested a blackout in communication for all but the most urgent matters as he traveled to Hamamatsu. In their last conversation, he'd mentioned a concern that the technology app Multima used to secure voice, text messaging, and videos might have been breached.

"While we've always believed that Signal provides us secure end-to-end encryption for our communication with

Multima users who've installed the app, my guy, Archie, in Vietnam, has connected some dots that raise some doubts. He's working on it. I hope to know more soon, but be careful what you say when you're using the app, and only contact me if you feel it's critically urgent."

She'd taken that admonition seriously, but she needed to talk with James. He answered on the first ring.

"Did you get a text from Serge about Signal?" she asked.

"Yes, I understand the concerns," he confirmed.

"Are you and Marie all right?"

"Neither of us was injured in the skirmish, if that's your question. Marie was rather devastated emotionally by it all. She's an Evangelical Christian woman who has lived a sedate life and has never experienced the ugly side. Can't say I'm enjoying all the madness either."

Suzanne detected an edge to his tone she didn't entirely recognize, so she changed her direction. "Do you feel secure in the new place?"

"It's better. I won't share the details, but the security guys get better views of the place—inside, outside, and the surrounding area. We should be secure here." James had clearly taken Serge's warning seriously and was choosing his limited words carefully. She waited to see if there might be more and was rewarded a few seconds later.

"I think it's safe to tell you that the guys here discovered a digital connection they found revealing. They're trying to find a secure way to get the information to Serge and are working with someone on his team who's apparently found another secure line to him."

It was rather vague news but moderately encouraging. She tried another approach. "Do you think Marie will be all right with you, or should we get the security folks to relocate her?"

"I think we can manage here."

Suzanne mulled over their conversation for a few

seconds. James's brevity might have been solely a result of the communication caution Serge had issued, but concerns lingered about his mental and emotional state after the trauma. He was usually a rock of stability, but these past few days were far different from the usual pressures of running a large corporation. She decided to close with some reassurances.

"I expect to talk with Serge early tomorrow morning. I'll give you a call after we speak to keep you in the loop, and if Marie wants out of there, just call. We should be able to do it within hours."

Back at the Hôtel San Régis, Suzanne felt a sudden pang of loneliness. Christmas was not a big celebration for her. Never had been. Usually, the period's greatest appeal was the outstanding store sales reports, bolstered by customers reveling in the spirit of the holidays and family get-togethers. Like most years since her mother had passed, with Serge now in Japan, she'd spend the next few days alone.

Never one to nurture the morose, she walked over to the large picture window in the center of the suite's living area and drew back the large dark drapes. The Eiffel Tower in the background immediately caught her eye. For the season, it was colorfully decorated with lights of all colors, many flashing playfully. For a moment, she appreciated the red lights highlighting the structure, creating a festive backdrop for the white lights that covered the rest of the surface.

The weather outdoors was unremarkable—about the same as she was accustomed to when she'd lived in Atlanta: cool temperatures and windy, but no snow in sight. Even at that hour of the evening, the streets in the area around the tower still brimmed with traffic in every direction, flooding each roundabout with vehicles wending in various directions at a snail's pace. Candidly, she preferred that picture to Montreal's bitter cold and deep snow, even though the neighborhood of her home in the nearby Laurentian Mountains would probably be Christmas-card perfect for festive scenery.

She glanced at her watch; it was late evening there in Paris, which meant early Christmas morning in Tokyo. Serge should have already arrived in Hamamatsu, and his mission there should be underway. She decided to order dinner to her room and relax with a good book until he called with his report.

Her meal was enjoyable, but the day had been a long one. She dozed off shortly after finishing, the ring of her phone awakening her sometime later her from a surprisingly deep sleep. Without checking the screen, she expected to hear Serge's greeting and was surprised when a male voice she didn't recognize asked if he was speaking to Suzanne Simpson.

She paused to look down at the screen, hoping to identify the caller, but there was nothing on the caller ID.

"Who is calling, please?" she responded with caution.

"My name is Antonio Primavera. I'm an agent on Serge's security team. I'm calling for Suzanne Simpson—is she available?"

Suzanne couldn't recall ever hearing the name, but that wasn't unusual. She had her regular bodyguards, and Serge seldom rotated them. Her personal number was considered highly confidential, so no more than a dozen people in the company had access to it. She concluded that Serge may have asked this fellow to call on his behalf and decided to take the risk.

"Yes, this is Suzanne—how may I help you?"

"As I said, my name is Antonio, and I work with Serge. I got your number from headquarters security in Montreal. Initially, they didn't want to give it to me, but Monique Boutin finally agreed that the circumstances warranted the breach in confidentiality." His use of the name of the

Montreal liaison for communication between the agents gave her a little comfort.

"Okay. I know Monique. What would you like to share with me?"

"I'll break it to you as gently as I can, ma'am, but Serge is missing."

She gasped audibly. She'd never entertained the possibility of such a call, and her voice trembled involuntarily as she asked him to explain.

"He divided our team of nine here in Japan into three groups to be less obvious on the train. At the Tokyo station, we boarded the last three cars of the train. Serge and the two women were in the very last car. Another team of three used the second-to-last car. I sat in the third one from the rear with two other colleagues."

She supposed it was essential for him to share all these details, but she silently hoped he'd get to the point quickly and explain what had happened to Serge.

After a pause for breath, he carried on. "Shortly after we left the Shin-Fuji Station—that's the third or fourth stop outside Tokyo and close to Mt. Fuji—one of my guys came running to explain that Serge's car had detached from the train. He noticed the car was no longer there when we pulled away from the station. I tried to call Serge right away, but the call went directly to his voicemail. I tried three or four more times with the same result, so I tracked down a conductor on the train and asked him what was going on with the last car.

"He didn't understand English, so I had to go back and get one of our guys who spoke Japanese. By the time we'd tracked the conductor down again, the train was arriving at another station, and the fellow needed to debark from the train to help the passengers. When the train pulled out again, the guy disappeared—he didn't get back on the train!"

She sat in silence, awestruck by the story. It seemed almost unbelievable, but she urged him to continue, regardless. "Then what happened?"

"I ordered my Japanese-speaker to debark again at the next station and find out what was going on with management there while I tried to track down someone to speak with on the train. Incredibly, the high-speed train didn't even slow down as it went through the Kakegawa Station. People were running away from the boarding area, thinking the train was out of control. In the end, our guy couldn't get off until we all arrived and left the train in Hamamatsu, the following station."

"What have you learned?"

"Nothing. There's no answer on Serge's phone or on those of the two women. Station management claimed to know nothing about leaving one car behind in Shin-Fuji or failing to stop in Kakegawa. It's like none of it even happened, and no one here seems to be at all concerned."

The story seemed almost a fantasy. The Japanese were known for their strict adherence to rules and protocols. Railcars didn't just disappear from trains. The Shinkansen rail system was one of the world's most admired networks. Where could she go with this mystery?

"Have you contacted the police there yet?"

"Not formally. At the Hamamatsu station, one of the agents we talked with called a police officer over to hear our story, but the guy showed no interest. Didn't even ask who we were or request identification. I had the impression no one involved had any interest in our concern, and I'm afraid that's usually a bad sign."

"Did you move forward with the mission without Serge?"

"We did what we could. It took our Japanese speaker a few minutes to establish internet communications once we arrived in Hamamatsu, but once he got us operational, we narrowed our bearings from the coordinates we'd received to identify the precise location where they were holding him. When we got there about midnight, we found the targeted warehouse empty." He paused for a moment and released a sigh of exasperation.

"None of the telecommunication equipment we discovered and tracked earlier on our monitors in Tokyo was there. We found nothing but a few stray power cords. Since then, I've been talking with Montreal to get permission to call you, while the rest of the guys divided up to see what they could learn back at the three stations before Hamamatsu. So far, we're drawing blanks."

Thirty-Five

Somewhere in Japan, Sunday December 24, 2023

He awoke woozy. They must have jabbed him with something. Serge's memory was also groggy, but he recalled someone bumping into him when the train had stopped, then stumbling toward Constance as though he were tripping. That was all he remembered.

His head ached. His muscles were stiff. He was lying on a cold, bare cement floor. When he turned his head, he saw Constance facing him, also lying on the floor, still asleep. He raised his head slightly. Another female form lay beside Constance. It must be Sheila, the other security gal who was traveling with them.

The room had only a dull light emanating from a dusty bulb sticking out from a receptacle mounted on the wall above his head. He detected the smell of gasoline or diesel oil; he couldn't be sure which.

"Are you awake?" he whispered to Constance.

Her eyes fluttered, then opened fully, looking at Serge with a mixture of bewilderment and fear. "Where are we? What happened?"

Their whispering and movement startled Sheila awake. She shifted her body in Serge's direction. Neither woman appeared injured, just groggy. Still, he inquired with a careful whisper after checking that the door opposite remained closed.

"Constance, you first—any injuries? How are you feeling? Do you remember anything?"

"I'm okay. Right after I saw a guy jab your upper leg, I felt a prick in my thigh. Before I could reach for the spot, I'd already lost my balance. That's all I remember. Now that

I'm awake, I'm just hungry and thirsty."

He nodded, first to Constance, then again toward Sheila.

"I was last. I saw you both slump to the ground, and I reached out to grab Constance. One guy shoved me downward and gripped his hand around my throat. Tightly. A few seconds later, another guy came toward me with a needle and jabbed my stomach. It's still sensitive. I remained conscious long enough to see him rummaging in my bag. I feel okay, too, but my throat is dry. Even whispering is painful."

Serge sat up and looked around the warehouse. His hands remained free, but he noticed all their legs were bound with black leather strips. They allowed for minimal movement but were latched together with a brass-colored lock. He kicked out his leg, but the strap only permitted movement of a few inches.

There were no windows in the room and no fan to circulate the air. He thought the gas and diesel fumes might be the cause of the slight headache he felt, but he couldn't be sure. It might also be an aftereffect of the drug the guy had injected.

He looked at his wrist and noted that his watch had disappeared. He checked all his pockets—they'd taken everything: phone, wallet, passport. If his pockets were empty and the girls' bags were nowhere in sight, the bastards must have seized all their belongings.

Stretching forward as far as possible, he was able to grasp the lock mechanism and pull on it, but the latch was secure. Before he could remove his hand, the door opened wide, letting bright light glare into the room. When his eyes refocused on the new brightness, he saw a large male with the physique of a sumo wrestler staring at them disdainfully.

The Japanese guy's lips curled with contempt, and his

shoulders hunched forward as though ready to attack with the flimsiest of excuses. He held his hands at the ready at his side, but his eyes appeared calm. They drilled first on Serge, then on each woman in turn. He said nothing, so Serge tried.

"Where are we, and who are you?" He took pains to keep his tone calm and respectful, then waited for a response.

The guy made no sound. Instead, he shook his head once emphatically and continued to observe them.

Maybe two or three minutes later, a woman joined him. Her form seemed comically petite standing next to the Japanese giant. Probably no more than five feet tall and weighing less than one hundred pounds, she looked like a child in comparison. But when she spoke, her mild manner disappeared.

In perfect English, and with a surprisingly loud voice, she commanded them to stand up and not say a word as they did so. The woman was not Japanese. Her skin tone suggested an Asian background, but her skin color looked darker, more like women from farther south in Asia, or perhaps from one of the mountainous regions like Laos, Myanmar, or even northern Thailand.

Serge obeyed her order and was first to his feet. He reached down to help pull Constance up, but the woman screamed for him to halt. "Stand still. Touch no one. Continue to say nothing. Don't give me a reason to have Abe here rearrange your faces."

When all three were on their feet, the woman motioned for the big guy to release the lock securing the straps around their ankles. Before he or the women could consider making a run for it, three more men appeared over Abe's shoulder, all carrying weapons, all pointed directly at them.

As the woman led them from the room, the three weapons tracked their path across the room and outside.

There, Serge realized the room was a garage, and the gas and diesel fumes made more sense. Two small SUVs waited for them on the short gravel driveway.

"You," the woman said, pointing at Serge, "climb into the first vehicle. Women, climb into the one behind it. Everyone, remain totally silent."

Before he could reach for a seatbelt in the rear, one of the men with a weapon yanked the strap into place and slipped a dark hood over Serge's head, almost in a single motion.

His vision blocked entirely, Serge heard the slam of a door in front of him, and the vehicle immediately left. Someone was driving the SUV at a high speed. For the first few minutes, there were a lot of twists and turns along the route, and his body swayed from side to side. Suddenly, the vehicle accelerated, sounding as if it was entering a freeway, its tires humming loudly.

Soon, Serge determined that they were passing other, slower-moving cars and trucks, given the swish of air movement. The driver and the other fellow didn't speak at all. There was no music on the radio. There were, in fact, no sounds but those coming from the engine and roadway. It was impossible to determine in which direction they traveled. Then, they started to climb. The engine strained, and their speed slowed slightly, indicating the slope was steep enough to suck power from the engine, reducing their speed. After a few minutes, Serge detected the sound of turn signals, and the vehicle's speed decreased to a crawl.

It wasn't long before the vehicle jerked to a stop, and both front doors opened. Someone wordlessly detached his seatbelt, then yanked him from the SUV with a powerful tug on his left wrist. Once he was out of the vehicle and upright, each guy grabbed an arm and hauled Serge forward. He was still unable to see from whatever was covering his head, and he stumbled on uneven ground before both captors gripped his elbows tightly to prevent a fall.

Soon, he heard the creak of an opening door. Inside, it felt like he was walking on a bamboo floor, with the distinctive creak of wood giving way to their weight. They shoved him into a leather chair and wound a strap around his chest, binding his arms tightly to his sides. They snapped a Velcro fastener behind his back, then stripped the hood from his head.

His eyes adjusted slowly as he blinked in the light of the room, and he looked around his surroundings. Already, the two guys had disappeared. He seemed to be alone in the silent room. He saw no sign of his two female colleagues.

The space appeared to be attached to a cottage or a home. The floor was tan-colored bamboo, and the ceiling was a simple white. The walls were slightly lighter than the floor and darker than the ceiling, painted in a subdued color. The lighting was equally muted, with a simple, wall-mounted lamp glowing partway up one of the walls. There were no odors that he could detect, nor were there distinguishing paintings or portraits on display. Instead, there were half a dozen colorful banners strung along the wall facing him, all with something on them written in Japanese characters he didn't understand.

From outside, he heard only the sounds of night insects flitting about. That probably meant a window was open somewhere, but none that he could see in the immediate room. He tried to stand up, but the chair was fixed to the floor, and they'd wrapped the strap beneath the seat, restricting his arm movement and inhibiting the use of his legs. He hadn't detected that earlier, so he tested the range possible, but it still only allowed for slight use of his arms, and his efforts resulted in only minuscule shifts.

He looked more intently at all the wall corners at ceiling height, looking for cameras. He didn't see any spots or anomalies that might be used to camouflage a device mounted there. There was no overhead lighting, and the only other fixture in the dark room was a tiny lamp sitting on the floor in one corner, unplugged. Beside it was the only other piece of furniture, a foam mattress about three inches thick with a plain black cloth covering. A temporary bed, perhaps?

He tested his ability to move within the restraints once more as he listened for any new sounds or footsteps approaching. With considerable fiddling and contorting, he was able to slide his right hand up enough from the strap confining it to hook his thumb between his belt and his jeans and grab the belt between his thumb and index finger.

Serge breathed in as he tugged and managed to slide the belt to the right a bit. He repeated the process a dozen or more times until his thumb finally touched a metal retainer attached to the belt in a spot above the belt-holes and well away from the buckle. Then, he pressed that metal strip until it gave way ever so slightly. He continued to press every few seconds over the next few minutes until he'd managed to return the buckle to its original position in the center and front of his jeans.

Again, he surveyed the room in every direction as far as he could twist his body, casting his view up and down the walls and across the floor, but found nothing unremarkable. Nothing he might use to try an escape. Nothing that looked like a camera or a recording device. From outside, he heard only the hum of night insects. That told him they were somewhere in the mountains, near Hamamatsu, Japan. He was also alone, with no sign of the women from his team. There wasn't even an indication that the armed guards were still somewhere nearby.

He couldn't recall a time when he'd felt so helpless and vulnerable.

Thirty-Six

Atlanta, Georgia, Saturday December 23, 2023

The last time Natalia checked her watch, it was past the dinner hour in Georgia. She thought momentarily about asking one of the security guys to order dinner for them all, then decided to hold off on the request for a few hours. If she planned to spend the entire night there in the office, it made sense that she should spread out the highlights of her night so she wouldn't become bored too early and waver in her determination.

She'd be damned if the assigned security guards were going to spend the night with her in the apartment—she'd rather starve before letting that happen. She settled into her comfortable leather chair and stared at a widescreen monitor that displayed new sales reports every hour with updates on how every store in the Multima universe fared with customer purchases as the hours counted down to Christmas.

The numbers were good. Suzanne would be pleased to see them. It bode well for a profitable quarter. Multima's fiscal year always ended on January 31 to be sure they captured all possible sales for Christmas, New Year's, and usually, some of the other holidays celebrated in North America. There were a few: Kwanzaa for African-Americans, sometimes the Chinese New Year, depending on when it occurred, and Orthodox Christmas for those transplanted from Eastern Europe.

In her short time with the Supermarkets' business, Natalia had found it intriguing how America thought of itself as a "melting pot" of cultures, yet its citizens often continued celebrating cultural occasions, even after two or three generations in the country. Those celebrations were essential to the supermarket industry, generating millions of dollars in additional sales as families prepared and enjoyed feasts.

That year looked particularly promising, especially on the eastern side of the country, where Multima Supermarkets had years of experience preparing and ordering goods for the lesser-known holidays. Some stores paid as much attention to the "lesser-knowns" as they did to Christmas.

Stores were always quick to point out to Natalia that it was Suzanne who had been the first to coach local store managers to talk to their customers and learn what kinds of meals they prepared for special occasions and the ingredients the stores needed to stock.

Locations on the West Coast weren't quite as well prepared, however. Multima had just completed the acquisition of Jeffersons Stores earlier that year, so management there needed some time to inch up the learning curve. Still, it was gratifying to see most stores report high single-digit increases compared to the previous year, and some had even experienced double-digit bumps.

A shiver moved up her spine.

Still in her early forties, she'd made it to the top of one of America's finest companies. Now, she needed to find a way to leave her mark on the company forever. She made a mental note to schedule a few minutes on her calendar every day in the new year to think about and consult with colleagues until she identified what that revolutionary concept should be. It wouldn't be wise to rely entirely upon Docket 2025 to come to fruition.

Before she could dwell more on that monumental plan, a text alert from Archie Begat sounded:

Just received an alert from Serge's tracker. Made Antonio Primavera aware of the coordinates somewhere in the mountains near Hamamatsu. Nothing yet from the women traveling with him. Thought you'd want to know. – A.

Natalia drew a deep breath. What should she do with that disturbing information? Constance Hope, her former direct report at Multima Financial Services, was surely one of the women. Archie had already reported that Serge had ordered her to Japan to join his mission there.

And what about Suzanne? Had they made her aware that her lover was in distress?

Natalia decided to risk any blowback from either Serge or Suzanne about her back-channel reporting arrangement with Archie and called. She woke her boss, as it took three rings for her to pick up.

"I'm sorry to disturb you in the middle of the night, but I have some unsettling news I thought I should share with you." She waited for her CEO to respond before continuing, giving Suzanne a moment or two to wake fully so she would be able to cope with the news she was about to receive.

"Go ahead, Natalia." Her tone sounded alert and neutral.

"I realize it might not have been entirely appropriate, but I arranged for my former guy in technology over at Financial Services to keep me in the loop with developments on the Asia project. Archie Begat's his name. Well, he just sent me a text alert that Serge's distress alarm just activated in Japan. Archie tried to reach him, but there was no response from Serge or the two women traveling with him to Hamamatsu. I thought you should be aware if you haven't already heard."

A rustling of sheets in the otherwise silent background suggested Suzanne was alert, awake, and prepared for action. "Was your guy able to reach Antonio Primavera?" she asked.

"So far I've only received the message that he texted Antonio. No other details."

"What time is it over there? Can you get him on the line?" Suzanne's tone suggested that Natalia act regardless of the time, but Natalia assured her it was about ten o'clock in the morning in that part of Asia, so she should be able to reach him.

It took a minute or two, but the connection for their conference call was crisp and clear. "Hello, Archie," Suzanne began after Natalia had made the introduction. "Were you able to connect with Antonio Primavera?"

"Yes. He called on a secure line after he got my text message. I just hung up. Somehow, the team got separated from Serge and the two women on the train to Hamamatsu and lost all communication. He confirmed the coordinates I received from Serge's alert device and said that the team would leave immediately for that location. He also asked me to text you a heads-up. That's what I was doing when Natalia called."

"How far is the location from Hamamatsu? Did he have any idea how much time they'd need?" Suzanne's tone grew more urgent with each question.

"On the map it looks like a drive of less than an hour, but Antonio reminded me they have no idea what might be waiting for them when they locate Serge. He cautioned that you shouldn't expect any further word for several hours, as he and his men would shut down all standard communication and use a private network until they rescued Serge and had him in a safe location."

It was Suzanne who closed the conversation by letting Archie know she understood and appreciated his help. She asked him to update her directly by text or phone as he received any new information. However, Suzanne made no mention of the back-channel arrangement Natalia had established with Archie before closing the line.

Might that be a reason for concern?

Thirty-Seven

Quepos, Costa Rica, Sunday December 24, 2023

James drew a figurative line in the sand.

"Get the Financial Services jet back here immediately. We're all returning to the States. Now. Never mind contacting Serge or your superiors in Montreal. Do it now, or I'll use your phone to call Suzanne Simpson and have her give you the order."

The security guy, Jacques Legault, understood the message, made the call, and reported back to James within ten minutes. "They're locating the pilots and giving instructions for them to pick us all up here. It'll probably be eight to ten hours before the pilots can get to the airport, fire up the jet, and fly from Montreal to here in Quepos. They'll give us an update when the planes are in the air."

James nodded. "Is the assailant conscious?"

"Yeah. He was only out for a minute or two. We've got him in handcuffs in one of the vacant rooms. He was bleeding a bit, but that's under control now."

"I want to talk to him."

James had gradually taken control of the situation. First, he'd persuaded Marie to stay inside and arranged for the English-speaking security guy, Alan, to park outside the suite they were using to assure her safety. Then, he huddled on the veranda of the suite closest to the complex entrance with the two other guards so they could all keep an eye on the electric gate and environs as they chatted.

"What do we know about the guy so far?" James asked both Jacques and Mateo.

Jacques deferred to his Spanish-speaking colleague with a nod.

"We're using the bad cop-good cop routine: Jacques makes the threats, asking me to translate. I deliver the messages and then try to develop a rapport. So far, he's shared no useful information—not even a name."

"No ID?"

"Nothing. He had the gun you saw and a one-hundred-dollar bill in his pocket. No wallet. No passport. No ticket. Just the money. We're guessing the money was his fee, and that he's from around here," Jacques said.

They went inside. James took a good look at the guy for the first time. He appeared only slightly older than a teenager, with a tiny mustache and just the outline of peach-fuzz beard growth. He wore a T-shirt that had seen better days and jeans worn out at the knees. His dark hair was long and unkempt. His lips curled into a surly, menacing look, like a guy who felt hard done by. He barely raised his eyes to look up at them.

James sat down on a comfortable chair, crossed his legs casually, and turned on the highest voltage smile he could manage under the circumstances before glancing at Mateo and asking him to translate.

"These men tell me you won't cooperate. You won't answer any of their questions. Will you answer mine?"

The guy gave no answer and showed no reaction.

James calmly posed another question. "I'd like to talk with you about your attempted attack on my companion and me. Will you tell me why you are here?"

The guy looked downward without uttering a word and held that position.

James tried another approach. "Will you tell us your name?"

The same response: neither a word spoken nor an emotion displayed.

James said nothing for a few moments, then stood up from the comfortable chair. For perhaps fifteen minutes, he paced around the living area of the suite, head down, deep in thought, intentionally ignoring everyone else. From the corner of his eye, he saw the assailant following his path, his body language gradually changing from hostile to accepting, maybe even relaxed.

The security guys said nothing. They, too, followed James's measured paces with their eyes.

When their assailant looked ready, James pulled a chair over from the nearby kitchen and placed it opposite the security team. He sat facing the two guards, with their captive to his right, then asked Mateo to translate his questions again.

The thug shook his head emphatically.

"Okay, then. I'm going to ask you to help me make a decision. These two men are not police officers. They are private security guards who are not bound by the rules and regulations of Costa Rica's laws. They're paid to keep me safe, and they'll follow the instructions I give them. So please, think carefully about your answer. Do you understand what I'm saying?"

He waited for Mateo to translate, then watched the guy nod slightly.

"Here's my dilemma: You are clearly a risk to me and my companion. Your country's president, Rodrigo Chávez Robles, is a close personal friend of mine. We studied economics together at university. I speak with him regularly and store his number in my phone. I'm going to ask you who paid you to attack us today. If you give me the name of that person, I'll ask these two guys to check it out. If you're telling me the truth, I'll tell them to let you go free."

James paused to give Mateo time to translate the message. He looked into the guy's eyes intently as he listened. There was a slight flicker of understanding, so James carried on.

"If you don't cooperate and let us know truthfully who put you up to this, I'll decide whether I should call your president and ask him to have his most capable police come to arrest you and prosecute you to the fullest extent of Costa Rican law. Or I could simply leave this room and tell these guys to do whatever they want with you. I'll give you a few minutes to decide."

James stood up from the chair the instant Mateo finished translating, delivered a single, fierce glare into the assailant's eyes, then spun on his heel and stepped out of the suite.

He returned to join Maria, enjoyed a strong cup of Costa Rican coffee—black, with no sugar—and chatted about where they should go when the plane arrived. After an appropriate interval for the intruder to consider his options, James returned to the front of the complex and re-entered the suite where the security folks held the assailant.

When everyone was seated comfortably around the guy, James simply looked at their captive and tilted his head to the right, expecting a response.

The fellow sat more upright in the chair and spoke for the first time. "I'll take you to the person who hired me if you give me four hundred dollars. That's the amount he agreed to pay me when I returned after doing the job."

James nodded to Jacques. "Give him the money. I'll go with you, Mateo, and the guy for the rendezvous. Tell Alan to stay with Maria until we're back."

Outside the suite, Jacques, of course, protested. It was too dangerous, he maintained. They needed to call the local police. What James was proposing was unlawful.

He listened patiently to the protests, considered his options, then declared, with a tone of finality honed over his forty years in the business world, "There have been two unlawful attacks on me in the past three days. The law isn't working. I'm not prepared to wait for a third attempt. If you don't follow my instructions, I'll simply get the four hundred from Marie's handbag, pay the weasel, and go with him to meet the culprit behind this, with or without you."

Fortunately, Jacques acquiesced.

Thirty-Eight

Paris, France, Sunday December 24, 2023

Suzanne usually discussed any significant change in her itinerary with Serge as a courtesy. Fear was rarely a component of her thought process. After all, she had traveled the globe for years without any security protection. But since she'd become Multima's CEO, she realized the dynamic had changed, and she appreciated having bodyguards with her.

It had been particularly helpful that time in Singapore when Jasmine Smith-Field had shoved her into a flowerbed to avoid a shot from a sniper outside the restaurant where they had all dined that evening. Her security partner, Willy Landon, had taken the bullet intended for Suzanne and was injured so seriously that he never returned to work. Multima's insurance company still paid him monthly benefits years later, although he was now mobile and improving with time.

The only good thing to result from that mishap was that Jasmine linked up with Willy as a life partner. Her dedication—visiting and encouraging Willy in the aftermath of his injury—had eventually morphed into love, and the couple had lived together for the past few years. In fact, when Suzanne moved Multima's headquarters from Fort Myers, Florida, to Montreal, Quebec, Jasmine had decided to stay behind with Willy.

That meant Jasmine was assigned to protect her only on occasional, overseas assignments, whenever Serge insisted someone from North American operations guard her, in addition to whatever local resources he assigned. This was one of those occasions, and Suzanne always enjoyed her chats with the female bodyguard during their free time.

Now, she sought confirmation that she was taking the right action from a security perspective. "You know Serge is missing, along with two women from his mission in Asia. James is in hiding in the Caribbean after a gunman was apprehended at their Costa Rica compound, and someone took a shot at Natalia in Atlanta. It seems there's some global coordination of these threats to our senior team. Am I wrong to suspect there might well be some attempt to harm me?"

Jasmine took a deep breath and shook her head slowly. When she spoke, she did so softly, and she chose her words carefully. "Suzanne, you know I never want to cause you alarm, and the team here in France is well-trained and conscientious. But I've always been apprehensive around the holidays. Sometimes, people get distracted or maybe drink too much wine the night before their shifts. If you told me that you were thinking about bailing out of Paris and flying back to Montreal—at least until we find Serge—you wouldn't hear a word of protest from me."

Suzanne nodded. If she returned to her home in the Laurentian Mountains, Serge's team of security experts could surely protect her better there than anywhere else in the world. Besides, her usefulness in Europe was now limited. She had the two surviving drivers talking with Interpol. It was time to let Edouard Deschamps perform his magic at the police agency. Gaston had developed a good working relationship with the guy as well, and she could lean on him to push Interpol should momentum lag.

"I'll call Eileen and ask her to prepare everything in Montreal. Please get the pilots to the airport. Tell them to plan for takeoff at about 8:30 this morning. I'll pack my things and check out of the hotel, so have your security detail ready with the car and whatever resources you think we need. I'll let Antonio know so he can bring Serge up to date as soon as they rescue him."

Jasmine pulled a phone from her jeans and started punching numbers in as she left the living room and headed toward the bedroom Serge had assigned her on the opposite side of the suite from Suzanne's.

Suzanne went through the same motions, dialing the secure number Antonio Primavera had given her to reach him in Japan. She expected a recording to greet her. Instead, he picked up.

"Suzanne? Bad news, I'm afraid."

He recounted how they'd traveled to the precise coordinates gleaned from the alert they'd received from the device hidden in Serge's belt buckle. About fifteen minutes before the estimated time of their arrival, the signal suddenly dropped. Luckily, they'd captured a screenshot on a laptop, so they were able to continue to the indicated coordinates.

However, when they arrived at the building where they expected to find Serge, it was vacant, still carrying the scents and debris of recent visitors. One or more had smoked cigarettes. An almost-empty paper coffee cup was still warm. Muddy footprints were evident. A flame still burned in the fireplace.

Antonio explained how he'd dashed to that fireplace, where he discovered a familiar brown belt, partially devoured by the flame. The buckle mechanism was charred and severely damaged. They'd lost contact with Serge permanently.

Thirty-Nine

Somewhere in Japan, Sunday December 24, 2023

It was broad daylight when Serge first detected an approaching vehicle. That realization sent a shiver up his spine. If his captors were so bold as to visit during the day, when anyone outside could see what they were doing, it suggested several possibilities, all of them dangerous.

If they ignored the potential hazard that private citizens might see what they were doing and report it to the police, it suggested the public knew and feared the perpetrators, so they dared not report them. Or perhaps that the police were in cahoots with the gang in some way. It might also suggest their location was so far away from other houses or buildings that his captors had little fear of being seen or reported. Finally, it might imply that those holding him had learned of some new development or danger and were planning to move him somewhere else . . . or worse.

He glanced around the room, searching for something he might use as a weapon, but he saw nothing. Preparing for their arrival, he flexed his muscles, twisting and stretching as much as his restraints allowed. If forced to defend himself, he'd need everything in working order.

A door unlocked, and three men entered the room, calmly and silently. It seemed to be a different crew than the night before. All three of them were tall, about the same height as Serge. They were all fit and muscular. Each wore a medical mask on his face, and at least one held something behind his back. Without hesitation, they moved toward Serge and shifted from single file to form a half circle, stopping a yard or so away from him.

With a curt glance in each direction, the one in the

middle, the one holding something behind his back, stepped forward and suddenly produced a needle. It looked like the one from last night. As Serge detected that the goon was about to move his arm, he shifted his hips to one side and managed to raise his feet enough to catch the guy on his knees and force him to stumble forward.

Angry, the thug lashed out with an open fist and struck Serge in the side of his face with enough force to almost knock his body off the chair. With his other hand, the guy jabbed the needle forcefully into the upper thigh of Serge's right leg, shifting his focus from the excruciating pain in his face down to his leg.

For good measure, the angry attacker slapped the other side of Serge's face, jolting his neck sideways enough to refocus his attention on yet another point of pain. It lasted only a few seconds. First, his vision blurred. Then, it faded to black.

~~~

Sometime later, a potent jolt shook Serge awake. They were moving. Lying flat on his back, he could feel the gentle sway of the vehicle, which traveled at a high speed. He shivered. The surface he was lying on was frigid and brutal, like metal. Sunlight entered the area from the windows on the rear door of a small van.

He looked to his left, saw a body next to him, and stiffened with recognition: Constance Hope. He raised his head slightly and saw that she was lying on her back—asleep or drugged—and completely naked. Startled, he glanced down and realized that he, too, was completely nude. He shifted his gaze to his other side and saw Sheila, asleep and also wearing nothing.

Reflexively, Serge touched his skin, hoping his eyes had it wrong, and he'd made some mistake. Maybe whatever they'd injected caused delusions or mirages. Or perhaps his
~~~

brain was malfunctioning after so many injections of who knew what drugs? He considered those possibilities for only a moment, but it was still apparent that whoever was holding them captive had stripped them naked and stolen their clothes. No doubt a precaution in the event they found a way to slip out of the handcuffs and ankle restraints.

He called out to Constance softly, in a tone barely above a whisper, but she didn't respond. He tried again, and on the second attempt, her eyes opened slightly. They were red, and it was apparent she'd been crying before she'd fallen asleep. Her voice was raspy, but she made no effort to clear it.

"They raped us. All three of the bastards forced themselves on us. Both of us. Three times." Her voice broke involuntarily as tears started to flow down one cheek.

What could he say? How could he help her cope with such a tragedy?

"Are you okay despite the trauma?"

"I don't know. I don't think I'm bleeding, but they didn't use protection. I can still feel them on me. One of them even entered from the rear a few times. All I can think of is getting my hands on something to kill any chance of pregnancy." She almost laughed as she spit out her concern, realizing the futility of her wish.

Their voices woke Sheila. "I know. There's little chance of a magic pill here, but I'll be watching for a knife. If I get my hands on one, you can be sure one of those bastards is going to lose his penis!"

Silence returned to the rear of the van. As he processed the women's misfortunes and fruitlessly sought words of comfort, he realized the implications. They hadn't raped *him. He* hadn't suffered any sexual humiliation or injury, but they'd taken his belt, so he could no longer send an alert. Those who might have received his precious signal could no longer track where he and his companions were.

A sole possibility remained. Perhaps the assailants had brought their clothes along. Maybe whoever was driving the vehicle had them in a separate bag up front, and the special belt buckle might continue to function. That appeared to be their only hope.

Forty

Atlanta, Georgia, Sunday December 24, 2023

The ring of her mobile startled Natalia for an instant—she'd dozed off sitting in the chair behind her office desk. From her computer screen, she noted it was 1:35 a.m. She shook her head to clear out any cobwebs, then pressed the green receiver icon on her phone.

It was Floyd Desmarais.

"The guys told me you're still in the office there. Everything all right?"

"Yeah. I just decided it might be more comfortable here." She considered whether she should share her concern or not. After the briefest of pauses, she continued. "I was okay with you staying in the apartment with me, but your colleague, Guillaume, is a little weird for my taste. I'm using the time to catch up here at work. How's everything with you?"

"Sorry to hear you're not comfortable with Guillaume. I know his manner can be a little off-putting from time to time, but you're safe with the guy. I hope you won't spend Christmas Day on the job."

It appeared that Floyd had no plans to return to Atlanta within the next few hours, so she probed a bit. "Was your trip to Palm Beach productive?"

"Somewhat. I had some news I'd like to share with Serge, but I'm not getting any response. I tried the security office in Montreal, but I'm not getting any answer there either. I've never known them to close for any holidays, so I was wondering if you'd heard anything."

"Serge is missing. He and two of the women on his team in Japan were hijacked from the high-speed train. Your colleagues over there had a lead on where they might be, but it didn't work out. Antonio Primavera is leading the efforts to track them down."

"Holy shit! Whoever nabbed them must be masters. There's nobody better than Serge. Is Suzanne aware?"

"Of course. When I last spoke with her in Paris, she was preparing to return to Montreal. She thought her overall security would be better there, with the whole team available." Doubt crept into her tone. If Floyd couldn't reach anyone in Montreal tonight, did it mean preparation for Suzanne's revised plans caused an abrupt change in staffing? Or might there be something more ominous going on?

Before she could decide where she might lead the conversation, Floyd volunteered some information.

"As I mentioned, I find it weird that no one from Montreal is responding to my calls. If Suzanne's heading there, we need to be sure she's not walking into a problem. I've got some non-security contacts in Montreal who might be able to help find out what's happening there. While I do that, can you reach Suzanne and let her know about the lack of communication? If we don't get answers, she might want to divert her flight to another destination."

Natalia agreed to call Suzanne. She voiced her support for his idea to try other ways to connect with security leadership in Montreal and was just about to end the call when something occurred to her: "Floyd, I realize I'm not part of security's line of communication, but I do have executive clearance. Share with me the reason Serge dispatched you to Palm Beach."

"Sure. No problem. Serge asked me to track down some coordinates he'd picked up from an intercepted message in Asia. That's why I was trying to reach him: to report on my findings. I can share them with you, but I'm a little bewildered by what I learned."

"Can you explain the issue in layman's terms so I might understand?" The security guys always preferred to channel everything through Serge, so she giggled to put him more at ease.

"Yeah. It's not that complex technically, it's just bizarre. The coordinates Serge sent me led to an old tool shed—literally, a tool shed: an old, weathered, nondescript, unpainted little gray shack. I had to check my device twice to be sure I had them right, but I was in the right place. I did a property search and learned that a numbered company based in New York owns the lot, and the owner's held it for almost a half-century." He paused, either for a breath or to reassure himself that he should go on.

"There was a lock on the door, but I was able to pick it. When I got inside, I found a row of garden tools hanging on a wall just inside the doorway. My first impression was that it looked exactly like one might expect a tool shed to look; however, when I walked down to the end of the wall, I found a passage behind all the hanging tools. I wandered down there and was shocked to find an elaborate bank of computers, monitors, and routers on the back wall. Everything one would expect to find in a highly sophisticated technology company."

"What was all that technology connected to? A home? An office?" Natalia asked.

"It didn't connect to anything. There were no hanging wires and no buried cables coming out of the building that I could track. There wasn't another building within a hundred yards, and the property surrounding it was just an unkempt, vacant lot." Floyd's tone conveyed his continued bewilderment.

Natalia tried another approach. "I think I heard a 'but' in your tone—is there more?"

"Only two things. First, inside the shed, besides all the technology, there was a walnut-finished desk that looked to be worth thousands, with a plush, matching brown leather chair that looked more expensive than any chair I've ever seen. But most perplexing of all: this shed, in the middle of a vacant lot, is right next door to one of the most famous resort properties around, one owned by a former president of the USA."

After she recovered from Floyd Demarais's revelation, a series of potential scenarios peppered her brain so quickly that Natalia had to take a step back to assess it all.

"We're talking about the Mar-a-Lago Resort, the same one owned by the family of a former president?"

"We are. I checked and re-checked the location before entering the shed. I even walked down the street a bit to be sure the sign at the entrance was indeed the one owned by the former president. The place is humming with activity. There are more limos in that parking lot than I've seen in one place for a long time." Floyd's tone implied he was impressed by such a collection of wealth and status.

"Why on Earth would someone locate such a cabin there? If they needed a secret area, why not just make space available *inside* that huge resort, or at least somewhere on the property owned by the family?"

"I wondered the same." Floyd paused for a moment, perhaps to decide how much he should share. "Over the past few hours, I've talked with a few people either living or working nearby. No one knew what the building was used for or to whom it belonged. None of the people I spoke to could recall seeing anyone coming or going. It just sits there, and the locals seem to pay it no attention."

While she listened to his comments and processed the information, she opened the resort's website and clicked through the dozens of photos highlighting the world-famous complex. After about thirty photos, she spotted one that included a shed like the one Floyd described, near a roadway and close to a fence that separated the resort's golf course from that vacant lot.

"I'm looking at some photos as we speak. I see a dark green shed with a dark brown roof that's partially surrounded by shrubs and miniature trees. Would that be the place you found?"

"Sounds about right," Floyd answered without hesitation. "From the roadway, all I saw the first time were the shrubs and trees. It's almost camouflaged, but enough of the building shows that I could spot it from the street when I looked closely. Clearly, whoever put it there wanted to attract as little attention as possible."

Natalia tipped back her head and tried to process all the implications. It almost overwhelmed her to the point that she wondered if her imagination was running wildly enough to play tricks on her cognitive reasoning. It was important to slow everything down.

"Okay, Floyd. As I understand it, you're trying to reach your team in Montreal both to share this information and seek guidance on how you should proceed—right?"

"Yeah. I'd really like to get some input from Serge, but if he's missing in action, I'll keep trying the Montreal office. The only problem is that I can't do it close to the shed. The equipment inside is so sophisticated that I fear any calls or conversations and perhaps even texts or emails might be intercepted. I'm calling you from a building about a mile away that I screened, inside a secure pocket I found. If I go back to keep an eye on that building for a few more hours, can you keep trying the Montreal security people for me?"

"Sure," she responded without hesitation. "How can we reach you?"

"If you need to call me back, just leave a message on my voicemail. I'll close my line when we finish. If you reach the folks in Montreal, they know how to reach me securely."

With a wish for good luck, she ended the call and hit the speed dial for Multima's corporate security.

Forty-One

Fortunately, the security guys slowed James down a bit. He'd been ready to tear out of the compound on foot with "Weasel," the guy they'd apprehended at their rented complex. They used that derogatory nickname whenever they referred to the intruder, confident he didn't understand enough English to know how insulting it was.

It was only a ten-minute walk down the hill, as Weasel had claimed. He insisted that he could point out where in town the fellow willing to pay five hundred dollars to wound—but not kill—James or Marie was staying.

Stimulated by his success at getting Weasel to confess his intentions, and then by the guy's offer to identify his sponsor, James admittedly experienced a bit of an adrenaline rush. It left him somewhat lightheaded, his blood pressure pulsing with excitement.

Jacques Legault's calm demeanor, his long experience in law enforcement, and now as a security specialist prevailed after a moment or two. He convinced James that walking was dangerous under any circumstances. They had no idea how many other guys might be with the fellow Weasel was about to lead them to, nor how many weapons they might have. At the very least, he needed to rent a car in the event they had to leave the scene quickly. It made sense.

Then, one of the guys mentioned that leaving Marie behind at the complex with only a single guard was not a great idea. She'd probably be safer in the vehicle they rented, and the guy guarding her could also serve as their driver in the event they needed to make a quick escape.

The third bodyguard also pointed out that they had no

idea how reliable Weasel was. Might he yell out a warning or tip off his sponsor in some other way, putting them all in jeopardy?

They had six hours before the plane would arrive from Montreal to carry them out of Costa Rica. Cool-headed Jacques formulated a plan, and everyone eventually agreed it was the best strategy possible. Even Marie had bought into the idea of sitting in the back of a van while all but one of the others followed Weasel to the guy who was the source of all their anxiety.

A critical component of their plan was to delay the entire exercise until about thirty minutes before the scheduled arrival of the corporate jet. Jacques estimated the drive downtown, an identification of the man behind the attack on James and Marie, a decision on how best to handle the information gleaned from that identification, and a high-speed drive to the Quepos Airport would fit inside a half-hour window.

The sun had set, and the sky had partially darkened. Everyone piled into a tall, long, narrow SUV Jacques had rented at the airport a few hours earlier. One of the security guys had removed the plates from the vehicle, and James stepped over them on the carpeted floor as he climbed in after Marie to the third row of seats. Jacques shoved Weasel into the middle row in front of James, then slid in beside him. The other two security guys claimed the driver and passenger seats up front.

Weasel was right: a steep, winding hill to the downtown area was less than a half mile from the compound they'd rented. The narrow paved road was well-maintained but sparsely lit. At that hour, it was also lightly traveled, with no cars ahead or behind them. Three minutes after their departure, they reached the bottom of the hill, where they made a sharp right turn onto a street more residential than commercial.

Only a few hundred yards along that narrow street, Weasel pointed to a small hotel that looked to have enjoyed better days. Sueño Tranquilo was the name on the dimly lit neon banner. Although the sign out front was easy to spot, James had to strain to find the entrance to the place. It looked more like a cement sidewalk that led from the roadway to a low-profile building surrounded by trees and shrubs.

The driver hesitated in front of the building until Jacques pointed out the entrance, then scooted further along the street. In a few hundred yards, he made a turn down a side street, then another left turn into a more tranquil residential area.

It was too quiet to park there, Jacques brusquely announced. They'd attract too much attention. It was better to return to the main street, find a tourist hangout, and walk from there to the hotel. It would take only a few minutes longer and would be safer for everyone.

In their earlier planning sessions, they'd already decided that Weasel was a liability as well as an asset. They couldn't just pay him the money he wanted, then let him go free. It would be too easy for him to tip off the other guy. Of course, they couldn't take him with them either. He could turn on them and create a nasty scene.

So, as the SUV came to a stop, James grabbed Weasel firmly by the shoulders while Jacques slipped another set of handcuffs over the pair already around his wrist and secured the new ones to the seatbelt anchor on the floor between the seats. James crawled out of the rear compartment, then turned to shove four one-hundred-dollar bills into the side pocket of Weasel's jeans.

"Not a sound until we return," Jacques ordered the man as he closed the door.

James, Jacques, and Mateo, the Spanish-speaking bodyguard, all walked back toward Hotel Sueño Tranquilo.

They strode casually, like tourists. Mateo told a couple jokes, and the others manufactured laughs to portray a relaxed demeanor. It was approaching the dinner hour, so they couldn't be sure their target would be in the room, but Weasel had insisted they'd find the guy there.

At the entrance to the hotel, they followed the cement pathway toward the inn. Up close, they realized it was actually a narrow driveway that small cars might use to cross a marshy area in front of the property. Despite a chance some passerby might notice, Jacques fished a retractable measuring tape from a pocket and asked James to grab an end so they could quickly measure its width. Thirty seconds later, Jacques nodded, waved for James to follow, and they headed toward the identified room.

The hotel office was exactly where Weasel had described it would be, and the windows were closed and darkened as he had also predicted. They spotted the room they wanted by its painted dark-blue wall, highlighted with a pale-green entrance on their left as they entered the compound. No other guests were in sight. Jacques held up a hand for them to stop and listen outside the target's den. They heard faint TV voices coming from inside, mixed with a buzz of insects and chirping from birds in the silent courtyard.

Jacques pointed James toward the side of the building, out of sight from the door to the room, then stepped in front of him before gesturing for Mateo to step forward and knock on the door.

It took only a few seconds before someone opened it. Without a word, Mateo lunged forward, grabbed the man standing there by the neck, and clasped his hand tightly over the guy's mouth. Jacques rushed into the room next and reached back with the needle to jab their unsuspecting victim, who struggled for only a moment longer before collapsing in a heap on the floor. It had all taken less than a minute.

James didn't have time to think about why a security guard assigned to him would carry such a potent, drug-filled needle. While Mateo shoved the unconscious body away from the door, Jacques closed it tightly with one hand and reached into his pocket with the other.

"Okay to drive through the cement entrance. The driveway is wide enough to accommodate the SUV," Jacques said into his phone. This part of their venture was unplanned because they were initially uncertain whether it would fit on the narrow cement driveway. "You should have enough space before the pool to turn and back up to the room's doorway. It's right where Weasel showed us on Google Photos. Open the hatch as you're driving so we can load him into the rear."

They dumped the unconscious fellow into the trunk of the vehicle as planned, but Weasel grew anxious and tried to loosen the handcuffs from the rear seat anchor. Apparently, he'd expected Jacques to unlock them and let him go once James had crawled into the rear.

"Not so fast," Jacques warned. "You're coming with us to the airport, too. I'll let you go free there."

They arrived at the airport within minutes and drove out to an area next to an office attached to some sort of garage. There, they parked outside a gate leading to the tarmac, where Multima's corporate jet sat, parked and running.

James wanted to know how Jacques planned to revive their unconscious victim. "Now that we've gone to all this trouble, I want to talk to the guy before we take off," he said as he slid out from the rear seat.

Jacques shook his head and responded, "We won't revive him yet. He's going with us on the plane." He pulled something from his pocket, flashed the cover of a passport at James, and rushed to the rear of the SUV. "He's

American. It shows a Florida address. He's coming with us."

"Help Marie up the steps. Alan and Mateo will bring our guy up the stairs."

"What about Weasel? Will you unlock his cuffs?"

"Nope. He's staying right where he is. Someone will find him when they discover the car."

Forty-Two

Paris, France, Sunday December 24, 2023

Japan and Serge suddenly popped into Suzanne's mind as she loaded all her belongings into the Multima limousine waiting for her outside the St. Regis Hotel in Paris. She hadn't heard from Serge for a couple days, and her worry grew as she wondered how and where he might pass Christmas Day. With the difference in time zones, she had fully expected to learn something from her missing lover or the team searching for him.

In fact, if a family with children that celebrated Christmas at all in Japan existed, they'd probably have already opened their gifts and be well into whatever other traditions and celebrations they included for the holiday.

Paris was damp, windy, and cold. Outside the hotel, the black limo waiting for Suzanne was the only occupied vehicle. A half-dozen other cars were parked in the street for the night.

A taxi passed as her car pulled out of the driveway, but otherwise, the city was quieter than she'd ever experienced. Even the church bells were silent. Perhaps a few people lingered inside places of worship, preparing the bells for a post-midnight serenade after the special midnight masses had finished, but it was still too early for those who observed the annual tradition to have left home.

Suzanne knew those customs well. When her mother was alive and living in Quebec, she and most others in the province observed the same traditions they had in France for the past few hundred years. Most people traditionally took naps after school or work, resting up for the big night and early morning to come. Preparations started midway through the evening. Women prepared extravagant meals while the men tidied up the living area, bringing out extra chairs from storage for their expected guests.

Those guests arrived toward midnight, often from out of town or other parts of the sprawling city. Minutes before Christmas Day had officially begun, church bells rang loudly from all directions, summoning people to the Christmas Eve services most of them thought of as compulsory. Priests and their many assistants prepared festive services with a lot of singing, positive religious messages, and seasonal joy.

Suzanne drew a deep breath as she remembered following that ritual for about the first twenty years of her life with both anticipation and excitement. But for her, the magic diminished as she gradually moved away from the religion, drawing on the critical thinking skills she'd learned at university and the frequent debates among her classmates about religion and its mystique.

For the next thirty years, she treated Christmas celebrations as a family obligation, a time to join her single mother for a few days of companionship and family love. However, since her mother had died a few years earlier, Christmas was little more than a day off to relax. After she and Serge had become a couple, they'd enjoyed two Christmases in the Laurentians. Clearly, no celebrations would be possible this year.

There were no gifts, and there would be no time with Serge. Seated alone in the rear seat of the limousine, she felt a tear escape from her right eye. She sniffled silently and wiped it away with her forefinger. Then, she felt a pang of regret. While she was feeling sorry for herself alone in the rear of the limousine, her bodyguard, Jasmine, sat in her usual position up front with the driver.

The woman was following Serge's long-established travel protocol, but she was also away from Willy, her guy, for the Christmas holiday. Suzanne should have invited her to spend the few minutes' drive to the airport in the rear compartment. It probably would have made the short trip more enjoyable for both of them.

There was also limited activity at Orly Airport. A few parked passenger jets were loading for departures, and a couple more either landed or were making their final approaches as the limousine pulled up to the private aircraft section. Her driver stopped momentarily at the gate, where an attendant made a cursory glance inside the car, but he'd already noted the special pass posted in the upper corner of its windshield because he waved the driver through the barricade once it had opened.

The jet engines were already running. Jasmine held the door open as Suzanne slid out through it. The other bodyguards had already fetched her bags from the limo's storage compartment and dashed up the aircraft stairs into the corporate jet ahead of her. Both pilots greeted her with waves and smiles as she entered the plane, wishing her a Merry Christmas.

One of the men was new. Suzanne paused and cast an inquiring look at Joseph Anderson. The senior fellow had worked with Multima for years and knew all the company executives well. He also read her intentions immediately.

"Jean-Paul Décoller here is filling in for this flight. I've known him since we both worked for Air France," Joseph said, giving his companion a nod and a broad smile. "Unfortunately, we needed to rush my regular partner, David, to the hospital with a fever a few hours before Eileen called me up. Don't worry—Jean-Paul is a better pilot than me, so we'll get you there safely."

Suzanne nodded and shook hands with the replacement pilot before wishing them both an enjoyable flight up front, and they returned to the cockpit. Finally, they said farewell to the French agents they'd leave behind. Only two of them were left in the jet's main cabin, leaving Suzanne feeling inexplicably ill at ease.

"Jasmine, let's leave protocol behind for the flight. Sit up here with me, and we'll celebrate the arrival of Christmas 2023 together." Suzanne flashed her most welcoming smile and opened her arms wide to indicate the seat closest to hers.

Jasmine glanced around the jet's cabin for a second or two as though seeking permission from someone else, then tucked her bag into a nearby compartment before sitting down in the posh, leather swivel seat next to the one Suzanne already occupied.

"I'm not sure how celebratory I'll feel." Jasmine laughed. "But I'll do my best to cheer you up. Did you get any word about Serge while we traveled from the hotel?"

Suzanne shook her head.

She fastened her seatbelt as the aircraft eased away from its parking spot on the tarmac. She checked that the Wi-Fi had successfully connected to her phone, and the signal for the satellite phone service glowed in standby mode. They'd barely reached cruising altitude when the first beep of a text caught her attention:

Have changed plans. Now headed for the U.S. Another attempted attack in Costa Rica. Marie and I are safely on the plane. Feel welcome to call me on Jacques Legault's secure line.—James

Her finger had almost touched the screen to look up the security guy's number when another alert sounded:

Have a new lead on Serge. Vietnam just intercepted a signal. We're following up now and headed back toward Tokyo. Will update you when we have more news.—Antonio

Suzanne leaned across to show the phone screen to Jasmine. She pulled it back and reached to dial the number for the bodyguard with James, but before she could find the number to call, another beep sounded. It was Natalia Tenaz.

Just got horrible news from Archie in Vietnam. The two resources Serge selected from Supermarkets have both been killed. They left their apartment this morning for breakfast at a ground-floor restaurant in the building across the street. As they were crossing, an SUV traveling at an extremely high speed hit them, killing both on impact. Unable to reach Serge. Please advise urgently on how I should proceed.

Forty-Three

Somewhere in Japan, Monday December 25, 2023

When the rear door of the SUV opened, Serge noticed the hint of a sunrise. The three fellows who'd captured them stood outside the vehicle, gazing inside, tall piles of blankets filling their arms. In the background, he heard the hum of a large idling engine. He looked beyond the middle guy's shoulder and spotted a windsock blowing gently with the wind: an airport.

Another group of men appeared from nowhere to gaze inside the van. One made a comment in Japanese that caused the others to laugh. Although he'd spoken in Japanese, he had a white, non-Asian appearance, of European heritage, perhaps. With broad shoulders and more body mass around his waist, he might be American. Before Serge could analyze more, the jerk who'd made the probably lewd comment reached in and yanked Serge's cuffed hands, dragging him from the back of the vehicle and forcing him upright. Another person reached down to unlock and release his foot chains.

The bully pointed for Serge to move toward a parked aircraft less than twenty feet away. At the top of the staircase of a small jet, yet another man stood, a rifle pointed toward Serge's head.

As he reached the base of the aircraft stairs, Serge glanced back at the SUV. A short Japanese guy was releasing Constance's leg chains while another fondled her breasts from behind. Serge took another look from the top of the stairwell to see her limping toward the aircraft, visibly sobbing.

The one with the gun shoved Serge into the plane

without saying a word and pointed to the first seat on the left. As soon as Serge was seated, he glanced out the window to see Sheila coming toward the jet, also crying, as yet another guard poked her bare buttocks with a rifle.

The guy holding the gun at the top of the steps first pointed toward Constance, then motioned for her to step farther into the eight-seat aircraft. She looked at Serge with despair in her eyes as she passed him, tears streaking down her cheeks.

When Sheila entered the doorway of the plane, the hoodlum with the gun ran the muzzle slowly over her body, from her breasts to her pubic hair, leering at her angst. Finished with his taunting intimidation, he pointed her toward another seat at the back, on the same side of the aisle as Serge.

A moment or two later, the guy with the gun barked out the command, "Seatbelts!" with a heavy, foreign accent. He watched as his victims buckled up, then motioned to a shorter fellow who'd entered behind them and closed the small jet's door. He was carrying the foot chains over his arm, and he moved toward Serge as if to rebind his feet. Although he knew it was probably futile, Serge tried to kick out at the guy with his right leg. The fellow gracefully avoided Serge's foot and rewarded his efforts with a prick to his thigh. The man administered the drug within seconds, and the plane went dark before he had moved on.

~~~

When Serge awoke later, it was to the buzz of an engine operating at high speed. He slowly opened his eyes and took a few seconds to focus. The drug they'd used felt more potent than the previous batches. Everything still seemed fuzzy and out of focus. His eyelids fluttered involuntarily from the intense sunshine flooding in from the window he
~~~

was facing.

He glanced down and realized they'd wrapped him in a wool blanket after administering whatever drug they used. It was tightly wrapped around his naked body, restricting his movements and secured with some sort of Velcro strap. His body was warm, but whoever these guys were, they were taking no chances that their passengers would cause a disturbance.

Serge listened. With the loud hum of the engines, it was difficult to discern other noises. Behind him, male voices engaged in conversation, but their dialogue wasn't loud enough for him to make out what they were saying or even which language they spoke. Regardless, it sounded harsh, even threatening.

He shifted his body, turning slightly away from the window. Across the aisle, the guy with the gun had dozed off, his powerful weapon sitting in his lap, casually secured by his left arm. Clearly, someone had failed to pay attention during his armaments training course, if he had, in fact, taken one.

The flight was smooth with little turbulence, but Serge had no way of knowing at what altitude they were flying, what their destination might be, or even the direction they were heading.

He leaned over the armrest as far as the blanket and restraint would allow. Constance, two seats back, was sleeping, her body pointed inward, also wrapped in a blanket. A second goon occupied a seat in the row in front of her. This one also had a rifle in his lap, only he sat up, erect. His eyes were also closed, his head nodding gently with the motion of the jet.

There was little Serge could do but listen and observe until the roar of the engines reduced, and the air speed diminished. A bell rang twice. The guy across from Serge jolted upright and released his seat belt with his free hand.

He glanced over before his expression shifted to menacing, and he stood, looked over Serge's head, and nodded to someone further back.

The guy then disappeared into the cockpit and pulled the door so it partially blocked Serge's view. They spoke for a few minutes in voices loud enough to detect that a conversation was taking place, but it was still partially drowned out by the noise of the jet engines, so he could not make out what, exactly, they were saying. He leaned as far forward as his restraints would allow, but eventually gave up and waited until the guy had closed the door and again faced the rear of the passenger cabin.

He motioned for his companions to come forward, and they gathered in a circle to Serge's right. At first, the man's voice was muffled, and at least one ruffian had trouble hearing—he kept pointing to his ear and muttering something.

The leader raised his voice and spoke more slowly.

At first, Serge didn't understand the language they used. Seconds later, he recognized a word: Vladivostok. A chill enveloped his entire body.

Vladivostok: the easternmost city in Russia. Serge leaned in further and strained to discern their words. Yes, there was no doubt: they were speaking Russian, and Vladivostok must be where they were landing.

Forty-Four

Atlanta, Georgia, Monday December 25, 2023

Natalia had tried Multima's Montreal security people every hour through the remainder of that night without success. She considered contacting Suzanne to share the bizarre information about the shed Floyd had discovered, but eventually decided that disrupting her CEO for a call about what might prove to be an irrelevant bit of information wasn't worth the risk. Instead, she chose to focus on the other crisis in Vietnam and wait for more concrete details from Florida.

Although it was already afternoon on Christmas Day, Archie Begat still hadn't contacted her with an important follow-up. Of course, Serge and the two women were of the greatest concern, but the callous murders of the two technology specialists on loan from her Supermarkets team also demanded attention. Without the details of their deaths by vehicular homicide in Ho Chi Minh City, Natalia had been hesitant about notifying their families. Passing on the news around the festive season was horrible enough, but to do so without any explanation of what had happened and why they had lost their loved ones seemed less than reasonable.

Archie answered after several rings. His voice was hoarse, and he formed his words slowly. Perhaps he'd been crying or was experiencing symptoms of shock. She decided to proceed with sensitivity.

"How are you?" She delivered the words in a tone just above a whisper.

"Alive. That's marginally better than my companions. The Ho Chi Minh City police just left my room here. They seized my passport, put an armed guard outside the door to my apartment, and ordered me not to leave. They warned that if I didn't follow their instructions precisely, my next stop would be a downtown jail."

"Why? Why are they taking such an adversarial approach toward you?"

"I'm not sure. The police claimed several eyewitnesses reported that the driver of the vehicle that ran over our colleagues, Regina and Phillip, was a white guy. More than one claimed the driver looked like me." Archie's tone was even more subdued than hers.

"That's absurd. What makes them think you would do such a thing?"

"It seems someone on our floor passed their apartment a few minutes before their deaths and heard shouting coming from the room. That person called the police, who didn't treat it as an urgent matter at the time of the call, but they recorded the report and dispatched a police car and officers just moments before the crash. It arrived shortly after the vehicle that killed them had disappeared."

"Was there some sort of dispute?" Natalia asked.

"None that I know about. Regina and Phillip always turned up the volume whenever they were watching TV. Serge had cautioned them about it when he was here. I heard excessively loud dialogue from my room next door, but always assumed it was coming from the TV. At least one resident thought the shouting was real, and they called the police. They asked me all sorts of questions about my relationship to them and what we were doing in the apartments."

"Oh, no!" Natalia whispered in dismay. "Did you divulge anything?"

"No. I think that's why they're holding me here. I didn't give them any information about our mission, and they're suspicious that I'm holding back information related to the murder." His voice dropped an octave, and she thought she detected a sense of despair.

It was time to rally his spirits, if she could. "Suzanne has powerful connections in the Vietnamese government. You might have met one of them the day you all moved into the apartment complex there. I'll connect with her and get wheels in motion to get you some legal help and released as quickly as possible."

She spent a few more minutes ensuring that his health was otherwise fine, his communication devices were all working, and his morale was, at least, stable. Then, she called Suzanne.

Oddly, she received only a recorded message, stating that the call couldn't be completed as dialed.

She tried again.

Same message, without a single ring or transfer to voicemail.

Suzanne was probably over the Atlantic, en route to Montreal. Maybe there was a technology malfunction on the plane. Perhaps a storm. The possibility even existed that Suzanne had simply shut off the phone to calls and messages. It was Christmas Day, after all.

Natalia dialed the number for Montreal security again. Still no answer, although she was prompted to leave a voice message, which she did.

Clearly, something was amiss, and she couldn't shake the feeling that the strange series of circumstances and communication gaps were somehow related. Serge had been captured and was incommunicado somewhere in Asia. Suzanne was probably in the air, traveling to Montreal, but without communication connections. Floyd Demerais had shut off his communications devices to monitor the shed in Florida. And the folks in security at headquarters weren't responding to calls.

That left only one option: she had to call the guy to whom she owed her entire success at Multima Corporation, even if it was still extremely early on Christmas morning.

She hit the speed dial for James Fitzgerald and listened for the rings.

Forty-Five

Chicago, IL, Monday December 25, 2023

Two beeps sounded before James was alert enough to realize it was his phone breaking the silence of their large suite at the luxurious Ritz-Carlton Hotel in the middle of Chicago. He fumbled in the darkness until he'd located it on the stand beside the bed, noticed that the incoming call was from Natalia, and pressed the screen to start their conversation.

"Have you heard from Suzanne?" she asked.

When he replied that he hadn't, she continued. "I haven't gotten any response on her lines for several hours. On its own, that wouldn't alarm me, but crises with Multima are occurring around the globe. I'm sorry to disturb your sleep so early on Christmas morning, but I need your advice."

James shook his head a couple times to clear the mental cobwebs from his belated deep sleep. They'd only checked into the hotel a few hours earlier, and it had taken some time for his heart rate to slow after the excitement in Costa Rica and the five-hour trip north in the corporate aircraft, so he'd probably only had an hour or so of sleep. He glanced over at the still-dormant Marie, who'd pulled the sheets up over her head to block any noise or distraction.

He slipped out of the bed and ambled toward the separate kitchen area as he processed Natalia's obvious alarm. "When did you speak with Suzanne last?"

"Yesterday. From Paris. She planned to fly back to Montreal because Serge was still missing in Japan, and we had two security employees brutally run over by a car in Vietnam. It all made her nervous. She thought Montreal was probably the safest place for her to be."

"What do the security people in Montreal say? Have they heard from her?"

"That's another problem." Natalia gasped. "I haven't been able to reach anyone in security since yesterday, either. Sometimes, there isn't even a recording, and I've tried all three numbers."

That caused his spine to stiffen.

Multima's security apparatus was as sophisticated as any in the corporate world. With Serge's experience and the acumen he'd gained with Canada's RCMP, Suzanne allowed him to acquire every device and known protocol immediately as they became available. His team's discipline was legendary. It was inconceivable that no one would answer Natalia's calls.

"There might be a problem with your communication devices or network. Let me put you on hold and try with mine."

James reached for a separate phone, found the headquarters' security number, and hit the appropriate speed dial. It rang twenty-four times before he hit the red "end" button with a grimace of resignation.

"I'm not getting an answer either," he reported upon resuming the call with Natalia. "It's Christmas Day, so I guess there's always the possibility that someone simply screwed up on staff scheduling."

"At first, I thought the same. But too many things are happening at once for me to accept that possibility. We know Serge was moved in captivity at least once in Japan. In addition to our two employees killed in Ho Chi Minh City, I heard from Archie—one of the other technicians over there—that the police had confined him to his apartment, under house arrest. Another security guy called me from Florida to tell me he'd discovered a shed with international communication devices just off a property owned by our country's former president. Now, that security guy, too, has gone incommunicado."

Natalia wasn't prone to overreacting. He'd known her and worked with her for years, nurturing her management prowess and analytical skills as she evolved to move into her current role as president of the Supermarkets division. If she was concerned, it deserved a second look.

"What do you think links all these events?" he asked as nonchalantly as he could muster on an hour's sleep.

"I don't know." She sounded frustrated. "I was hoping you might have a suggestion or two."

"Do you feel safe there in Atlanta?"

"Marginally. The office here seems safe. The two security guys Floyd left behind for me are outside my office, although one of them gives me troubling vibes. I just have this feeling that we need to find out what has happened with security at headquarters in Montreal. Once we know the answer to that concern, I might be able to relax more."

"Let me send the corporate jet down to pick you up. I'll send along a couple of the security specialists here with me to ease any concerns you might have with the team there. Come up to Chicago on the jet. Spend some time on Christmas Day with your mom. We can try to put the pieces of this puzzle together." He wasn't sure he'd avoided sounding either paternal or condescending, but it was the best he could do at three in the morning.

She thought about it for a long moment before replying in a tone just above a whisper. "Okay. That might be the best solution. I'll pack a bag and be ready to meet the plane at Hartsfield-Jackson. When would you guess—in about three hours?"

"Make it three and one-half to be safe. They'll need to refuel there anyway."

After thinking about his protegee's concerns, he decided to travel to Atlanta on the jet. The extra time would allow him a shower and a farewell kiss for Marie as the guys fired up the plane for departure.

By the time he arrived in Atlanta, he guessed that he, too, might feel a need to check out what was happening with Montreal's security department.

Forty-Six

Over the Atlantic, Monday December 25, 2023

Mid-flight, Suzanne dozed off to a restless sleep, twisting and turning in her seat. At one point, she woke abruptly, startled by the jet's sudden drop from cruising altitude. Her stomach tightened, pressing upward. She gulped for air, and her throat seemed to close off momentarily. The drop must have been substantial.

The aircraft vibrated, then hit turbulence as the jet bounced in the air. Reflexively, Suzanne grabbed the arms of her leather seat and squeezed tightly to steady her jostling sway despite having the seatbelt tightly secured at her hips. She glanced to her left and caught Jasmine reaching for an airsickness bag with one hand and clapping her mouth shut with the other as if to hold in the vomit.

Suzanne reached into the side pocket of her own seat, grabbed the bag stored there, and whipped it open with one deft swoop of her hand. Jasmine grasped it and raised it to her mouth as the bile building inside her started to escape. She expelled the waste from her upset stomach with two violent gasps, then leaned her head backward against the seat to regain her composure.

Suzanne fished a tissue from her handbag on the side of the seat and offered it to Jasmine with a shrug and smile of sympathy as the jet continued to bounce erratically, its engine sounds vacillating with the bumps and grinds of the aircraft.

The turbulence and discomfort continued for several minutes before a slight crackling noise and the louder sound of the engines caught Suzanne's attention.

"Sorry, ladies," the pilot said. He paused for several

seconds as the next few violent bumps in the air caused him to lose either his concentration or his voice. "This storm is far worse than the mild turbulence air traffic control told us to expect. We're changing direction slightly and climbing a little higher to see if we can't find a smoother space. Please don't move around in the cabin until we get better stabilized. I'll let you know as soon as I can."

Suzanne glanced over at Jasmine, but her bodyguard's eyes were squeezed tightly closed, and her large hands gripped the arms of her seat in desperation. Her airsickness had apparently subsided, but her chest heaved with either discomfort, fear, or both.

"Anything I can do to help?" Suzanne mustered as much compassion in her tone as the constant bounce of the aircraft allowed.

Jasmine shook her head with a resigned expression on her face and body language that conveyed only trepidation. Her eyes drooped downward. Her shoulders slumped forward tentatively. Her hands trembled visibly.

Suzanne let Jasmine cope with her fear and discomfort in silence. However, the storm outside the aircraft thwarted that good intention. The jet's engines roared one moment and idled the next. The turbulence shook the cupboards and compartments in the cabin, causing a cacophony of rattling, shaking, and creaking. Accustomed to flying, with thousands of air miles under her belt, even Suzanne began to grow concerned.

After over an hour of continuous disruptions, Jean-Paul Décoller, the pilot who'd been recruited as a last-minute replacement, emerged from the cockpit, tightly grasping both the wall and the door into his work area. He stretched upward, pressed the palms of his hands against the interior roof of the cabin, and walked toward Suzanne, delicately putting one foot before the other to maintain balance in the still-buffeting aircraft.

"We have some issues of concern," he started with a poker face and a calm tone of voice. "We've learned from other aircraft that the storm might worsen as we approach the North American shoreline. We've used more fuel than expected with the stronger headwinds, and our air pressure indicator signals suggest we need mechanical attention. We think we should take the plane down in Gander, Newfoundland."

"Why are you consulting with me?" Suzanne offered the most reassuring smile she could manage under the circumstances. "You're the experts. If you think we need to land, we need to land. Don't worry about getting permission from me."

He nodded but broke eye contact before he spoke again. "I just want you to know that we should be able to land in Gander all right. I expect we can manage a safe and smooth landing, but we might be stuck there for a while. If the air pressure indicator needs maintenance, being Christmas Day and all, we might not be able to get either a technician or parts quickly, and it could be a day or two before we get out of there."

Suzanne nodded her understanding and offered another smile to put him at ease. "Do what you think is best. Jasmine and I will adapt."

The co-pilot shifted his body direction gingerly, preparing to return to the cockpit. He offered a final nod before working his way delicately back up to the front. As the door to the cockpit closed, Suzanne reached for her phone in the pouch on the left side of her seat. She raised the screen toward her and realized there was no internet. Upon closer examination, she discovered there were no signals from either the plane's satellite connection, the jet's Wi-Fi, or a cellular connection.

Moments later, she felt the plane's direction veer slightly and the engine slow before she noticed the tiny hint of the plane's descent. It took over an hour, with frequent, impatient glances at her phone, for the descent to become more pronounced. Finally, with what felt like a desperate lunge toward the runway, the wheels bounced upon impact, then settled into a whine and a roar from the engines as they slowed the aircraft.

A glance toward Jasmine reassured Suzanne that her bodyguard had survived her personal ordeal, as her skin color had returned to normal, and her eyes sparkled with relief. A few seconds later, her device came to life, lighting up and sounding alerts. One message, from Antonio Primavera, caught her eye:

> *Just received a message from Sheila on Serge's team using a stolen device. Got location coordinates where they're being held in Russia. All are alive and okay. Arranging transportation there now. Contact me when you can.—A*

As the jet taxied toward the small terminal, Suzanne pressed her speed dial and, moments later, was rewarded with the comforting sound of a clear ring. Antonio picked up the call within seconds. There were no pleasantries to start the dialogue.

"Tell me more," Suzanne begged as soon as Antonio had identified himself.

"Somehow, Sheila managed to grab a phone for enough time to capture their GPS coordinates, and send me a message with their exact location. Said that would be her only communication as she'd have to destroy the phone so their captors couldn't track her message. She begged for help in her sign-off."

"No word about Serge or the other woman with him? Her name was Constance, I think."

"Nothing. Clearly, she was rushed and focused on

letting us know where we could rescue them."

"What is your plan?" Suzanne kept her tone calm, despite being disappointed that there was no new information about Serge.

"I've connected again with the Keisatsu-chō, Japan's national police force. Serge wanted to keep them out of our activities here, but I felt we needed their help. They've agreed to lend us some resources and a jet. We'll leave within minutes for Russia. I'll be incommunicado until we complete the mission in Vladivostok. I'll let you know what happens."

The jet pulled to a stop as Suzanne pressed the screen to end their call. Tears threatened to burst out, but she refused to succumb. Instead, she drew a deep breath and turned toward Jasmine. Her companion looked better: composed but not refreshed after the hour or so of tension during their harrowing descent. Suzanne filled her in with the scant details from Antonio's call.

They gathered up their belongings while waiting for the pilots to exit the cockpit, open the door, and lower the staircase so they could leave the plane. It took more than a few minutes. Suzanne glanced at her watch. It had already adjusted to Newfoundland time, a half hour ahead of the Atlantic time zone used by the other Canadian Maritime provinces, which was, in turn, an hour ahead of the Eastern Time Zone in New York and Montreal.

It was just after three o'clock in the morning on Christmas Day.

Suzanne peered out the nearest window and saw only blackness. She detected no movement on the runways. From that side of the aircraft, she had no view of the airport buildings, but she could see that a light snow had fallen to the ground.

She'd never visited Gander, but she knew its name from the heroic efforts of the townspeople in 2001, during the

9/11-related crisis. Back then, the tiny airport and population of less than ten thousand people had received thirty-eight commercial flights that were unable to land in American cities. They wound up accommodating over six thousand passengers and crew in public places or private homes, with food and refreshments, for up to two days. Her spine tingled just remembering the events.

Impatient to leave the aircraft, Suzanne made small talk with Jasmine as they waited for one of the pilots to give them the "all clear" and help them off the plane. It took longer than usual before the replacement pilot slipped out of the cockpit.

"We let air traffic control know we were coming with enough time for them to round up a ground crew under normal circumstances," Jean-Paul Décoller explained, "but it's Christmas, and they still haven't been able to find staff willing to come in at three in the morning to let us into the airport. We can keep an engine running for heat and electricity, but that's all we can do until a ground crew arrives. They're expected in a couple hours, at five."

Suzanne sighed in resignation. At least Jasmine wouldn't be throwing up every few minutes as she had during the turbulence of the storm. She settled back into her seat to try for a few hours' sleep but was interrupted by the alert of an incoming text message from Natalia Tenaz— it wasn't yet two in the morning on Christmas Day for her.

> *Received a text from Archie in Vietnam moments ago. He just intercepted a message from Vladivostok to an IP address in Palm Beach, Florida, confirming they had the three prisoners and would start interrogation immediately. The message requested authorization for unconventional methods if necessary.*
> *~ Natalia*

Forty-Seven

Vladivostok, Russia, Monday December 25, 2023

Serge awoke to brilliant sunshine beaming through a window high above. He glanced to his left and saw Constance and Sheila, sleeping, huddled together under one colorful, thick blanket. He sighed with muted satisfaction. They'd yanked Sheila from the room earlier for who knew what sort of blatant impropriety, but had at least returned her to their group while he'd slept.

His eyes focused more clearly. He rubbed them, then raised himself to a sitting position on the wooden floor. Clearly, their accommodations were no more than a shed. The roof and walls were constructed from the same type of wood as the floor, and neither had insulation nor a finish. He shuddered with a combination of the thought and the cold.

The decrepit building looked like it had once been used as a workshop or tool shed, though no tools remained that he could see. It had electricity, and a portable heater was plugged into a socket a few feet away, blowing warm air in the direction of the three captives. Someone had left a single bottle of water on the floor just a few feet beyond his reach, but with his hands cuffed behind him, he didn't know how he could drink from it, even if he found a way to open it.

There was no doubt the women were still asleep. When they awoke, perhaps they could connive a way to reach, open, and drink from the bottle. He swallowed hard to suppress his immediate thirst in the meantime.

He tested his legs and feet. Though both were cold, neither showed evidence of frostbite either during transportation or so far in confinement. Everything seemed to work all right.

Pangs of hunger followed. They had fed the three captives a single, small bowl of rice after their arrival, having released their hands so they could grasp the bowls. One of the masked guards stood directly over them as they ate, his high-powered weapon pointed at one of their heads as a warning.

His thoughts shifted to Sheila. He remembered her silently teasing one of the guards with her eyes and tongue before they dragged her away from the shed after their feeding. When he saw it, he swallowed hard but said nothing, fearful that any words or actions would make it worse for her. He also remembered momentarily wondering if that would be the last time he would see her face.

Seeing her huddled there with Constance relieved a modicum of the guilt he felt about endangering them with their fateful mission.

Constance had remained subdued, terrified of the men and the circumstances. She hadn't uttered a word since they'd dragged her, naked, onto the private jet in Japan, and her eyes remained downcast whenever she was awake. He couldn't recall her making eye contact since they'd been thrown on the floor of the shed.

Suddenly, he detected voices and movement outside. At that moment, the women stirred from their places on the floor. A few seconds later, the door swung open, and two massive hulks lowered their heads to enter the doorway, stepped inside the shed, and pointed their automatic weapons. They looked angry or possessed and screamed something, which Serge inferred to mean that they should move or maybe stand up.

After a few seconds, one of the thugs realized the futility of his command, lowered his weapon, and moved forward, bending his knees and back lower. With one quick motion, he reached out with his massive left hand, gripped the back of Serge's head, and yanked him fully upright, like he might a petulant pet. The other guy waved his gun, signaling for Serge to follow him despite the zip ties that limited each of his steps to only a few inches. They offered no other help, stayed a few feet away from him, and ambled toward the open door of another nearby structure.

When they got closer, Serge could see it was a European-designed recreational vehicle. "Dethleffs," a small insignia beside the door confirmed. There was no way to mount the three steps from the ground to the floor of the elevated RV, so the guy following him laid down his weapon and lifted Serge, depositing him firmly on the floor of the vehicle, while the guy inside helped steady him.

The man at the top of the stairs stepped aside for Serge to enter the vehicle, where he saw a small kitchen with a counter and a sink. He took two more tiny steps and turned to the left, where he could see the rest of the interior. There was a black, U-shaped sofa wrapped around a table which was secured to the floor by two metal pillars.

At the edge of the sofa, almost within reach, sat another massive hulk, holding a long cigar in his left hand and smiling gratuitously. He looked familiar: long, dark, wavy hair, a creased forehead, a full beard covering most of his face, and a crooked nose that had probably been broken several times. His broad shoulders filled the entire corner of the sofa the guy occupied, and his fat belly took up almost all the available space between him and the table.

It took more than a few seconds to put a name to the face. In his last mugshot, the fellow hadn't had a beard, but the piercing black eyes and overgrown eyebrows hadn't changed. He was undoubtedly the long-time enforcer of The Organization, Lazzaro Grasso. He was the personification of his last name.

"Sit there," he said in perfect American English as he

pointed to a corner of the sofa opposite him. For a few moments after responding to his command, the fellow said nothing. He just stared, assessing his latest "project."

Serge surveyed the tight quarters uncomfortably and silently. The RV's motor idled harmlessly to generate power for the heater. Warm air blew toward Serge's ankles from a vent that had been cut into the dull gray carpet, which helped hold adequate warmth despite the freezing air outside. Birds communicated in a tree only yards away from the vehicle on branches long ago stripped bare of their leaves, but it was impossible to determine the sort of feathered creature, as the closed doors and windows blocked all but a trace of their tune.

When he finally spoke, Grasso's voice boomed, although he appeared to exert almost no effort. "Why were you in Japan?"

It seemed like an odd place to start since his outfit—or someone working with them—had gone to so much trouble to detach a train car and transport them to a mountain hideaway, then fly them from Japan to Vladivostok in Russia. Still, it was always better to accommodate than infuriate.

"My team was following up on some tips we received about possibly illegal activities that might impact my employer."

"Do you mean your employer, Suzanne Simpson, or the Multima Corporation?" The thug asked this question without a trace of a smirk or other suggestion that his question might be intended to lighten the tone or temper the environment.

"I think you know that, to me, they are the same. Suzanne is my boss. She runs Multima."

"That's right. I expect she is much more to you than a boss. So, when I ask you a question, I want a full and truthful answer, or something unpleasant might happen to her." He reached into a pocket, pulled out a phone, pressed the screen a few times, then leaned forward to show him a photo. It was of Suzanne's borrowed jet, parked near a runway, with a sign in the background: Gander International Airport.

"How do I know that photo isn't doctored?"

Again, Grasso pressed his phone screen and brought up a locator application, identified as FlightRadar24. It showed the live location coordinates for an aircraft carrying the identification number N247365 parked on the ground in Gander, Newfoundland. It was the number Suzanne had personally chosen to signify that her stores were open twenty-four hours a day, seven days a week, every day of the year.

"She's on the aircraft, but it's not going anywhere soon. It has a mechanical problem, and we control how quickly the required part gets to her. In the meantime, we also have resources at the airport, assuring she stays within our span of control until we decide otherwise. Now, answer my question. Why were you in Japan?"

Serge took a few seconds to consider his response. Almost any answer he might give could cause The Organization to act against Suzanne, Multima Corporation, or himself. He decided to answer with a version of the truth.

"Multima feels threatened. No one has made a formal demand to Suzanne or anyone else in senior management, as far as we know. And you might be aware that we recently lost the president of our Supermarkets division under suspicious circumstances that remain unsolved. We want to find out who is making these threats and why."

Grasso listened impassively and made no movement signaling understanding, sympathy, or surprise. Instead, he drew a smoking cigar to his mouth and inhaled a long drag, releasing it through his nose and mouth some seconds later. The stench was powerful enough to irritate the throat of anyone sitting in the same confined space. When he chose to respond, his tone was threatening.

"I've taken people out for less. Your arrogant law-and-order mentality has cost The Organization millions of dollars. The people I work for have tried to buy your company for a fair price. We tried as long ago as the days of John George Mortimer and as recently as last year with Suzanne Simpson. Multima has repeatedly rebuffed The Organization's reasonable proposals to share in Multima's success with a posture nothing short of puritanical. Now, you come poking around Japan and our friends in the Yakuza. You made them nervous enough to hijack a train and put you and your team on the sidelines. That's embarrassing for The Organization."

His manner and apparent mindset left little room to maneuver. And the thug looked deadly serious despite the irrational premise he outlined. Still, it seemed possible to test his resolve, at least slightly.

"Does The Organization have something specific for Suzanne to consider?"

"She can decide whether it's worth protecting Multima Corporation or her own life. The people I work for are willing to either pay her a fair price to buy controlling shares in the corporation or to simply drop her in the Atlantic Ocean." Grasso paused and let a disgusting sneer form. "A chopper is ready in Gander, and The Organization is out of patience. If you're not willing to cooperate, the big boys outside would love to dismember you and the naked women ... piece by piece."

"Why is Multima so important to The Organization?"

"I don't know and don't care. The folks I report to are the most powerful people in America. It's not my job to understand why they make their decisions. I'm only here to carry them out. Shall I tell them you'll cooperate? Or ask them how they'd like me to snuff you out?"

There was no point prolonging the discussion. Clearly, Grasso was following orders and willing to carry out any he received. If it were only about himself, Serge might be inclined to ignore the risks and accept the outcome. But there was much more at stake. Suzanne, his companions in the nearby shed, the Multima Corporation and its shareholders around the globe—and who knew how many more people in the business community.

Serge drew in a deep breath. He was about to succumb and agree to cooperate when he heard a barrage of bullets outside the RV. Instinctively, he lunged across the table toward Grasso, who'd already reached into his pocket for a weapon. As the noise and gunfire outside surged, he grasped desperately for Grasso's massive hand with his own cuffed wrist.

Grasso was far too strong. The guy's unencumbered hands moved fluidly as they resisted whatever meager pressure he could muster. The mobster's powerful right hand eventually shook off Serge's desperate lunge, and he yanked a weapon from a pocket or holster. From the RV's doorway, a hail of gunfire followed.

It only took a few seconds for everything to go dark again, this time with a searing pain in the back of his right shoulder.

Forty-Eight

Atlanta, Georgia, Monday December 25, 2023

When Natalia first asked the security guys to walk with her to the rented apartment in Atlanta to pack her bags and prepare to meet James at the airport, all seemed normal. Guillaume gave her space, and Jack Smith walked well behind them.

At the apartment, she quickly gathered what she'd need for a few days in Chicago. It was cold there, so she found sweaters and leggings for warmth and skirts that Mom would accept in equal measure. When the bag was full, she opened the apartment door, ready to call an Uber—there was no reason to disturb her assigned company driver on Christmas Day.

As she reached into her pocket to retrieve her phone, Guillaume put his hand on her elbow forcefully, then yanked the phone from her hand.

"I've got a better service. He'll get us to the airport quicker and cheaper."

Before she could respond, he sprayed something foul-smelling into her face, and everything darkened.

~~~~

A bump jolted her awake. She was lying on a coarse black carpet in a stuffy, confined space. The darkness was total, and it took a few moments to realize that she was in the trunk of a car. Panic set in. Would she be able to breathe? How long had she been there? Where was the car going? Who'd captured her and why?

Before she could discern answers to any of those questions, the vehicle slowed, the engine's whine reduced,
~~~~

and her body's swaying with the movement of the car became gentler. The rhythm suggested they were on a winding path with many curves—a residential subdivision, perhaps, or maybe a country road.

Because she'd lost consciousness temporarily from whatever Guillaume had sprayed in her face, it was impossible to know how long she'd already spent in the trunk of the car. So it was impossible to determine where they might be headed, given the scant facts she could muster.

The car came to a complete stop, and the engine shut off before she could worry more.

"Be careful," a voice called out. "I didn't have anything to secure her in there. She's physically fit and probably quite strong. If she's awake, she might resist."

"My gun is ready if she tries anything."

The trunk latch released. It was still dark outside, but a beam of light flooded in as the lid swung slowly upward, forcing her to momentarily look away. She tilted her head at another angle, and her eyes adjusted again. Sure enough, outside the car, a large Black man stood next to Guillaume, staring at her, pointing a weapon directly toward her face. She screamed despite the earlier warning.

Guillaume lashed out with a stinging slap across her face.

She cringed in response but resisted making any further noise or trying to communicate. Satisfied, he hoisted her out of the car and stood her upright, facing the Black guy. He was taller than Guillaume by at least a foot and looked like he might have once played football, with broad shoulders, a massive chest, and a face that showed no emotion.

He studied her with his eyes, silently and critically. He blinked only once as he stared up and down her body and finished his inspection with a simple twitch of his closed lips. Then, still pointing the gun at her, he addressed his partner. "She looks too young—is she really Multima Supermarkets' president?"

"We've got the right bitch. I've been assigned to her for a few days now. There's no question that she's the right one. You're probably thinking about the CEO. She's ten or fifteen years older and already under our span of control elsewhere."

Their voices had calmed somewhat. Their bodies relaxed slightly, and the Black fellow pointed for her to start moving in the direction of a building a few yards to the side. It was a modern reddish-brown brick building, with ceiling-high windows along the front. A large white logo with the numbers 2975 embedded in the wall above some windows caught her eye, but there were no other signs or banners to identify the company. Only two other cars were parked in the lot, both of them late-model luxury cars, but she couldn't identify the brands from her position.

The Black fellow rattled some keys as they approached the building and leaned around her to unlock the door. Like the windows, the doorway used dark-tinted glass, blocking any view inside. He nudged her forward, where another man waited for them to enter the building.

Seated on a casual chair, with his feet hoisted on a desk in the back corner of the room, the man yawned. He dropped his feet to the floor as they moved toward him. The new guy was brown, maybe Latin American in heritage, and very well dressed in a dark-blue suit over a brilliant white shirt with the collar open enough to expose the curly hairs on his chest. He sported a well-trimmed beard and appeared to be about her age. When he stood up, he was about as tall as the Black fellow.

He pointed them toward another corner on the opposite side of the room, occupied by a well-worn leather sofa. As they passed, he stepped forward and handed Guillaume two plastic restraining devices and nodded, studiously avoiding eye contact with her.

Once she was seated, Guillaume wrapped the restraining devices, first around her wrists and then her ankles. Satisfied, he stepped away, lit a cigarette, and exhaled the smoke in her direction as a final gesture of defiance or arrogance; she couldn't be sure which.

The three men huddled around the desk and chair, where the Latino guy appeared to ask all the questions. The other two responded in tones low enough that she couldn't discern what they were talking about. After a few minutes, the Latino dismissed the others and pointed at the outside door.

Once the pair had gone and the door was securely locked, he ambled over to Natalia, dragging a chair with him.

"Merry Christmas," he said with a warm smile and polite nod of his head, a marked contrast to the treatment she'd received from the other pair. "My name is Mauro Alvarez. I'm a shareholder in the Multima Corporation, and I plan to become an even larger shareholder over the next few days."

She made eye contact, meeting his dark brown pupils that drilled uncomfortably into hers. Despite the polite demeanor, there was no sense of friendship or personal interest. Those eyes could easily be mistaken for a robot's: probing, assessing, and calculating. She waited to make any comment.

After his visual assessment of her—or maybe it was an attempt at intimidation—he looked away, reached inside a pocket for a cigarette pack, and lit one with a large flame from a small lighter, seemingly dragging out the process. He spoke again after exhaling a large quantity of smoke over his shoulder and away from her face.

"You've enjoyed an impressive career with Multima so

far. We've watched you climb the ladder at Financial Services and congratulate you on your recent appointment as president of the Supermarkets division. You've shown outstanding business acumen and extraordinary leadership ability."

His tone suggested that he was genuine with his praise, but she was still in plastic handcuffs. She seized upon a pause to make that point. "Thank you, but I'm not accustomed to having business conversations with my hands and feet bound by zip ties. What's going on?"

He laughed loudly and inhaled more smoke from the cigarette. "They told me you were a spirited one. They also warned me you were very fit and might even be able to take me out with your hands and feet—is that true?"

She hadn't actively participated in judo since her days in high school, though she'd achieved the level of brown belt back then. How much more about her did they know? She chose to laugh off his question rather than reply.

He gave her a moment longer, then decided to move on, leaving her confined. "I'm related to Abduhl Mahinder, the chief executive officer of Bank of the Americas. You know him as a director on Multima's board. He's my father-in-law, and it was he who recommended that we meet for a chat." Alvarez paused again for a drag on his cigarette to, no doubt, give her some time to process the connection and its importance. It still didn't excuse her treatment.

It was time to test him. "I was working in my office all day and evening, only a phone call away. With a brief introduction, I would have been happy to meet with Abduhl's son-in-law for a few minutes. Why was it necessary for you to kidnap me and bring me here in the trunk of a car?"

"Good question." Again, he paused for dramatic effect and inhaled deeply on his cigarette as though relishing his ability to make her wait longer. "You see, I'm here conducting a job interview. If you answer my questions correctly, within a few days—maybe even a few hours—you can become the Multima Corporation's chief executive officer, but if you fail to impress me with your answers to my questions, we want you to be comfortably subdued for an alternative destination."

Once more, he stared into her eyes with a clear warning that gradually morphed into a demeaning sneer.

Forty-Nine

Atlanta, Georgia, Monday December 25, 2023

James became more concerned when he couldn't connect with Lori, the gal who oversaw the security team at Multima's corporate headquarters in Montreal. From the company jet, en route to Atlanta, he dialed her personal mobile number since calls to the office still proved fruitless.

Mateo and Alan, the guys in his personal security detail, had finally found her private number and were confident she'd be reachable. She had three young children, and both fellows knew her well enough to expect the kids would have her out of bed and opening gifts unusually early that morning. It was disconcerting that his repeated calls didn't go through to her voicemail so he could at least leave a message. Instead, the calls rang for minutes before they simply dropped off.

James and each of the guys in turn continued to dial the corporate office every few minutes, hoping someone would eventually answer the lines. None of them could recall a similar incident occurring previously, and all began to wonder if there might be more than a technical glitch at play.

He also tried Suzanne's personal number repeatedly, but all the calls went directly to voicemail, implying she had blocked her calls. In all the years he'd known and worked with Suzanne, he couldn't recall a single instance when she wasn't immediately available. It was something she took pride in and assured her direct reports and fellow management colleagues that their calls were always welcome at any time of the day or night.

As the aircraft started its descent into Atlanta, James

called Natalia to let her know they'd arrive within a few minutes. When he dialed her number, it too immediately transferred to voicemail. Perhaps she was making another call at the time. He tried again as the plane touched down with the same result.

"Mateo," he called across the seat. "Try Natalia's security guys to find out where they are and why she doesn't answer my calls."

The fellow followed James's instructions and, a few moments later, turned toward him with a bewildered look on his face. "I tried Guillaume—the call goes immediately to his voicemail. I'll try his partner, Jack Smith."

A few minutes later, Mateo waved to get James's attention. The color had drained from his face. Mateo unbuckled his seatbelt and advanced toward James despite the roar and high speed of the jet decelerating on the runway. When he was close enough to James's face to touch it, he practically shouted, "I've got a nurse on Jack Smith's line. Says she's from the Grady Memorial Hospital. They're treating him for some kind of drug overdose."

James accepted the phone from Mateo, identified himself by name and corporate position, and asked who he was speaking with.

"I'm Jeannie Winslow, a nurse practitioner on the emergency ward here at Grady Memorial. Are you related to Jack Smith?"

"I'm a colleague of his at Multima Corporation. Jack is one of our security specialists. Can you tell me what happened?"

"All I know is that Jack was dropped here about one hour ago, unconscious. The doctors tested and treated him, and he's now awake, but we're keeping him a while longer for observation. Can you notify his family? We haven't been able to reach anyone."

"I'm sure we can," James replied. "Is Jack well enough

to talk with me?"

There was a pause. Muffled voices conversed in the background. A male voice came on the line and spoke in a hoarse, feeble tone. "Hello?"

"It's James Fitzgerald. I'm currently the president at Multima Financial Services and serve on the board of directors. Do you recognize that name?" He did, so James carried on. "What happened to you?"

"I was just getting ready to leave Natalia Tenaz's apartment in Atlanta to take her to the airport when I felt a sudden prick on my thigh. When I turned to see what it was, someone smashed me in the face. I fell and immediately lost consciousness. I just woke up here a few minutes ago. A doctor told me they'd performed tests and discovered a large amount of heroin in my body, but I don't use anything, man."

"Where was your partner when this happened?"

"I'm not sure. Had said he was stopping for a piss while we waited for the elevator. That was the last time I saw him."

"Was it your partner who called the ambulance?"

"I have no idea. I haven't seen him since."

"Wasn't he also supposed to accompany Natalia to the airport?"

"Yeah," Jack replied. "We were both assigned to her and planned to meet you at the airport. She used your name."

James passed the phone back to the security guard Mateo, telling him to gather all the necessary information to alert Smith's family of the incident and make any necessary calls and arrangements. Mateo nodded and started to speak into the phone.

The jet came to a full stop during the call. One pilot stepped out of the cockpit as James finished speaking. He waved for the fellow to come over as he unbuckled and stood to engage with him.

"Let's leave the doors to the aircraft closed for a few moments." He used an authoritative tone but kept the volume subdued. "Some strange things are happening right now. I can't share all the details with you because I'm simply not certain what is happening and where. The woman we were supposed to meet here is incommunicado, and one of her assigned security guys is in a hospital recovering from a drug administered by injection. His partner is also missing in action."

The pilot nodded and replied calmly, "Shall I get air traffic control to connect us with the airport's security folks who oversee private aircraft and ask them to locate that woman?"

"Her name is Natalia Tenaz," James replied with a nod of dismissal, then turned to Mateo. "Any luck reaching Jack Smith's family?"

"I reached a brother. They all live in Connecticut, but he'll get a flight to Atlanta as soon as he can. Even though it's Christmas Day, he expects to get out from a nearby airport."

"Work with the hospital to keep Jack there until his brother arrives. Multima will cover all additional expenses. Make sure the brother keeps you informed about his flight details, and see if you can track down another Multima security guard. I know it's tough with central control inoperative in Montreal, but check your contact files and phone records to see if you can reach someone in the Atlanta area and get them to watch Smith until we find out what's going on."

James leaned down to peer out a window of the plane on the side closest to the private jet terminal lobby and offices. It was light outside, but he saw little activity. Scanning the tarmac around the terminal, he counted a dozen aircraft. Most seemed parked with no engines running. Three or four jets away, a Bombardier Global

7500—the same type of aircraft Suzanne normally used—was backing away.

James quickly keyed the aircraft's identifying details into the Notes app on his phone and walked toward the cockpit. Without knocking, he swung the door open and pointed through the front windshield at the departing aircraft.

"Ask air traffic control where that jet, N9246Z, is headed, and see if they'll give you any information about the owner or current passengers."

The pilots both nodded, and one gripped the microphone before James ducked back out of the cockpit. He looked up to see the other security guy, Alan, waving wildly for his attention.

"I have Antonio Primavera on the phone from Japan. They've snatched Serge from The Organization in Russia and are on their way back to Tokyo. He wants to speak with you."

Fifty

Gander, Newfoundland, Monday December 25, 2023

A glance at her watch indicated sunrise was approaching in Newfoundland, though it was still dark outside. Suzanne had found it impossible to sleep after the cryptic and disturbing message from Archie they'd intercepted several hours earlier between Southern Florida and Vladivostok, Russia. While details were scarce, the text seemed to imply the party in Russia had Serge and his female companions and sought permission to interrogate using torture if necessary.

In the hours following, she'd desperately tried, without success, to reach any of her security personnel in Montreal. Jasmine, too, had tried all the numbers for team members from the Montreal area she could find in her phone. Meanwhile, the airport looked deserted, and communication between the replacement co-pilot and air traffic control produced no new information.

A knock on the aircraft's door caught her attention, and Suzanne jumped from her seat to approach the window next to the doorway. She'd taken only two steps before the cockpit door swung open, and Jean-Paul Décoller filled most of the doorway space. His right arm appeared from behind his right leg as he raised and pointed a gun directly at Suzanne's face from a distance about five feet away.

He glared a warning and jerked his head for her to retake her seat as he addressed Jasmine. "I know you're carrying, so get your weapon out of its hiding place, slowly and gently." He paused while Suzanne's protector followed his instructions. "Place it on the floor and slide it toward me with your toe. Otherwise, don't move, or I'll fire."

As he spoke, he eased sideways toward the aircraft door, where someone was banging with a fist. Satisfied that Jasmine had moved her weapon out of easy reach, he felt behind himself for the door's release handle and swung it open. Next, he stepped forward and scooped up Jasmine's gun without removing his gaze from the women. He continued to point his weapon directly at Suzanne's face.

As the co-pilot returned to lower the stairway to the ground, a slight movement in the cockpit caught Suzanne's eye. Her assigned pilot, who was slumped forward over the aircraft controls, twitched as though in troubled sleep. What had happened to him?

"Will, are you all right?" she cried out to Will Andersen, her regular pilot, as loudly as possible.

"Quiet!" the co-pilot commanded with an equally loud shout.

Damn. She should have probed more when Will had introduced the new guy as they were boarding in Paris. Also frustrating was her naïve, unquestioning acceptance of her trusted pilot's explanation that the guy was substituting for his regular partner, the fellow who'd supposedly fallen ill hours before their departure from an undetermined ailment.

Two hooded men climbed the few stairs from the ground to the aircraft's entrance. Their hoods were attached to thick winter jackets to help cope with the extreme cold outside the cabin. Once inside the jet, they both pulled handguns from their pockets and pointed them at Suzanne and Jasmine.

The co-pilot diverted his attention to the cockpit. He stepped back inside and yanked on Joseph Anderson's hair, pulling his head upright. He held it there while he leaned around to inspect his victim's condition. Satisfied, he let go, and Joseph's inert body collapsed back on the control panel again with a thud.

A woman appeared at the top of the stairs, carrying heavy wool blankets. She looked Latina and had clearly not dressed for the occasion like her male counterparts. Her jacket was zipped tightly, and there was a scarf around her neck, but her hands were bare, while the men wore gloves. She seemed dressed more appropriately for a winter day in the southern United States than one in Newfoundland.

The woman stepped into the airplane and passed in front of Suzanne to hand a blanket to Jasmine. She reached around her security protector's shoulder, wrapped it around her shoulders, then pulled it down to cover her feet. She fidgeted for a moment or two before leaving the blanket. Jasmine's left leg twitched slightly before the woman turned toward Suzanne.

The woman repeated the process, covering Suzanne with a large wool blanket, pausing again to fidget with how it fell around Suzanne's feet. When she was done, Suzanne felt a prick and watched her right leg involuntarily twitch. Alarmed, she turned toward Jasmine and saw her head already slumped to her chest.

Suzanne tried to throw off the blanket and lurch forward, but she couldn't move. Her legs seemed frozen. Her vision went fuzzy, and then there was nothing.

~~~~

The next images were hazy and blurred. Her throat was dry, and an attempt to swallow proved painful. Her tongue felt swollen. When she blinked her eyes, she saw only darkness. She tried to reorient herself. She felt the heavy wool blanket on her face, the one the woman had covered her with before doing something that had caused her to lose consciousness.

Suzanne realized that she was lying prone on her back, but she felt as if she were moving. There were sounds. Music played softly in the background. It sounded festive, so it was still probably Christmas Day. Some of the other
~~~~

sounds came from the wheels of whatever she was lying on, probably a stretcher. Whoever moved her stretcher did so at a brisk pace. The bumps were frequent and occasionally severe.

Even with the heavy wool blanket, it was cold. Frigid, even. She trembled involuntarily from it and tried to pull the wool blanket more tightly around her. As she tugged, her stretcher changed direction and dropped suddenly downward, first below her head and then, a second later, her feet. The blanket opened slightly, exposing her to the outside air, and she saw snow blowing and a large building off to one side.

She felt another chill as her hands fumbled under the blanket, searching for a railing or something else she might grip onto. As her right hand passed across her chest, it caught momentarily on her blouse, which was open almost to her waist. Her bra was missing. She yanked one corner of the open blouse to cover herself, then fumbled discreetly around inside the blanket, trying to locate it, but was unsuccessful.

A vehicle approached, its tires crunching loudly in the snow, its engine purring in protest against the frigid air. Suddenly, all movement stopped. Four hands grabbed her prone body and hoisted her into the rear of an SUV, where they dropped her on the floor. One pair of hands dragged her, headfirst, toward the rear of the vehicle. She kept her eyes closed until she heard the slam of the car door and footsteps retreating outside.

She tugged a corner of the blanket away from her eyes and looked out of the vehicle's rear window. It made a sudden turn, and she saw a modern, large, gray building with no sign of windows. A few seconds later, the SUV turned out of the parking lot, and a large sign identified that they were leaving Wabush Airport.

Wabush. The name sounded remotely familiar. It took a few moments, but her memory produced the results she sought. Wabush was a town of less than two thousand people in the province of Newfoundland and Labrador. It was located almost at the province's border with Quebec in Canada's far north. Although she'd never actually visited there, there had been a small, unprofitable store in the Canadian supermarket chain she'd managed located in that town before Multima had acquired it. She'd ordered its closure a few months before becoming president of Multima Supermarkets, more than a decade earlier.

The ride from the airport to the next stop took no longer than ten minutes. As she peeked through the tiny opening in the wool blanket to preserve the impression she was still sleeping, a tall brick building came into view, perhaps an apartment building or a hotel.

She pulled the blanket up tightly around her head again and feigned sleep as the doors to the SUV opened and closed, then one opened at the rear. Almost immediately, she heard the metallic rattle. Probably it was a stretcher dropped with a jolt from the roof of the SUV to the snow-packed pavement below. Feet crunching loudly suggested there was considerable cold snow on the ground, enough snow to prompt what sounded like cursing in a foreign language as her attendants tried to maneuver the equipment.

Two sets of doors opened and closed before immediate warmth reached her extremities, and she heard a conversation taking place in a language she didn't understand. Not daring to move, she focused on the conversation, which sounded Slavic. When she heard the word "*davai*" used several times in the conversation, she became certain. Someone had once told her it meant "let's go," "come on," or "okay."

There was little doubt that the people who'd snatched her from the plane and brought her to this remote part of Canada were Russian.

Fifty-One

Tokyo, Japan, Monday December 25, 2023

The pain in Serge's head and shoulders was indescribable. At first, the throbbing caused him to gasp uncontrollably, his entire body squirming and shaking. It felt like a tremendous weight, crushing him and making it almost impossible to breathe. And it continued for some time.

When his eyes finally focused, he saw a room with white walls, a ceiling, and smelled a distinctive medicinal odor. Some equipment hummed, and something was attached to his arm. He tried to raise his head for a look around, but the pain was too great, and things started to swirl. After his groan of discomfort, he sensed movement: someone had come in and stood next to his bed.

A man leaned over the bed, gazing downward. He looked familiar.

"Hi, Serge. It's me, Antonio."

The name also sounded familiar, but from where?

"Do you hear and understand me okay, Serge? I'm Antonio, your security colleague. They told me you might not recognize me right away. Can you understand?"

Serge tried to speak, but words were slow to form. He nodded instead, then reached for a glass of water he'd spotted on a tray beside his head. Another searing shock ran down his neck and shoulders, and he slumped back on the bed in resignation instead.

"Here, let me help you." Antonio brought the glass of water to Serge's mouth and placed a hand gently behind his head to help him drink.

He could only manage a sip before the searing pain in his head and neck caused him to choke, and his entire body shook violently.

"Where am I?" It took some time to ask the question.

"You're in a medical center operated by the Japanese military and used by the national police force. They brought you here after they helped us rescue you in Russia—do you remember anything about that?"

He shook his head, causing another jolt of pain and a tremor throughout his body.

Antonio lowered his voice an octave and spoke more slowly. "The National Police Agency loaned us a jet and two officers to get you out of Vladivostok, where the Yakuza took you and the girls after they seized you from the train. Do you remember that?"

He shook his head; more pain.

"No problem. They hijacked the railcar you were on and eventually flew you and the women to Russia. We got you out, but it was messy. The guy in charge of it all used you as a protective barrier when we first attacked. He tried to shoot with his weapon, but one of the Japanese guys used a karate move to knock you away from him. You lost consciousness. Sorry, but the guy really had no choice. He saved your life because the guy was trying to shoot you."

A picture formed. The experience sounded familiar. But any response still caused him pain, so he chose to wait for Antonio to carry on with his story.

"The doctors here say you'll need a few days to recover, but there's no long-term damage. You should be able to fly after forty-eight hours without further risk of harm to your brain, but it might be painful. The doctors recommended we wait a week, then you should be good to go to either Vietnam or Montreal, whichever you prefer."

It took some time—several minutes, he guessed—before those names made sense to him. Vietnam came first: something related to his job. Montreal followed soon after: Suzanne, then Multima. He blurted out one word: "Suzanne."

Antonio's eyes dropped, and he made no reply, either misunderstanding what Serge wanted or hiding something.

Serge repeated Suzanne's name before the guy replied.

"They told me it was better not to tell you, but you're my friend as well as my boss. You need to know, even if there's nothing we can do immediately. Suzanne is missing. Someone snatched her and our security guard, Jasmine, from her jet when they were forced to land in Gander, Newfoundland, as they flew from Paris to Montreal."

The pain returned with another violent surge, but he was determined to prevail this time. He formed the words slowly and finally blurted them out as he forced himself upward with his arms and tried to swing his legs from the bed.

"Must. Go. Now. Help me." The effort caused him to collapse onto the bed again.

Antonio placed a firm hand on his chest. "No, Serge. It's too dangerous for you to leave the hospital. Trust us. We're working to rescue Suzanne as soon as we learn where she is. There have been no demands for ransom yet, or any other threats. James Fitzgerald has taken temporary charge of her corporate responsibilities. Unfortunately, someone— probably the same thugs—has also seized Natalia Tenaz. As soon as I can get in touch with Montreal, I'll tell you more."

Fifty-Two

Natalia answered Mauro Alvarez's questions. It took only a few seconds to assess the probability of leaving the building alive should she fail to cooperate, and a promotion to the position of chief executive officer of Multima Corporation was not the worst possible outcome a gal could imagine. More honestly, hadn't Abduhl Mahinder secretly implied earlier that this was the ultimate goal, the real purpose of the still secret Docket 2025?

His first questions dealt with her background, education, and upbringing, such as a legitimate inquirer might use during a job interview. She adopted a cooperative demeanor and a friendly tone, telling him the truth, but only as briefly as she dared. He'd need to show her where they were going, and clearly, before revealing details she considered sensitive or somewhat private.

Alvarez had obviously done this type of thing before. He was handsome, and he knew it. He turned on the charm from the moment she showed an interest in his proposal. Like her, he was Latin American, and he underscored the importance of that reality by posing the first question in Spanish. She'd anticipated it and replied to him in Spanish but pointed out that she'd been raised and educated entirely in the US. So her second-language skills were more suited for family or perhaps social dialogue than business. She said this with a smile as broad as she could manage and a suggestive tilt of her head.

He bought it and switched back to English for the questions that followed. His body language relaxed as their conversation progressed.

He seemed to like what he was hearing, so she tested his mettle. "I think you can see that I'm interested in our conversation and your suggestion of a different role within Multima. Is it really necessary to keep me bound like this? With zip ties on my wrists and ankles? I really need to pee. Could you release me to do that?"

His smile disappeared, and his brow furrowed. She might have surprised him with the request, or tripped some form of concern. He looked her squarely in the eyes and said nothing for a few moments as he mulled over her request. Glancing around the room as though checking if someone might be watching him, he reached inside his open collar, and she heard an audible click. A microphone, perhaps? Or a recording device?

"I'll walk with you to the toilet, take you inside, release the zip ties there, then wait outside the stall while you piss. As soon as you're finished, I'll put them back on while we talk. Got that?"

She nodded and felt her face redden with either discomfort or embarrassment. She couldn't be sure which was more powerful.

As promised, once they were inside the restroom, he expertly cut both of the zip ties with a sharp knife he'd pulled from a side pocket. During that process, his eyes barely left hers as if searching for any sign of rebellion.

Still feeling warm and uncomfortable, she escaped inside the door to the cubicle and did her thing. After a suitable lapse of time, she called out to Alvarez.

"Sorry, I need to do more than pee. It'll take a moment or two, but something else is calling. It might smell a little unpleasant, so you might want to wait outside. Don't worry—I'll do it as quickly as possible and submit to the zip ties right after you hear me flush the toilet."

He did what she suggested. She did what she needed to do, then pulled up her panties, touching the tiny pouch on her outfit's belt for an instant at the same time. Slipping them into place she let them sit a little lower than usual but still comfortably near her hips. Gingerly, she pulled up the black slacks she was wearing and positioned her belt an inch or two lower on her waist than usual. Then, she flushed the toilet.

As expected, Alvarez didn't come back inside the restroom, so she took an additional few minutes to wash her hands thoroughly—using a lot of liquid soap—and let the hand dryer complete its entire cycle before opening the door. He was waiting outside for her as she expected. The moment she stepped through the doorway, he motioned for her to hold out her wrists.

When they were seated in the larger office area, Alvarez reached inside his collar, and again, she heard a click before he resumed his interrogation.

He started with a loaded question. "What's your relationship with Suzanne Simpson?"

It was clearly a trick question. There could only be a right or wrong answer, and she needed to be sure she delivered the one that was right.

Natalia took a minute to make eye contact with him before smiling and leaning in toward him suggestively. "I'm grateful that Suzanne had the confidence to elevate my role in the company to the position I now enjoy as president of the Supermarkets business. Clearly, she recognized my leadership strengths. But we're business colleagues. I may be appreciative, but I don't feel indebted. In my opinion, the woman just used her good judgment wisely. If you choose me to replace her as CEO, I imagine that I might feel something greater than appreciative."

He liked the answer. He reached inside his collar and clicked once more. Then, he reached out and squeezed her right breast. His eyes bore down on her as he fondled it until he found her nipple. He squeezed the nipple roughly and grinned with satisfaction.

"You get it. You'll become the CEO, but you'll be the CEO of Multima at my pleasure and for as long as you *give* me pleasure." His black eyes became cold, and his smile disappeared before he reached back under his collar and clicked again. This suggested the guy was playing with a recording device. He wanted her to know that he'd keep the information he wanted for later.

"Where is James Fitzgerald today?" he asked.

"I was scheduled to meet him at the Atlanta Airport over one hour ago. I don't know if he's there, or if he's moved on."

Alvarez recoiled in anger, then swung his fist violently against her jaw. "Why didn't you tell me that earlier, you stupid bitch? Now, we'll have to find him before he screws up the entire project!"

This time, he muttered something into his collar before Guillaume and two other guys ran into the office area from the outside, weapons in hand, looking for trouble.

"Take her to the airport and try to find Multima's private jet there," he screamed at the men. To Natalia, he shouted, "If Fitzgerald's there, keep him on the ground"—he now suddenly pointed a gun at her face—"or you're finished."

Guillaume and one of the other guys grabbed her by the arms and half-dragged, half-carried her out of the office. Back in the SUV, they pricked her with another needle, and the world again went dark.

Fifty-Three

Montreal, Quebec, Monday December 25, 2023

The moment the security people from Japan told him about Serge, James Fitzgerald realized he needed to be in Montreal with the corporate security team, even if it meant leaving Natalia behind. From the air, he repeatedly tried calling the security offices and individual company cell phone numbers issued to the various members of the elite team protecting Multima, but all attempts failed. Were they blocking his calls in Montreal, or were the bad guys somehow diverting attempted calls elsewhere?

Three hours later, he touched down in Montreal and persuaded an attendant in the airport's office to let him use the airport's landline. First, he tried to reach Lori, the security team communications coordinator. Instead of her office number, he tried the cell phone number she'd shared with him at the last Multima get-together after a board of directors meeting.

She answered on the second ring. "I'm with my family in Sept- Îles in Quebec," she shouted into the phone as music blared in the background. "What's the problem, sir?"

"There's no one responding at your security headquarters in Montreal, Lori. What's going on?"

"I'm sorry, James. We set up everything according to company policy. What do you mean, no one's responding?"

He explained the issue. There was simply no answer when people tried to connect.

She put him on hold while she tried it herself. Minutes later, she returned to the line, apologetic. "You're right. I tried every method I know, and nothing happened. What should we do?"

James switched gears "Do you have any way of tracking the senior team? Suzanne, Natalia, Serge, or me, for that matter?"

The woman took a moment or two before she replied. Her breath increased and the music faded, as if she were walking away from the festivities with her family. "No, for Suzanne. She refuses tracking. But Natalia has a device, if she chooses to use it."

"I'm in Montreal now—how can I access the security floor at headquarters?"

There was a long pause as she probably considered alternative responses. "There's no code I can give you. Serge had the entire system revamped last year, and access is only possible with a fingerprint. We'll have to find someone on the team to meet you at headquarters and let you in."

There was no point in scolding, threatening, or expressing frustration. He'd have to play according to the rules Serge had established.

"Start calling. Let me know as soon as you find someone who can come immediately to the office." There was one more bit of information he needed. "Before you start those calls, text me the phone numbers for Serge's entire team in Asia. Although it's late over there, someone must be reachable."

Before her text arrived, he received an unexpected call. His phone screen announced that the caller was none other than Abduhl Mahinder, the chief executive officer of Bank of the Americas and a fellow member of the Multima board of directors. James let the phone ring a few times. It was more than odd that Mahinder would be calling on Christmas Day, even if he didn't observe the holiday personally. Still, he touched the green button on the screen just ahead of the expected transfer to voicemail.

"Merry Christmas, James. In what part of the world are you enjoying your holiday today?" Mahinder's tone was cheerful, suggesting a genuine interest in James's response. But he still felt uneasy. Since the fellow had been named a director several years earlier, he'd never quite been comfortable with the man despite his stature as CEO of one of America's largest banks. It stemmed from Mahinder's demand to become a director as part of a multi-billion-dollar loan his bank had provided when Multima had run into some financial challenges years earlier.

James chose to ask his own question instead of directly answering the guy's opening query. "I'm enjoying a quiet day. I don't have a lot of family left, so it's a good time to read a suspense novel and stay out of the cold. How about you? What prompts your call today, Mahinder?"

"Well, as you know, I don't celebrate, so I'm in the office skimming the news from around the world and checking out the recent performance of some of the equities we hold. I don't know if you've checked lately, but Multima is getting pummeled in the pre-markets. Our shares are down about twenty-five percent in Singapore and in the pre-markets of Frankfurt and London. And there's been a concerning amount of activity. It looks as if some shareholders are losing faith in the company."

Although he paused for a moment to take a breath, probably for emphasis, he repeated the startling amount again when he resumed. "More than five million shares have been offered up for sale at prices up to twenty-five percent lower than the close on Friday afternoon. I'm truly worried that it'll get worse when investors on this side of the Atlantic finish their turkey dinners and see the trend." Mahinder's friendly tone had become more than concerned, perhaps restraining a touch of anger.

James mulled over the implications silently, seeking to make some sense of the threatening circumstance. He decided a question was the best path forward. "Have you been able to determine any reason for such a dramatic drop?"

"I suspect it has to do with a post on that site 'X' or Twitter that thousands have seen already. It's a photo showing Suzanne Simpson seated in a comfortable chair, a full glass of wine on a table beside her, partially undressed, with a woman's head filling the space between her spread legs." His condescending tone oozed disdain. "I tried to reach her to find out what it's all about, but my calls go directly to voicemail. I've been trying out here since early this morning, and it's always the same result."

James drew a deep breath. Surely, there was more going on than he'd realized earlier, but he needed to cool the situation with this alarmed director before anything else. "Before we jump to conclusions, let's remember that it's easy to create or doctor photos these days with artificial intelligence or Photoshop. Let's locate Suzanne and get her side of the story."

"I realize that what you say is true—I thought of that, too—but it doesn't matter what we think. If users on Twitter assume the photo is legitimate, and they decide to sell their shares at a substantial discount to market prices, we have a crisis. And our CEO is missing in action."

Again, he paused. Then, speaking more slowly and in a slightly louder tone, he carried on with his rant. "If the prices continue to plummet, the company's financial future is at risk. I've already heard from members of the consortium I put together back when we had to make that loan to Multima—you should remember them—they're already making noise about the agreement's provisions for the CEO's personal conduct. One in the Middle East suggested they might take legal action to recall their portion of the loan."

Plunging share prices were never desirable for any corporation. With a CEO demeaned and out of action, such a crisis could seriously injure Multima Corporation's business reputation. If many shareholders piled on, the damage could be severe. What did the influential director on the board intend to do about it?

Before James could ask the question, that powerful director provided the answer.

"Since Suzanne is unavailable, and the board has not yet agreed upon who should be named the person in charge in her absence, I'll contact Alberto Ferer when we end this call. As general counsel and secretary for the board of directors, he can convene a meeting of the board later today. We can meet via Zoom and discuss how best to deal with this attack on the share price. Somebody from Multima needs to make a formal statement—the board can decide who that person should be."

Of course, Mahinder was correct—he knew the corporate rules as well as anyone in the company—but it all seemed to be happening too quickly. Suzanne hadn't been missing for days; instead, it had only been a matter of hours since she had become unreachable. With Serge now rescued in Japan, maybe he could track down and resolve the company's security communication issues, then find Suzanne. James decided the best strategy was to buy some time.

"I already tried Alberto's company phone, but the calls disconnect before anyone answers. I tried a private number, and it went immediately to voicemail. Alberto is away on holiday in Aruba, and he probably doesn't want to be disturbed until later in the day. I'm also guessing that it might be difficult to reach many of the other directors today as well. Most are celebrating the Christmas break, and several had exotic trips planned. You might have trouble getting a quorum for a decision, even if Alberto is eventually able to round up a few."

Mahinder had obviously already anticipated the suggestion to slow it down. Within a second of hearing

James's caution, he blurted, "I've tried Alberto's private line, too. Someone at the hotel where he's staying is tracking him down to have him call me. Stay reachable if you want to participate in the call. We should be back to you within the hour."

There were no goodbyes before the call disconnected.

Fifty-Four

Wabush, Labrador, Monday December 25, 2023

They must have drugged her again. To Suzanne, the world appeared foggy, and her vision blurred as she awoke. It appeared to be the same hotel suite. The ceiling was still a dull white color, matching the equally bland walls. The temperature seemed comfortable on her skin, so she tugged back the heavy wool blanket they'd left covering most of her body.

Plastic restraints still bound her ankles and wrists together, but she found enough mobility to shift her position to her left so she could look away from the wall and into the living area outside her doorway.

When she glanced up, what she saw was shocking at first, and then, bewildering. At first, she thought she was experiencing some of the drug's aftereffects, but no, it really was Jasmine. There was no mistaking her large, muscular physique—she was on her knees, facing a standing man, and appeared to be actively engaged in oral sex!

After a few otherworld moments, no doubt remained. Her long-time bodyguard and friend was sexually satisfying one of their captors. Her body bobbed forward and back in a rhythmic motion, her hands holding his large, erect penis as she inserted it repeatedly into her mouth, eyes downcast.

She must have felt Suzanne's fixed gaze on her body because she suddenly raised her eyes from the floor and made visual contact. Her eyes conveyed no message, but she glanced away and looked upward for a moment or two. Then, she yanked suddenly down on the guy's penis with one hand and forcefully chopped the back of his knees with the other, causing him to fall to the floor, his shoulders dramatically sagging.

In a move so fast Suzanne almost missed it, Jasmine sprang from the floor like a gymnast and used her free hand to grab the big fellow's neck, gripping him just below the ears and squeezing. The pressure she exerted caused her own cheeks to swell with the effort. She grimaced but continued to glare at her victim with equal measures of hatred and satisfaction until his body collapsed on the floor.

Jasmine reached for the man's waist and pulled a knife from the pouch attached to his belt. With a graceful wave, Jasmine sprang open the knife and reached down to cut the plastic restraints binding her feet, then abandoned it on the floor. A second or two later, she energetically bounced to a standing position, dragged the guy on the ground toward the suite entrance, and parked his limp body against the door.

Satisfied, Jasmine ran back to the knife, grabbed it, and severed the plastic restraints around Suzanne's wrists and ankles before yanking her upward with one powerful tug. She almost lost her balance when Jasmine drew her CEO by the wrist so she'd follow her bodyguard out of the room.

"Another one, and maybe more, will be coming to the suite soon," she whispered. "I assume they have both video and sound monitoring, so we have only a few seconds."

Jasmine motioned for Suzanne to remain standing behind the open door. "Slam it shut as soon as both move inside the room," she whispered a little more loudly to emphasize what she wanted Suzanne to do.

Seconds later, they heard a key enter the lock and a rattle of the door handle. Someone tried to open the door, but it resisted due to the weight of the guy lying against it. Voices talked with each other, followed by several attempts to force open the door. It opened only an inch or two more each time they tugged and jarred it. After another consultation in Russian, there was a sudden, massive bang on the door, loosening it from its hinges. It terrified Suzanne.

She started to move away from it, but saw Jasmine seize the outstretched leg of one man as he entered the room. Her protector delivered a series of rapid kicks and chops, causing his body to somersault across the carpeted living area. Stunned by the impact with the floor, the man collapsed in a heap, immobile.

Seconds later, another person opened the door and entered the room. As soon as he became visible from her vantage point, Suzanne slammed the door closed with all the force she could muster.

The guy who had just entered the room swung his body toward Suzanne and raised his handgun so it pointed at her face. She screamed as Jasmine reached out from behind him and karate-chopped the guy's throat. He dropped the gun, and she applied pressure to his neck with both hands until his body also sagged to the floor.

Behind her, the first thug was regaining his senses and slowly reached for the holster on his chest. Before his hand could reach his weapon, Jasmine jumped on his arm with full force, fracturing something enough for Suzanne to hear the crunch across the room.

For good measure, Jasmine chopped twice at his vocal cords and landed a sideways kick to his face.

"Follow me," she ordered, grabbing Suzanne's arm and forcing her to change direction. Barefoot, they ran along a silent corridor to its end. At the doorway, Jasmine held a single, upright finger to her lips and mouthed, "Silence." She listened until she heard the sound she apparently wanted, nodded, and motioned for Suzanne to stand in the corner behind the doorway again.

Within a moment or two, they heard the quickly approaching clank of shoes on a metal stairway. When the doorway burst open, Jasmine kicked out, catching the person approaching at the knees, causing him to stagger and momentarily lose balance. She stepped forward, jumped on his hand as it moved for his weapon, and chopped the back of his neck at least five times before his form appeared lifeless and slumped on the floor.

"Grab his other one," she ordered, and she started pulling on the guy's left shoe. "Follow me," she commanded a moment later. She passed Suzanne the extracted shoe for her to carry. "Put these on your feet and stay here until I come back for you. I'll check the stairs at the other end." She stepped out into the stairwell.

It was probably only a few moments, but it seemed like an eternity before Jasmine returned, wearing a pair of leather boots. She held her index finger against her closed lips as soon as she opened the door, then listened intently at the top of the stairwell. Apparently satisfied with the silence, she nodded for Suzanne to follow her and led the way down.

There were only three floors in the hotel, so they reached the bottom quickly. Once there, Jasmine again signaled for Suzanne to wait in a corner and slipped into the main lobby. Soon, she heard someone shout out in surprise, followed by a commotion that sounded like a physical altercation. She closed her eyes and hoped that Jasmine would maintain the upper hand, as she had with all her targets so far.

When Jasmine called out for Suzanne to enter the lobby, she had to step around a body just inside the doorway. The man's neck was entirely twisted so his head faced backward, his face contorted in an expression of shock.

Suzanne looked up from the body to find Jasmine standing there with a gun in her left hand. She used it to wave for Suzanne to join her at the door of a small room. "This is the hotel's communication center. Go inside and start calling numbers until you get us some help. Start with security communications in Montreal, and keep dialing until you reach someone we can trust. Let them know we're on the ground floor of the Wabush Hotel." She held up a piece of paper with a few numbers scrawled on it. "Here are the location coordinates, if anyone needs them."

"Shouldn't I start by calling the police?" Suzanne asked.

"Nope. We don't know if they can be trusted. They'll certainly want to disarm me, and I'm not prepared to take that risk unless we absolutely must."

"Aren't there other guests in the hotel? Won't we be discovered by other people, maybe even more gang members?"

"I checked the registry. No other guests are registered in the building. This hotel is used for business customers, and they're all probably celebrating the holidays at home." Jasmine's logic made sense, but she seemed to hesitate for a moment, probably doing a mental check to see if she'd missed anything.

"Lock the door when you get inside. If you hear gunshots or someone banging on the door, call 911 then."

Suzanne followed her security guard's advice and reached for the first phone she found on the desk in a corner. She'd already keyed in the numbers for Multima's security headquarters in Montreal before she sat down.

Fifty-Five

Tokyo, Japan, Tuesday December 26, 2023

Despite Serge's protests, the hospital staff must have slipped some sedatives into the intravenous drip connected to his arm. He came to gradually. He remembered the white ceiling and walls but struggled to recall more about his whereabouts and physical condition. Finally, he lifted his head from the pillow and peered around the room.

A member of his security team sat in a corner reading his phone. Serge couldn't determine who it was from the angle of the bed, but he called out a hello anyway.

The fellow glanced up as he stood. When he noticed Serge was awake, he moved closer.

Serge recognized the guy as Tony, one of the new recruits they'd brought to Asia.

"Where's Antonio?" Serge asked.

"He left for a few minutes to take a call. Said he'd be back shortly. Should be here any minute now," Tony replied. "You need anything?"

Serge shook his head no, then reached for a glass of water on the tray beside his bed. He lifted his head and left shoulder and tried to reach out, but collapsed on the pillow in exhaustion instead, his head and neck in excruciating pain. Tony stepped forward to help, the way Antonio had helped that first night after they'd pulled Serge out of Russia. As he finished swallowing the gulp of water, Antonio himself strode into the room wearing a grim expression.

"We have some news, and it's not good." Antonio's manner was always abrupt and to the point, the way Serge liked it. He waited for the guy to continue. "Archie Begat contacted us from Vietnam. We lost the other pair of resources from Financial Services. Someone ran 'em down in the streets of the complex where we were all staying. Killed 'em both."

Serge squirmed in his bed at the news, then tried again to sit upright. Their mission had never once anticipated the loss of life, and two young people murdered for simply doing research was more than shocking.

Antonio looked away for a moment, giving him time to absorb and process the news. When he looked back, he offered Serge an outstretched hand and helped him to a seated position, then tossed another pillow behind his back for good measure. Only then did he carry on.

"Now, Archie's in a bit of a pickle. Somebody in the building claimed he was the driver of the car that hit our colleagues, and the Ho Chi Minh police authorities have subjected him to intense interrogation. He's created enough doubt that they've got him under some form of house arrest. They seized his phone, left an officer outside his apartment door, and ordered him not to leave the suite."

"How did he contact you?"

"The burner phone. They didn't find it when they searched his room. Calls can't be traced, recorded, or intercepted with the software we added to all of 'em. He said he was calling from the bathroom, with the door closed and the shower running just to be sure."

"Has he heard from Đại Dang, the government official? The guy we met that first day." When Antonio shook his head, Serge continued his thought. "Get him on the phone for me. I don't know him as well as Suzanne, but if she's still out of the loop, I'll need to exert some influence."

"Sure, but before I do that, can I share a couple more details we've learned?"

Serge nodded in reply.

"James Fitzgerald is in Montreal. He's got the

communications system at headquarters up and running again. Somebody knocked out the entire platform for hours, but he rounded up some resources, and everything started back up after he got into the corporate security offices."

"What took him to Montreal in the first place?" Serge needed to know.

"He ended up there after making a trip to Atlanta to pick up Natalia Tenaz, but she didn't show. After repeated attempts to get help from Montreal, he realized something was wrong and checked it out in person."

Antonio flashed a brief grin of satisfaction with the executive's sound judgment before continuing. "On the way to Montreal, he got a troubling phone call from Abduhl Mahinder on the board of directors. He learned Mahinder was trying to get the board together to oust Suzanne from the CEO role and appoint new leadership for the company. But, it seems he needs Alberto Ferer to make it all happen and is trying to locate him as well."

What a way to start a morning! For most, the day after Christmas was a time for relaxation, time with the family and recovery from celebrations. Instead, he was lying helpless in a hospital bed in Tokyo. He couldn't imagine a more annoying, complex, and dangerous beginning to his day. Regardless, he took a deep breath, determined to show leadership despite it all.

"First, tell James we need him to sit tight in Montreal as our anchor for all communication until we can get this issue under control. Next, Natalia agreed to wear a tracking device when she assumed the role of president at Supermarkets a few weeks ago. Check with Montreal to see if she's active and traceable, then ask James to deploy whatever resources he thinks appropriate to track her down and rescue her if needed."

He paused a moment as Antonio nodded his understanding of both issues. Satisfied, he moved on to the next challenge.

"Try Alberto Ferer, too. I think he might be on vacation somewhere in Europe or the Caribbean. See if he has any suggestions about thwarting any funny business Mahinder might try. If he's amenable, you might see if he's willing to rent a jet wherever he is and return to Montreal. Anything Mahinder might try will surely require the involvement of Multima's chief legal officer."

Antonio simply nodded to acknowledge his understanding of the instructions. Subtly, the fellow raised his eyebrow slightly, as if to show that he was anxious to get started on the string of commands.

"Two last things," Serge added. "Try to reach Đại Dang for me before you do all those things. Then, get a doctor down here right away. I need him to release me."

With that final note, he nodded to dismiss Antonio, shifted the sheets away from his legs, pivoted his body ninety degrees, and sat with his legs dangling over the edge of the mattress. The pain was excruciating.

A nurse arrived. She was petite, but her physique displayed strength, and her manner was polite but insistent.

"You need to lie back down," she instructed with adequate English. "You aren't going anywhere on my shift unless a doctor instructs me to assist with your release. In my opinion, even walking is too dangerous for your condition at this stage. Leaving the hospital is not a good idea at all."

He felt dizzy while seated and had to admit the nurse was probably right. He allowed her to ease him back into a lying position while he waited for a doctor.

He had no idea how long it took for someone to return, but his patience dwindled by the minute. Finally, Antonio popped his head around the corner of the door and blurted out new information.

"We've located Natalia. She was wearing the device, as

you suspected, and we were getting the signal in Montreal on the computer system there until it crashed. Now that it's back up, the folks there have determined she's probably in an aircraft headed northeast from Atlanta. The rate of speed is too great for an automobile, and a train is unlikely, so they're checking with air traffic control now to see if they can determine which plane she's on and where she's headed."

Fifty-Six

On an airborne corporate jet, Tuesday December 26, 2023

When she regained consciousness, Natalia first noticed that her hands were bound with some form of plastic wire. She twisted her wrists, glanced at her watch, and realized she'd been out of it for some time. The big holiday for Yuletide had passed, and it was very early in the morning on the day after Christmas in North America.

It was clear she was on a luxurious private jet. The engine's groan sounded familiar, and the dark brown leather seats were plush and very comfortable, even more elaborate than those on Multima's corporate jets. She opened her eyes wider, trying not to attract any attention with her movement, and glanced at her surroundings.

Lighting on the jet was subdued, probably set low by the crew to allow the passengers to sleep. The temperature in the cabin was chilly, though not cold. Someone had thrown a blanket over her, probably so she wouldn't notice the drop in temperature and wake early.

There was no music nor voices. She tilted her head toward the front of the plane and noticed that nothing was projected on the wide screen mounted on the wall. Probably everyone was sleeping. Now, who was "everyone"?

She looked down at her feet and noticed they, too, were bound, but loosely enough that she could separate her legs a foot or two. She squirmed upright as quietly and as gently as possible, still adamant about not attracting any unwanted attention.

No one occupied the spaces beside her or across the aisle of the private jet. She raised herself so she would sit more upright and peered over the top of the seat a few feet in front of her to see that four tall men were sitting in the front of the cabin around a table, two on each side. All of them had their eyes closed.

She didn't recognize any of them but noted that they all wore black jeans and black sweaters, and all looked Latino in complexion.

Natalia squirmed a bit to her left and tugged against the armrest. She stretched her head to look around the seat and behind her enough to see that two men sat in the rear of the cabin and off to the left. Their seats were in a reclined position, so they were entirely flat, and both men were partially covered with bright red wool blankets. Plush cushions supported their heads. Neither of the men faced in her direction, so it was impossible to identify who they might be.

But she needed a restroom urgently.

Natalia decided to risk it. She tossed back the blanket and placed her feet on the floor. It was cold even though she still wore shoes. She unbuckled the seat belt and slid forward in the seat until she was able to stand, using the armrest for balance. Once fully upright, she tried to maneuver out of her seat and found that movement was possible if she used the tiniest of steps. More confident, she turned to locate the lavatory and spotted it between the entrance door for the jet and a doorway she supposed opened into the cockpit.

She moved gingerly forward, leaving behind the balance of the armrest, and took about three steps before there was slight air turbulence, and the plane swayed. As she tried to compensate for the shift, she lost her balance and tumbled to the floor of the aircraft in an awkward heap.

The two men in the seats closest to her jumped into action. They grabbed Natalia by her elbows and hoisted her to her feet with one forceful jerk.

"Where the fuck do you think you're going?" screamed

one in Spanish as he leaned menacingly into her face.

"The toilet. I need to use the toilet. And let go of my arms!" Natalia shouted back in English, equally loud by design, and in only a moment, jerked free of their grip.

"Let her use the toilet," a calm voice instructed. She turned toward the voice. Shockingly, it was Abduhl Mahinder, perhaps the most influential person after Suzanne on Multima's board of directors. "Go ahead. They'll see you get to the door of the toilet okay. No one will hurt you."

His presence there raised dozens of questions, but nature's call was increasing its urgency, so she resumed her tiny steps toward the aircraft's lavatory. Sitting there while she relieved herself, countless possibilities surfaced and flooded her mind. It seemed all too much to process at one time. When she'd finished, she checked the belt on her outfit. It felt secure, so she headed toward her seat. Abduhl was already seated again, the space next to him vacant. He motioned for her to take that spot.

On her way toward the seat he'd indicated, she glanced to her right and recognized Mauro Alvarez, the guy who was probably responsible for all this. He smiled faintly, but said nothing as she worked her way to Abduhl and the seat beside him.

"I'm sorry they treated you this way, but don't worry. You're in no danger. We'll have you home again soon, and I'll be with you in the meantime. May I ask one of the guys up front to make you some coffee while we chat?"

Natalia simply nodded. She watched him stand again, then heard him issue instructions in Spanish. The fellow who'd first yanked her up from the aircraft floor unbuckled his seatbelt and moved past her to an area behind their seats. Abduhl Mahinder didn't wait for his coffee before he began.

"Mauro over there told me about his conversation with

you back in Atlanta. He said you were interested in our proposal to make you Multima's chief executive officer." Abduhl used his trademark calm tone as he spoke, looking directly into her eyes as if searching for something.

She answered as deferentially as she dared. She still didn't know who or what the guy now represented. None of this seemed at all like his earlier descriptions of Docket 2025… a covert possible restructuring of Multima that she'd sworn to keep secret.

"What Multima executive wouldn't be interested in the CEO role if it were offered?"

His eyes didn't waver from hers as she responded, although he did blink. He paused long enough to create some discomfort, but she was determined to maintain her demeanor. Finally, he glanced away, but only for a fraction of a second.

"We've located Suzanne. You know we lost contact with her, but we learned she encountered a mechanical problem with her corporate jet and is now on the ground in a remote town in Labrador. Do you know where that is?"

She said nothing but nodded as she waited to hear more.

"Mauro already explained to you that he represents both shareholders and holders of corporate debt who want to see a change in leadership at Multima. I've tried to help her understand how strongly they want to see that change, but Suzanne has resisted so far. However, Mauro has reason to believe she's ready to make a deal, so we're going to meet up with her in the small town of Wabush in another hour or two. Hopefully, we'll have a brief meeting with her to negotiate the details. We'll get her resignation agreement without delay and recommend you replace her as CEO. I have a media release already drafted."

He continued to probe her eyes as if looking for any sign of her willingness to cooperate or perhaps not to play their game. She did the same to him.

Again, he glanced away for only an instant before he continued.

"Suzanne currently earns ten million dollars per year and has a performance bonus that can potentially add another ten to fifty million dollars, depending on the company's profit. I'm confident the board of directors will approve a similar structure and amounts for you." He waited for a response, still staring into her eyes as though trying to peer into her conscience.

She swallowed. That salary and bonus program was over ten times the amount she could earn currently, even with the new compensation structure she'd negotiated with Suzanne only weeks earlier!

"Wow. I don't know what to say. What executive wouldn't be interested in learning more about a proposal for that kind of money?" She took care not to gush or appear overwhelmed, but it was hard. "I'd like to understand why there is such a rush to make this change in leadership and why all the drama of snatching me from a hotel in Atlanta, drugging me, and transporting me to somewhere in the wasteland of Labrador to make this all happen."

His black eyes turned cold. His lips tightened. His jaw hardened. He broke eye contact to look across the aisle toward Mauro Alvarez. She followed his gaze and saw that he was suppressing either anger or dismay; she couldn't be sure which. It was he who spoke next.

"Go back to the seat you were in before. We'll discuss it with our colleagues and make a decision. You'll either go home as Multima's CEO on our terms, or you won't go home."

He waved her off with obvious disgust.

Fifty-Seven

Montreal, Quebec, Tuesday December 26, 2023

James felt as if he were living in something close to a whirlwind. Almost from the moment a technology specialist by the name of Pierre Lachance told him that the security communications system was up and running again, the messages pinged and information gushed. It was almost impossible for the pair to keep up with the developments, let alone make complete sense of it all.

During the night, they'd received the message from Antonio in Japan, relaying Serge's requests and creating more actions on more fronts. Archie Begat then sent several messages from Vietnam, reporting bizarre communications between entities in Russia and Palm Beach, Florida. With all the activity, James instructed Pierre to reach out to his colleagues to get more help at the office.

Within minutes, the guy had rounded up three more security specialists, who jumped into the fray quickly upon their arrival. With a phone propped on his shoulder and keying data with his other hand, one of them waved excitedly toward James.

"I have a fix on Natalia. She's on a private jet that just left Atlanta, Georgia. According to air traffic control in Canada, the plane is headed due north, toward a remote town called Wabush in Labrador. ETA is scheduled for three hours and seven minutes."

James moved to another vacant computer screen two desks over, flashing bright green alerts. He clicked on one alert, and a message appeared on the screen:

Unusual amounts of activity coming from the shed near the hotel. Impossible to tap in, but data I can access suggests messages from Russia, Atlanta, and Vietnam, all within the past hour. Duration of calls up to thirty minutes. Has anyone been able to reach Serge for instructions?—Floyd

Before James could find out what the security people knew about Floyd's message, a female specialist waved to get his attention, mouthing that she had Suzanne Simpson on the line. He rushed to the woman's workstation.

"Where are you, Suzanne? Are you all right?" He fought to keep his voice calm despite the chaos around him.

She responded in a tone just above a whisper. "Jasmine and I are still okay. She's certain we're being held captive by some Russians at the Wabush Hotel in Wabush, Labrador. The hotel may be closed for the holidays, and Jasmine also thinks that up to six people are guarding us. I'm calling from the hotel's communications room, and Jasmine is guarding me from the check-in counter. Have you heard from Serge?"

Her manner was calm, but her discomfort and worry came through. He chose his words carefully. "First, I'm glad to learn that you and Jasmine are okay. Good news on Serge. I spoke to him. With the help of the Japanese, they got him out of Russia, and he's back in a Tokyo hospital with some sort of head and shoulder injury. It seems they have it all under control, but recommend he not travel immediately."

"Good. I've tried the communications center every fifteen minutes since Jasmine freed us from the room where they were holding us. Why couldn't I get through?"

"Something took down the entire system for several hours. We don't know yet why it was unmanned and inoperative for so long, but we'll deal with that later. Do you have your phone? How can we reach you?"

"No," Suzanne said. "We're dealing with a well-organized gang here. They placed one of their people on the plane as a co-pilot when our regular guy took ill. They took out Joseph Anderson before or after they diverted the flight to the Wabush Airport. When they moved us from the jet, I saw him slumped over the control panel in the cockpit. Here at the hotel, they hustled us from an SUV through a back door. Jasmine thinks at least two others are searching the hotel for us right now. All the men have been armed with sophisticated weapons."

He left the call on speaker so they could all listen intently—for information, surely, but also to detect her state of mind. The female security specialist who'd received the call motioned to indicate that she had a question. James nodded for her to go ahead.

"If the hotel appears to be closed, have you or Jasmine been able to check if any of the doors are unlocked?"

"Good point," Suzanne responded. "Jasmine tried the front doors nearest and the locks don't operate manually. She's looking for an electronic release but there are switches and buttons everywhere. If someone comes to rescue us, they might have to break down the doors. I'll let you know if Jasmine finds any way to open them."

"Let's not finish. The team here is already setting the wheels in motion to get there as quickly as they can. Let's keep the line open while we try to reach the guys in Japan so we can let Serge know. The same woman you spoke with before will monitor your call while I attend to a couple new crises unfolding here."

"Only until Jasmine tells me she found a way out the doors. The moment that happens, I'll sign off and do what we can to escape the hotel and seek help on the ground here," Suzanne replied in a forceful tone.

By the time he got back to the desk where they were

trying to reach Floyd Desmarais in South Florida, the guy there was shaking his head in frustration—they couldn't reach him.

James darted toward a destination three desks away, where they were trying to reach the folks in Japan. Before he was halfway there, he heard a noise on his line with Suzanne, and he spun around to listen. Voices were yelling and screaming, but too muffled to understand. Suddenly, there was a loud gunshot, followed almost immediately by a crash that sounded like wood cracking or splintering and the clanking of boots.

From the speakerphone, Suzanne's voice screamed out in shock before they heard a male voice with a Russian accent shout, "On the floor! Now! On the floor!" Seconds later, the telephone line fell quiet.

It took a moment for everyone in the communications center to recover.

From the end of the bank of computers, an excited techie from the batch of new arrivals called out that he had Serge on the phone from Japan. James rushed to the monitor, put on the audio headset when it was offered, and briefed Serge on the latest news. Surprisingly, the chief of security remained calm.

"Okay, is our security gal, Lori, reachable?" When he heard James's affirmative grunt, Serge continued, "She has access to my contacts app on Multima's computer system. Have her search for an RCMP officer, a constable named Gagnon in Labrador City, just down the road from Wabush. Contact him right away and use my name. Let him know we need his help rescuing Suzanne at the Wabush Hotel. Let him know there's a high level of danger, and he should bring support. He must let us know as soon as he extracts her from the hotel."

James asked for a moment to relay the command before he returned to the conversation with Serge, who carried on with his instructions. "We'll need to provide additional manpower. Work with the team there to round up four other security field experts and get them on a jet to Labrador. It's less than two hours' flying time from Montreal. I'm planning to be on my way soon."

It was truly only a few minutes, but it seemed like an eternity until an operator at the workstation on the other side of the room from the desk James had commandeered called out that she had Constable Gagnon on the line.

James jumped right into the issues. "Constable Gagnon, a former colleague of yours, Serge Boisvert, gave us your name and asked us to seek your help. We beg you to rescue Serge's life-partner and Multima Corporation's chief executive officer."

Succinctly, and as calmly as he could manage, James recounted the alarming events happening to Suzanne, while ever so briefly recounting why Serge himself was not making the call. He ended by pleading with Gagnon to get to the hotel to rescue both Suzanne and Jasmine.

"It sounded like Suzanne is in grave and immediate danger. Can you please get a team together quickly and get over to that hotel?"

"On my way. Write down the following phone numbers. Call those numbers and speak with the person I mention for each. Let them know you're calling on my behalf and that I'm responding to a code four situation at the Wabush Hotel and need their immediate support—no sirens or lights. Tell them to contact me for instructions on the secure conference line from their cars. Keep this line open for further communications and instructions."

James watched for a few moments to be sure the security team was following the officer's orders, then wandered back to the desk of the guy tracking Natalia. He was about to ask how the flight was progressing when the guy jumped from his seat, still staring at the screen, incredulous.

He shook his head several times, shrugged his shoulders in exasperation, then spread his arms out wide in amazement before he turned to James and said, "They've just veered ninety degrees off course. They're now headed west.

It looks like they're flying toward someplace in the States."

Fifty-Eight

Wabush, Labrador, Tuesday December 26, 2023

This time, they didn't bother to sedate her. Instead, the two thugs hoisted Suzanne up from the floor and roughly half-dragged, half-pushed her out of the communications room. They had to step over Jasmine, who lay immobile and face down on the floor. When Suzanne paused to see if her security guard was alive, unconscious, or injured, one man jerked her onward before she could make any determination.

The men shoved her into an elevator, pushed the button for the top floor, and, moments later, she found herself slammed into a sofa in the same room where they'd held her before.

A surly gang member yanked from her feet the shoes she'd confiscated from one of his companions earlier, then threw them across the hotel living room in disdain. Without a moment's hesitation, he slapped the plastic zip ties around her ankles again, only tighter than before, restricting all movement of her feet. He leered at her as he applied the same restraints to her wrists and drew them tight with a quick jerk of his wrist.

As a final insult—or maybe a threat—he grabbed her top and yanked it downward, exposing her partially bare left breast, almost to the nipple. He left the torn cloth dangling over her restrained wrists and gave a snort of satisfaction. Leaving the room, he slammed the door shut as a final warning.

More than a few hours passed before another Russian hoodlum unlocked the door and strode to face Suzanne, still immobile on the sofa. The guy was huge, well over six feet tall, with shoulders as broad as an American football player and hands so massive they made the phone he drew from a pocket look about the size of a lighter. With two fingers, he opened his phone and spun it around to show her.

She groaned in shock and dismay. The photo showed the entire front of her nude body. Her eyes were closed, but both breasts were entirely bare. She had her legs splayed indecently wide, and someone's head was buried in her vagina. She squinted in disgust. It took a few seconds, but she recognized the back of the head—it was the woman who had burst onto her aircraft with the thugs when they'd seized control of the corporate jet in Gander.

They must have undressed Suzanne after drugging her, taken the photo on the short flight from Gander to Wabush, and dressed her again before they landed. That would explain why her bra had been missing since their arrival at the hotel.

The shock left her speechless and numb. When she looked upward from the repulsive photo, she met the eyes of her captor. They were black and sparkling with unexplained glee. He made no effort to camouflage his delight with her disgust and discomfort.

With a snort of satisfaction, he spoke to her in English through a Russian accent. "In a moment, I will make you a proposal. I will explain it once. You will have a few minutes to consider it. If you accept what I suggest, I will delete this photo from my phone. No other copy exists. It will be fully destroyed."

He held the phone directly in front of her eyes as he paused before carrying on.

"Should you not agree to our proposal, this photo will arrive on the desks of the editors at *The Wall Street Journal*, *The Globe and Mail*, *The Financial Times*, *Handelsblatt* in Germany, *The Business Times* in Singapore, *The Nikkei* in Japan, and *El Economista* in

Spain. They'll also appear on Facebook, X, and TikTok, posted by a woman who will claim she is the person pictured giving you sexual pleasure. She'll claim you didn't pay her the five hundred dollars you promised her when she satisfied your disgusting sexual urges."

He paused again to let the message fully sink in. They intended to destroy a business image and stellar reputation she'd worked decades to build. Her instinct told her to cry tears of desperation and humiliation, but something more substantial stirred her hope. There must be an offer that followed, something they wanted from her, and she needed to fight off her despair and listen to what they had to say.

She held back for as long as she dared before muttering, "Or . . ." That's all she'd give him, along with a tilt of her head and a questioning expression.

"He said you were a smart one," he whispered. He showed her the outline of a cruel smile as he continued to stare into her eyes. "You are the controlling shareholder of Multima Corporation. You own fifty-one percent of the one hundred million shares outstanding. Tomorrow, there will be five orders placed, one hour apart, offering to buy 10.2 million shares at $132. That's two-thirds of the current listed price. You will agree to sell your shares to those five offers at precisely the prices they request."

His manner softened as he paused again, then he put away the phone with the incriminating photo on it, shrugged his shoulders, and carried on.

"When you've sold the last batch, I'll delete the photo and return you to your corporate jet. Your people can find a couple pilots to fly you home. You'll continue in your role as CEO of the Multima Corporation, Serge Boisvert will be returned to you to recover from his current poor health, and you'll still be one of the richest people in the world."

He smiled with some degree of satisfaction as he finished his spiel. Then, he sat down in the chair at a right angle to the sofa and looked over at her as though he was ready to engage in a casual, friendly conversation while he waited for her answer.

She tried to buy some time. "I need to use the restroom. I can't think clearly or give you an answer until I've relieved myself."

Much to her surprise and blip of satisfaction, he produced a sharp knife from his pocket, sprang open the blade, and slashed the plastic restraints around her ankles.

Fifty-Nine

Tokyo, Japan, Tuesday December 26, 2023

Serge's team needed to use subterfuge—if not outright deception—to spring him from the Japan Self-Defense Forces military hospital in Tokyo. He remembered Antonio Primavera being reticent when he gave the non-negotiable order to get him out of there, insisting they be in the air aboard Suzanne's corporate jet within the hour, but he recalled only sketchy details.

Antonio had come back with a new nurse, one Serge hadn't seen before. As she prepared a syringe, Antonio had watched her every movement. She'd muttered in barely understandable English that Serge needed sleep to avoid making matters worse. That was all he remembered until he awoke with a start when their jet encountered turbulence.

It lasted for several moments. The plane's engines groaned in protest as it bounced in the air like a basketball on a polished wood court in the hands of a player evading a close-checking opponent. Serge had to force himself to swallow multiple times to keep down whatever was in his stomach, rebelling against the turmoil. Some of the dramatic drops took seconds for the pilots to stabilize their flight pattern.

Occasionally, the frame of the jet not only shook violently, but it also creaked ominously, as if it might break apart. More than once, Serge reached down to his waist to yank his seatbelt increasingly tighter.

It seemed like an eternity—but was probably only a few minutes—before the pilot made an announcement on the intercom.

"Sorry, folks. We went through an unexpected storm

back there. It appears we're past the turbulence for now, and you can be sure I'll let the Tokyo airport authorities know we're not happy with their failure to provide better weather guidance. I've checked other resources, and we should be relatively free of turbulence for the remainder of the trip." The intercom grew quiet as they experienced yet another tilt of the aircraft and a steep descent that brought Serge's stomach momentarily to his heart.

"Sorry again, folks. I spoke too soon. Let's just say it should get better before long. Most importantly, the communications system is now back up and running. Digital records show Montreal security tried to reach us several times. You're okay to connect with them now."

Serge raised himself higher in the leather seat to determine which team members were nearby. He caught Antonio's eye in the partially reclined seat opposite him and to his right, and he waved for him to come closer.

"Where are we?" he asked when Antonio was crouching beside Serge's partially reclined seat.

"About three hours out of Tokyo. The pilot has us heading toward the Labrador town of Wabush, as you requested. Our plane can't make it without a stop for fuel in Anchorage, so it's probably about another twelve hours before we touch down there."

Serge wanted to check his mental alertness. "So, we have about another six hours until we arrive in Alaska?"

"Yeah, more or less. I've arranged for medical staff to meet us at the airport there and fly with us to Labrador. We're all concerned about the amount of time you've been sleeping since the nurse in Tokyo gave you that sedative. It might just be your injury from the violence in Russia, but we don't want to take any chances."

Serge nodded. "Who's handling communication with security in Montreal?"

"Sheila's on the line now." The turbulence had

disappeared. Antonio waved for her to join them.

She unbuckled her seatbelt and stepped toward them with her phone to her ear.

"They've lost Suzanne again. Someone interrupted their communication several hours ago, and the team still has not been able to re-establish contact. They haven't been able to reach Jasmine either."

Serge took a moment to process the significance of each piece of information. "Get James on the line."

It took more than a few minutes, giving Antonio ample time to let him know that Floyd Demerais had made some startling new discoveries in Florida. "There have been some weird communications. Floyd intercepted one message between Palm Beach and Moscow that suggested someone there was following the developments out of Vladivostok yesterday. They know we got you out."

When Sheila raised a finger and mouthed that James was on the line, Serge reached for her phone. "Any new developments there?"

"Yeah. We got a bead on Natalia. A flight originally destined for Wabush, Labrador, suddenly made a forty-five-degree left turn over Pennsylvania with no route notification to air traffic control. The speed of the aircraft has dramatically reduced, suggesting a possible landing in Erie, Pennsylvania, on the south coast of Lake Ontario."

"What about Suzanne? Have you been able to re-establish communication?"

"That's a negative, I'm afraid," James replied. "Communication from the Wabush Hotel has come to a complete stop. We can't even connect with their switchboard. The good news is that we've contacted Constable Gagnon. He's on the way to the hotel and has roused several members of his contingent there. He says they'll have four officers surrounding the hotel within minutes."

He relayed the information from the earlier call with Floyd Desmerais. Clearly, there was more going on in the U.S. right now than he'd expected. The big question remained.

"Who's behind all the turmoil?"

Sixty

Montreal, Quebec, Tuesday December 26, 2023

James found it odd that Alberto Ferer's wife came on the line when the team had reached his room at a hotel in Aruba. "He left a few hours ago. He told me he received a message about an urgent matter to address, and it could only be handled in person. He said the company was sending a jet to meet him at the airport for a quick trip to Montreal. He'd be away for only a short time and would return within twenty-four hours."

James sensed a touch of worry. He didn't want to alarm her further, so he spoke slowly and tried to appear as nonchalant as possible.

"Yes, I understand he's trying to get a quorum of directors for an urgent matter. I received the same call and just arrived in Montreal, too. I tried to reach him on his phone, but got no answer. Do you know whether he took his phone with him?"

She didn't know, but she did agree to check around their room while James waited on the line. It took longer than expected. When she returned, her tone was one of exasperation. "I can't believe this. I found his mobile phone sitting here in a drawer. I looked around for mine and couldn't find it. He might have taken that phone instead. That's never happened before!"

"No problem. If you can give me your number, I'll call him there. He should be able to answer a call without your password." He wrote the phone number on a scrap of paper as she dictated it to him. "But he won't be able to make any calls without the password. Can you give me that to relay to him as well?"

James leaned back and stretched his arms high above his head in the only executive-style chair in the security department's Montreal office. He couldn't stifle a sense of satisfaction at his good fortune to think of asking that second question and getting Alberto's wife's password.

Sure enough, when he tried the number she'd given him, Alberto Ferer responded after a few rings. He was on a jet with a lot of background noise, but they had a brief— though strained—conversation. Alberto told him Mahinder had sent the plane to pick him up, and that he was en route to Montreal for an urgent meeting of the board of directors. Mahinder had insisted that Alberto attend the meeting in person to sign the actual written documents despite the legal expert's insistence that electronic signatures would suffice. However, Alberto had strangely resisted providing more details about the issue until they met in person at Multima's Montreal office.

Despite Alberto's expectation that he wouldn't need to use his wife's phone before landing in Montreal, James insisted that he make a note of her password, just in case. Sure enough, moments later, he called James back.

"Something is going on, James." Alberto's voice trembled with alarm. "Abduhl Mahinder told me the jet was taking me to Montreal. We've landed, and I just realized we're not in Montreal. I saw a sign over the doorway to the terminal that says, 'Erie International Airport.' I've just activated the executive digital tracking device Serge gave me, which I've never used before. Let the security team in Montreal know and get them to track me. I've got to go. The pilot's headed for the exit door."

While waiting for Alberto to get back to him, James reached Serge, who was in flight from Japan. Between the two groups, they had a team of eight of Multima's armed security people on flights to the remote town of Wabush, Labrador.

"Have we been able to reach Floyd Demerais down in South Florida again?" Serge asked.

The answer was negative. Members of the security team had tried to reach their colleague several times, but Floyd's phone was still off. Calls over the past several hours had gone directly to voicemail.

Serge urged James to push the team in Montreal to try to locate Floyd.

As they spoke, another security specialist poked her head around the corner and mouthed that Constable Gagnon was on the line from Labrador. James patched Serge into the call for a conference.

"The hotel is completely locked down. We've tried all the doors without success, called all the numbers we have available as contacts, and walked around the entire building exterior twice. There are two cars parked in a corner of the hotel parking lot, but the license plates show they're registered to a car rental company. Anyone in the town could be using that parking lot."

"Is closing up entirely like that a normal practice for the hotel? Are they still in business?" James asked.

"The heating and electrical systems all appear to be working okay. I've never known the hotel to close before. Usually, it operates twenty-four hours a day, like every other hotel. My people tried to reach the manager at the number we have on file, but there's no answer, and the guy actually lives on the top floor of the building. My team is trying to reach other staff members for whom we have numbers. While we legally have probable cause to break into the hotel, I need to be sure we don't put any of the Multima people or my team at unnecessary risk.

The constable's tone of voice didn't sound confident. Serge wanted more. "I googled the ownership of the hotel. It seems new owners took over just a few months ago. Do you know anything about that, Sergeant?"

"Yeah. That was big news here for a few days. The previous owner was about to declare bankruptcy last summer when there was a sudden announcement about an investment outfit from Argentina buying him out. I don't recall ever hearing anything more about that transaction, but I had lunch there last week, and everything seemed to be operating normally."

"How many folks do you have in your RCMP contingent there?" Serge asked.

"A dozen people. Ten officers and two support staff. But I know four of them are away on holiday leave right now. Besides the five of us surrounding the hotel at the moment, there's only one other gal. She had her phone turned off when I sent out the alarm."

Serge changed his tack. "We have information that another flight landed in Wabush a while ago with at least one Multima executive on board. She's wearing a digital tracking device that indicates she's already at the Wabush Hotel. Can you get a court order to have a locksmith open the doors for you and your people to get in?"

The constable paused for a long moment. When he answered, his tone was subdued. "I won't need a court order, but it will probably take some time. It's five in the morning here, and I know the town's only locksmith was at a party last night. I'll try to reach him, but I can't guarantee this will be quick."

"I understand," Serge said. "Do your best, buddy. And keep trying to reach your missing gal. If you can roust her out of bed, I'd appreciate it if you would dispatch her to the airport. We'll be landing there within an hour and could use some help."

The constable signed off, but James asked Serge to stay on the line. "Something's brewing. I just received a text from Abduhl Mahinder. He provided a link for a Zoom call scheduled an hour from now. He's asked for an immediate acknowledgement, which means he'll follow up in just a few minutes with any director who fails to acknowledge the alert. We're running out of time."

Sixty-One

Why did the corporate jet she was on suddenly reduce speed, veer sharply to the left, then descend with a pitch steep enough to cause the aircraft to shake violently and rattle? Natalia couldn't be sure. She glanced in all directions around the cabin.

The thugs seated in front of her tried to feign calmness. Behind her, both Mahinder and Alvarez remained deep in conversation, but each displayed some level of irritation with the bumpy ride. Alvarez even resorted to pointing a threatening finger toward the high-powered executive at one point. Though the conversation was surely animated, their voices never rose to a level where she could discern what they were talking about. Sooner than she expected, they made a half circle over a large body of water and landed, tires screeching, on an empty runway.

"Erie International Airport," read a huge white sign with blue lettering mounted over the doorway that the jet jerked to a stop directly in front of. All the thugs released their seat belts—almost as though coordinated—and checked the weapons stashed inside their oversized jackets. Apparently satisfied, each performed a series of stretches using their fingers, hands, legs, and necks before bouncing to their feet and spreading out in the aircraft, with two of them facing the plane's door. No one spoke.

The moment something metal grazed against the side of the jet, the two facing the doorway yanked their weapons from the holsters below their left shoulders and pointed them at the door. One of the guys moved to the window closest to the exit and peered outside for a moment before releasing the lock mechanism so someone outside could raise the doorway open.

Several footsteps clanked loudly up metal stairs as the door swung open, and three figures came into view. The one in the middle was shouting in protest and trying to resist the iron grips of two on either side, forcing him into the jet. Although his face wasn't entirely visible, she had no doubt the voice she heard belonged to Multima's chief legal officer, Alberto Ferer.

With a final, potent shove, the men outside released their prey, and Alberto stumbled into the aircraft. He looked directly at each person inside the airplane in total silence for several long moments—until he recognized her, and his expression of fear morphed into puzzlement.

"What . . . what is going on?" he finally managed to spit out. A touch of anger seeped into his voice. He glared directly at her, unblinking.

Before Natalia could decide how best to respond to the question, Abduhl Mahinder stood up behind her and replied in his trademark calm voice, "Relax, Alberto. Don't make any sudden moves or do anything foolish. They're not here to hurt you. Walk back here with me—slowly—and take a seat with me and Mauro Alvarez."

The moment Alberto took his first step forward, one of the thugs knocked loudly on the door of the pilots' compartment. The door opened, and the co-pilot stepped into the main cabin. His eyes searched the interior until he fixed his gaze on Mahinder with a nod.

"Close the door, and get the engine started immediately," the board member and CEO of Bank of the Americas ordered, barely above a whisper. "Get us in the air toward Wabush as quickly as you can and try to make up some time. They have complications that need to be dealt with urgently."

They were in flight within moments, and the engines

roared in protest for what seemed like an hour or more. Throughout the flight, Natalia strained to grasp even a tiny morsel of their conversation, but it was fruitless. Mahinder and Alvarez did all the talking, and with their backs to Natalia, she couldn't make out what either was saying over the groan of the engines.

The jet descended more quickly than she'd expected and soon touched ground. The thugs in front of her repeated their same landing ritual as soon as the plane came to a full stop.

She reached down to release her seatbelt when the guy closest to her wagged a warning finger, shook his head, and shouted for her not to move.

Natalia froze, then glanced behind her to see if the men seated there were preparing to leave. All three had unbuckled their seat belts, gathered their papers and personal belongings, and looked prepared to deplane. She felt a pang of unease. When she looked back toward the front, the dude who had warned her not to move now hovered over her so closely that he blocked her view.

She spotted his right hand heading for her lap before she felt a sharp prick in her upper thigh and realized that she'd remain conscious for only a moment or two longer.

Sixty-Two

The restroom delaying tactic proved only modestly helpful for Suzanne. She stretched out her time in the lavatory until the Russian banged on the door and demanded she finish up. The few minutes she'd bought for clear thinking wasn't enough. She saw no immediate alternative but to agree to sell her block of shares in the company and accept their conditions ... with only the tiniest possibility remaining for an escape. To buy a little more time, she insisted on reviewing a draft of their proposed legal agreement in a feeble effort to maintain a shred of control.

Extreme fatigue took over and she dozed off after that, likely compounded by the stress of them physically dragging her back to the room from which she and Jasmine had escaped earlier and her confrontation with the Russian. As she slowly became aware of her surroundings again, she scanned every corner of the room, looking for her missing bodyguard.

Things had changed in the suite. All the dark-blue drapes were fully closed. Earlier, they'd only been partially closed. The bulky, royal-blue sofa that matched the curtains now blocked the doorway to the second room, the one they had assigned to Jasmine when they'd first arrived at the hotel. All the drawers from the cupboards in the tiny kitchen had been emptied and thrown in a heap on the tiled floor.

As she lifted herself off the bed, she checked for possible injuries or damage to her clothes after the rough handling of her captors. She reached for the light switch on the table beside the sofa—it didn't work. The Russian had snapped new restraints around her ankles despite her partially positive response, so she slid from the couch and tested how much movement the zip ties around her ankles allowed—she guessed she had about fifteen inches or more when she tried to spread her feet.

Moving gingerly, slowly, to maintain her balance, she went to the doorway and tried the light switch there, but there was nothing despite her frustrated flicks. The only light came from small battery-operated devices located in each corner of the suite.

With some trepidation, she inched her way toward the closed drapes and peeked outside. A massive snowstorm raged. It was only then that the howling winds caught her attention. She pulled back the drapes for a better view and saw the intensity of the storm. From her third-floor suite, it was almost impossible to see the ground. Instead, she saw only a wall of blowing snow. It caused a shiver to run down her spine.

From the window, she moved toward the sofa blocking the doorway to see if she might be able to move it enough to open the door. They'd secured her hands with a zip tie again, but more loosely and in front of her. Twice, she tried to budge the sofa from its location, but she couldn't nudge the corner a single inch.

Thirsty, she moved cautiously toward the kitchen and opened a cupboard—it was empty, as were all the other doors she could reach. Deciding to improvise and drink directly from the tap, she turned it to the open position, but nothing came from the spout. Veering toward the refrigerator, she opened the door and peered inside, but there was nothing. No food. No water. Nothing.

Knowing it was probably fruitless, Suzanne tried the door to the hallway, grimacing with the realization that her situation had become more dire. Rather than panic, she opted to scrounge around the darkened room, checking closets, drawers, and mostly empty bookshelves. They must have her shoes, phone, and handbag somewhere else, making an escape in the raging snowstorm impossible even if she found a way out of the room.

Finally, she decided to conserve energy, so she returned to the royal-blue sofa blocking the doorway. On a whim, she knocked on the door before sitting down, then recoiled when a muffled voice called out from behind the locked door.

She knocked again.

Once more, the voice called out, this time closer and louder. Dare she respond?

Before she had the time to make a decision, the door handle to her left rattled slightly. She realized that if someone was trying to open the door from the other side, they must think the door was unlocked. She tried the latch mechanism on her side of the doorway and was relieved to see it slide slightly. The door almost immediately banged against the sofa, opening only an inch or two.

When Suzanne peered through the opening, Jasmine peeped back, only a few inches away from her face, startling both women. Suzanne told her bodyguard about the heavy sofa blocking their progress.

Jasmine asked Suzanne to tug hard on the sofa while she pushed on the slightly ajar door. Nothing happened. Jasmine coached her to try pulling from an angle slightly closer to the door. With Suzanne's restrictive zip ties, she couldn't spread her legs enough to leverage her leg strength effectively. As a result, the weight was far greater than the women could manage with the door and sofa in their current positions.

Jasmine brought her forefinger to her lips and signaled for Suzanne to stay silent before moving out of her limited view. She returned a few moments later, holding a screwdriver that she gently slid through the open crack of the doorway. "Take this and try to remove the screws holding the hinges in place at the top of the door. You might need to climb up on the sofa to get enough torque to loosen them."

Suzanne completed pulling the screwdriver through the opening. She assessed the challenge for a moment before she sat on the sofa. Seated, she swung her feet upward, then twisted and shuffled her arms and legs until she was upright on the leather surface of the sofa, despite her bound feet.

It was firm, and she found a way to brace one bare foot against the armrest for better balance. It took several tries, each seemingly futile, until she saw a movement, no matter how tiny. She tried again, and the screw loosened more. With each subsequent attempt, it became easier, and then a screw fell into the gap behind the sofa and landed on the floor.

Encouraged, Suzanne repeated the process two more times until the third screw fell to the floor, and the top hinge popped loose and hung harmlessly from one side. Jasmine motioned for her to step down from the sofa and away, then she gripped the door at the top and pushed with enough force to slightly jar the sofa.

"Step around to the end and tug on the sofa hard when I tell you," Jasmine whispered.

Suzanne stood where her security guard had pointed, spread her legs as far as the restraint allowed, and bent her knees. When she heard Jasmine's whispered "Now," she pulled with every ounce of strength she could muster. Unbelievably, with Jasmine shoving on the dangling door, the heavy sofa groaned and shifted a few more inches across the hardwood floor.

Jasmine coached her three more times, each of which resulted in a tiny movement that eventually created a gap of about two feet.

"Let me try now. Stand to the side." Suzanne stepped to the side a few feet, where her view was unrestricted. On the other side of the door, Jasmine drew a deep breath, then squatted as close to the sofa as possible from her side of the gap in the doorway. With a loud, unrestrained grunt, Jasmine lifted the rear corner of the sofa and heaved it upward. It shifted another foot away from the doorway, enough for Jasmine to squeeze her muscular body through the opening.

Suzanne hugged her companion's shoulder tightly and brought her into an awkward embrace of congratulations, appreciation, and relief. Then, with an unexpected laugh, she blurted, "Where did you find that screwdriver?"

Jasmine giggled in return. "I poked around the bedroom and found an enclosed electrical box in a closet. When I opened it, I found that someone had left behind the tiny screwdriver. I took it with me but realized the door hinges were mounted on the other side, and I had no way to use it. When I heard you, I immediately wondered if we might have an opportunity."

Then, more seriously, Suzanne asked, "What can we do now?"

Before Jasmine could respond, they were distracted by a commotion in the hallway outside the main doorway to the suite. It sounded like feet stomping, and then the door swung open, and one of the Russian thugs stepped in and looked to his left. Shocked to see both women standing just feet away, he grasped for the weapon in his shoulder holster and called out something in Russian before pointing the weapon menacingly at them.

Two more Russian thugs burst through the doorway, their weapons already drawn, encircling both women, who stood frozen in shock.

When one of the Russians shouted, "Okay," two more men entered the room, still brushing snow from their windbreakers and rubbing their bare hands to warm them from the cold outside.

The first through the doorway was a tall man of Latin American heritage who walked with a confident swagger despite his obvious discomfort from the cold. Behind him followed a face familiar to both of them—Abduhl Mahinder. He spoke first.

"Ladies, it appears you've upset your watchdogs." He surveyed them up and down, then looked beyond them to the hanging door and royal-blue sofa before a cruel smirk appeared on his face. He turned to face Jasmine.

"I'm impressed. Great ingenuity for a bodyguard, and formidable strength. The fellows thought you'd be secure in here until we needed you, so they used their last pair of leg restraints on the wrong captive. We'll need to keep you both here for another few hours, and we'll also need both of you alert when we're ready, so we'll have to modify our procedures."

With a wave of dismissal toward Mahinder, the tall Latin American spun on his heel and headed toward the doorway, shouting out to the Russians as he reached the door. "Zip ties, top and bottom on both ... and tight."

Sixty-Three

In the airspace over Labrador, Tuesday December 26, 2023

The violent turbulence lasted almost an hour. Earlier, the pilot had warned that everyone should remain seated to avoid possible injury. So, Serge was surprised when that pilot peeked around the open compartment door and braced himself against a wall with one hand as he moved tentatively toward Serge.

The fellow swayed twice and had to catch his balance against other seats before he plopped down with relief in the seat across from Serge. "They've closed the airport in Wabush. Air Traffic Control has instructed us to land in Gander instead. About another hour in the air. Apparently, the storm has weakened there."

He took a moment to think about the alternatives while the pilot waited patiently and silently. Serge swung his chair around to face the fellow and locked eyes with him to gauge his depth of conviction. "If we can get them to open the airport, can you bring us down safely?"

"If we have enough visibility to see the runway, we should be okay. The plane's built by Bombardier. They test the planes in this kind of weather, so I have no concerns about the plane's mechanical operation, structural integrity, or balance. It handles well in even very high winds. But I need to be able to set the thing down in the middle of the runway for all those things to apply."

Serge nodded his understanding. "How about stopping it before the end of the runway?"

"Again, if visibility is adequate enough to identify where the runway starts and ends and there is no ice or icy buildup, the brakes will perform without issue."

"Okay. Say visibility is good, and we get them to open the airport—is there anything else we should worry about?" Serge asked.

"Takeoff. To take off again, we'll need to be sure that the runway is cleared enough to see the markers and warning signs. We'll need to have the plane de-iced. And we'll also want to be sure the wind velocity is not much greater than it is near the ground now. Candidly, if you're thinking about pulling some strings to get the airport open for landing, I'd be more worried about getting out again than going in."

"We still have about thirty minutes until we're over Wabush?" Serge waited for the pilot to nod before he continued. "Check every resource you can from up front. Suzanne is in danger, maybe others, and time is of the essence. But I'll leave the final call to you."

With the pilot dismissed and struggling to get back to the cockpit, Serge dialed a number. As soon as Constable Gagnon identified himself, the instructions flowed.

"We're about thirty minutes from Wabush. The airport is closed, but I'll need you to contact your people out there to get an exception for us. Our pilot will abort if he deems landing or taking off again too dangerous, but I want *him* to make the call, not ATC."

He waited for the constable to agree, then carried on. "I need one heavily armed officer from your detachment stationed out there to meet us when we land, plus two cars that my eight security guys and gals can use to get to the hotel. Anything will do."

The officer repeated his understanding of the request, as RCMP officers are trained to do, then offered his own brief update. "I found a locksmith, and he's on his way to the hotel. That extra resource you requested would be my gal, Marjorie Laplante. I've reached her, too. She's a little hungover, but she sounded like you can rely on her. I've already asked her to stop by the station and pick up a C8.

She knows how to use it well."

Satisfied, Serge ended the call and immediately dialed James Fitzgerald in Montreal. After a quick briefing on their plans, Serge asked if there were any new developments. There were.

"When you called, I had just hung up from a call with Floyd Desmarais in Florida. He's okay. It turns out that he lost his connection to us because someone imposed a telecommunications blackout for the area around the resort. In addition to the two guys who were working inside the hut next to the resort, three more drove up in a golf cart, all decked out in bright lights, which they dimmed just as they reached the building. One carried a portable transponder as they slipped into the cottage. One was heavily armed, and he surveyed the terrain in all directions as they wended their way into the house. The third guy was the one they were protecting. Floyd couldn't see clearly enough to identify him positively, but his build and walking manner very much resembled a former US president."

Serge drew a deep breath. There had to be more, so he remained silent.

"Floyd was able to work his way closer to the shed after the men were all inside. He noticed one of the only windows in the place was cracked open enough so that he could hear voices. When he finally got close enough in the darkness, the voices grew clear enough to catch bits of the conversation." James swallowed audibly.

Serge tapped his armrest in anticipation but stayed silent as the experienced executive carried on with his story.

"The guy who looked like the former president did most of the talking. It sounded like he was apologizing to whoever was on the other line, explaining that it was just taking a little longer than planned. There was a snowstorm in the area. A flight was delayed so they could meet up with the lawyer. The guy said that, at first, the asshole refused to cooperate drafting the documents until they'd rearranged his face enough to get his cooperation, that the bitch and her bodyguard had connived to escape and almost did, but that it should all be done within a short period."

Serge had a ton of questions, but he knew it wasn't the time to bombard the executive, who was operating under unfamiliar and stressful circumstances. He focused on one issue.

"Did Floyd make any mention of money, money transfers, or payments?"

"Yes, I was just about to give you that information. I had to ask him three times to be sure I heard it correctly, but Floyd distinctly recalled the American asking whoever was on the other line where the ten billion dollars were. Apparently, the guy had been expecting such a huge amount to be transferred to an account or accounts somewhere." James's tone was incredulous as he relayed the amount in a voice barely above a whisper.

"I realize Floyd could only hear one side of the conversation, but could he deduce anything more about the money or the purpose of the money?" Serge probed.

"No. The guy was apparently satisfied with the response because the call ended abruptly soon after. The only other thing Floyd heard before the men left the shed and took off on the golf cart was the fellow who apparently talked with a similar vulgarity to a former US president, swearing that they were dealing with a fuckin' bunch of Commies."

"Where is Floyd now?"

"He's still outside the complex, waiting for further instructions."

Serge asked James to relay his thanks to Floyd and asked him to keep them posted with any new developments.

Before Serge stashed his mobile, the plane's engine noticeably slowed, and he felt a slight dip as the aircraft continued to bounce and sway with the high winds.

In fact, it only took a few minutes. But those minutes seemed like an eternity. The engine roared occasionally and sputtered at other times. The wings often tilted so dramatically that the passengers across the aisle from Serge seemed physically higher or lower as the pilots delicately countered the fury of the storm and winds.

The dips and bumps were too frequent to count. Serge found lumps in his throat that made it difficult to swallow more frequently than anything he had ever experienced. After first touching the wheels to the ground, the plane jolted them with four more hard bumps before the engines slowed further and the speed decreased dramatically.

As soon as it appeared safe to do so, Serge detached his seatbelt and called out for everyone to join him, motioning for them to stand in a semicircle before him for their last-minute instructions. He started with a confirmation that they wouldn't be burdened with taking care of him.

"The moment you leave the aircraft, Antonio will take charge. I'm not mobile enough and would only drag your rescue efforts down. Follow the plans we discussed until Antonio changes them, should that become necessary. I'll stay here at the airport with the plane and the pilots, making sure we have everything ready to take off the moment you guys get back with Suzanne, Jasmine, and whoever else from Multima you might find there. Good luck!"

With that command and counsel, Serge switched his focus back to Florida. It was becoming increasingly clear that some form of defensive action was necessary. The bigger question was related to the scoundrel there. What action might Serge take from Labrador? And how could he be assured that neither he nor Suzanne would be sucked into the morass? It would take some creativity.

Sixty-Four

Wabush, Labrador, Tuesday December 26, 2023

Natalia couldn't recall a time she'd felt so disconnected and alone. It was more than just being the only person in a locked suite. She'd tried the door several times, but it appeared securely fastened from the outside as well as inside. An electronic device controlled access and, of course she didn't have a card. Normally, the inside lock would release, but this one seemed programmed to open only with a card on one side or the other.

The handle didn't budge, no matter how much pressure she exerted. Although she had no intention of jumping from the third-floor window into the winter storm, she tried all the windows, and they were all tightly sealed, impossible to open.

Her pursuit of growth and success at Multima had occupied almost half of the years of her life, so she never focused large amounts of time on curating a social world. As a result, virtually every moment of her hours away from the office she'd spent on her own, so she was accustomed to not having other people around.

What she wasn't accustomed to was the void that having no access to the outside world with her electronic devices left. Who didn't spend a few hours a day checking news feeds, responding to emails, or touching base with social media contacts? Stuck there, alone in the comfortable suite, none of those things were possible, and it felt extremely odd—it was disconcerting. She'd had more than enough time on the plane and in the few hours since they'd unceremoniously stuffed her into the confined environment for her to think.

She was clearly at the mercy of some very disreputable people. It was hard to imagine a scenario in which things ended well. Abduhl Mahinder continuously emitted vibes suggesting she act with caution. His manner in both individual personal interactions and meetings had always created doubts about both his motive and his method, but the guy was the chair of Bank of the Americas, after all. He also seemed to be the main driver behind Docket 2025, though she had no evidence of that. Each of those factors should make it prudent to mingle with caution.

Where did Mahinder fit in among the hierarchy of the gang he was hanging out with? Mauro Alvarez seemed to be the one giving the orders, and Mahinder always appeared to follow them, whether he might agree entirely or not at all. She had no way of knowing. And their manner suggested both might defer to some unknown power with whom they communicated frequently by text or phone.

Their offer to install her as Multima Corporation's CEO was perplexing. Any objective analyst would probably agree that Suzanne Simpson was approaching the end of her tenure at the helm of the massive corporation. It didn't appear that she'd made any unforgivable errors in either judgment or execution, but she was aging. Shareholders and boards of directors always became more wary as energy and passion waned. It seemed a normal and natural eventuality.

However, Suzanne showed no signs of lost passion or energy. The woman worked incredibly long hours in multiple time zones and traveled the globe constantly. Her direct reports still showed not only respect but admiration. Natalia still studied her every move with appreciation, wonder, and almost a sense of reverence.

Logic suggested that the only reason these folks had offered her the top job, seized her, and transported her to some small town in the frozen barrens of Labrador was to accomplish some nefarious goal. The same logic implied that she herself would soon become as dispensable as Suzanne.

Only minutes after she'd decided that she must cooperate but not succumb, the door to her suite was unlocked and opened. Her chair faced the doorway, and she saw Alberto Ferer standing there, his shoulders slumped forward. Some papers were rolled up in his hand, and the expression on his bruised and battered face was beyond sheepish. To describe it as shame seemed more appropriate. Their eyes made contact for an instant before he glanced downward and stepped tentatively into her room.

Abduhl Mahinder followed behind him. His eyes were also cast downward, and he made no attempt to connect with hers. In comparison, Mauro Alvarez appeared almost buoyant as he pulled the door closed behind him and grinned at her with an expression suggesting satisfaction and perhaps even triumph. No one spoke for a moment, and the prolonged silence caused her heart to beat noticeably faster.

When he finally looked up, Alvarez nodded to Mahinder, who then spoke with a resigned tone. "Despite the hiccups, we still want you to become Multima's CEO, under the same conditions we discussed earlier, effective as soon as today. Alberto has prepared an employment agreement to confirm all the details, but we need you to sign another agreement first."

Alberto shifted his weight from one leg to the other but continued to gaze downward. A few more seconds of uncomfortable quiet elapsed before he raised his head tentatively toward Mahinder, who simply nodded in return.

"It's a confidentiality agreement," Alberto mumbled as he moved toward her, flattening the paper in his hand as he progressed. Only slightly louder, he said, "You'll want to read it carefully before you sign it because the terms and conditions are stringent. You'll be agreeing to limit your interactions with all media going forward. You'll need to seek permission and approval before you release any company information, financial or otherwise. And you'll notice the consequences are severe should you violate the terms or the spirit of the agreement you sign."

He reached out to hand her the document and peered directly into her eyes. His expression wasn't difficult to read, with his lips pursed tightly together, his nostrils flared, and his eyes pleading for forgiveness. The deep creases in his forehead were familiar—they appeared whenever he was distressed.

She snatched the papers and broke eye contact with Alberto, turning to face Alvarez instead. "May I take a few moments to read it as Alberto counselled?"

He nodded in response, then turned toward the men. "Give her some space alone."

They all shuffled toward the door and filed out in silence.

It took a surprisingly short time to read and understand the entire agreement. They demanded that she agree to operate essentially as a puppet, performing the tasks they ordered for as long as they chose to have her serve in the role of CEO.

Sixty-Five

James didn't dare leave the hi-tech control room of Multima's internal security office in Montreal. Throughout the night, he'd devoured coffee to stay alert and found that a new morning brought with it an unusually intense hunger. He ordered one of the junior colleagues to find an open restaurant in Montreal on the Boxing Day holiday. It took her only minutes to find one both open and able to deliver promptly.

As the morning became brighter, a young woman hustled through the doorway. A colleague held the usually locked door open with his foot as he reached to take one of the bags stuffed with breakfast food strapped over her shoulder in the type of gray canvas sack used by professional delivery folks. She surely had enough for everyone.

The technicians sat at their desks, frequently checking their banks of widescreen monitors as they wolfed down the food in silence. James sensed the tension in the room—he felt it personally, too. Events appeared to be converging in Wabush, Labrador, and the elite communications team in Vietnam continuously updated reports of electronic messages and bundles of data through Vladivostok in Russia.

In Montreal, one of the technicians tracked the data reports from Vietnam on a massive map of the world displayed on an electronic screen hanging from the ceiling. Green lights flashed in Monaco, Cyprus, Luxembourg, Singapore, and Hong Kong. A new one started flashing in Jakarta while James swallowed a bite of his sandwich.

Before he'd completed a sip of coffee to wash it down, another started flashing in the Cayman Islands. According to the technician, each flashing green light indicated a location that Vietnam's sophisticated technology had detected receiving electronic transfers of one billion dollars or more from a single bank located in Vladivostok in Russia.

James wanted to understand better why the folks on Multima's security team were monitoring that particular bank, and why they'd focused on that specific location. As soon as he swallowed the last of his breakfast, he reached Archie Begat over in Vietnam. The day was winding down there.

"Acting on a hunch, Serge asked me to find a way to penetrate the computer systems used by the Russian SDR—that's the acronym for their Foreign Intelligence Service. It took several days after we arrived, but one of our guys stumbled upon it, found a way in, and has been monitoring it 24/7 for the past few weeks. The signals we're intercepting are all from a site in Vladivostok that's controlled from a private address in Moscow."

"Who owns the site?" James asked.

"We can't be one hundred percent sure, but it's definitely someone very influential in the Russian government. Over ninety percent of the signals we intercepted were from that private residence to the Presidential Executive Office of the Russian Federation.

"The gal on our team who spoke Russian was killed in that traffic crash here in Saigon a few days ago, so we don't know exactly who they're going to or what the messages said."

James recalled hearing about the tragic accident that had killed two security team members on the street in front of the apartment building they were operating from. "Where else are these messages going?"

"The single most frequent address is in Vladivostok.

From there, the most frequent destinations after Moscow are Palm Beach, Florida, and Haneda, Japan. Messages out of those locations are primarily sent to spots in North America from Palm Beach and Southeast Asia from Haneda. There are dozens of them every day." Archie paused for a moment, then added, "Our gal who was killed said the overwhelming number of messages she saw dealt with issues only an organized crime outfit would deal with: collections, punishments, amounts of money, and what appeared to be coded instructions."

James shook his head, admiring the technical whizzes' expertise. He understood the basics and even grasped the concept of some of the new, emerging technologies related to artificial intelligence, but he never envisaged that a company he worked for would have the ability to tap into such secret servers and services. How much more was he missing?

"Anything else you're working on over there?"

"That's all we can do over here. Now, we're relying on the new connection we just added out of Inuvik."

"In Canada's Northwest Territories?"

"Yeah. Serge just called a few minutes ago and asked us to link to an address in Canada's far north. Someone related to CSIS, Canada's Secret Intelligence Service. We just linked everything to a computer there that uses artificial intelligence to translate from Russian to English. Serge expects we'll know exactly what's going on from those sites in Russia within hours, maybe even minutes."

James froze. He'd spoken to Serge only minutes before—why on Earth hadn't he shared that critical information?

Sixty-Six

Wabush, Labrador, Tuesday December 26, 2023

Hours had elapsed since the thugs had bound the hands and feet of both Suzanne and Jasmine in their zip-tie devices. Inexplicably, the Russian guy who'd so forcefully demanded she sell her Multima Corporation shares at a fraction of their actual value had abandoned the hotel suite. He'd received a call, spoken a few words in Russian, then stood up and glared at her before spitting out a warning:

"Don't either of you try to move. Keep thinking. I'll be back with the documents for you to sign and expect your signature immediately."

Time elapsed. It was far longer than she'd expected, and the Russian guy hadn't returned. Nor had anyone else. Bound and left to lie on the carpet in the suite's larger bedroom, she saw light through cracks in the drawn curtains.

The unpleasant interaction with the guy and his minions left her exhausted. She'd tried to rest, but it proved elusive with her limbs bound uncomfortably, and her brain racing to cope with it all.

Serge had always counseled a siesta under such circumstances. While he never bombarded her with security advice or made her worry about her risks, on a few occasions, he'd quietly and calmly shared his expertise. Adequate slumber was essential for anyone being held captive—sleep-deprived people made more mistakes, he claimed.

He maintained that fatigue affected people's judgment and critical thinking skills, which, in turn, often led to poor decisions, irrational behavior, and sometimes fatal risks, so she had tried, but sleep had proven impossible.

The howling wind outside had subsided. That suggested the snowfall might also have abated somewhat. Or perhaps not. When she lived in Quebec City, snowfall sometimes continued for days after the winds decreased.

Although the entire affair was unpleasant, it was too early to panic. Logic suggested they would keep her alive until she signed the documents they'd threatened her with but had not yet produced. Dead, she would be unable to sign anything, and her estate would take charge of the disposal of her assets. It was hard to imagine how criminals could outfox a team of expert lawyers to somehow suggest they were entitled to a share of the fortune Suzanne would leave behind.

Torture was an option. Their treatment of her had been somewhat rough, but nothing had suggested they'd harm her to wring a signature from her. Jasmine was probably in greater danger. Might they force her to witness her bodyguard's torment to induce Suzanne to sign their documents? Russian thugs were notorious for their racial prejudices. With a woman of color who'd already caused those hoodlums some grief in the equation, she needed to brace for such a dreadful possibility.

Still, the whole affair didn't make rational sense. If they forced Suzanne to sign their documents, the moment she was free, she'd tell the authorities what had happened. If they murdered her, the bad guys would still need to deal with the lawyers for her estate if they wanted to get their hands on paper copies of the shares she supposedly sold to them for a fraction of their real value. It would be a hard sell.

For whom were these guys fronting? There had to be someone or some organization behind them. And where did Abduhl Mahinder fit in the scheme? She'd never trusted the man, but her father, John George Mortimer, had named him to Multima's board of directors after Bank of the Americas had provided him with a massive loan years earlier. Since she'd become the chief executive officer and inherited John George's controlling shares in the company, she'd thought about replacing Mahinder but hadn't made it a priority. In retrospect, that was clearly a mistake.

And why were the Russians involved at all? The Japanese might have made more sense. After all, she had wrangled ownership of Jeffersons Stores from the Yakuza. If anyone should be seeking retribution, they were the logical suspects, but none of those involved so far showed any sign of involvement with the notorious Japanese criminal outfit. Instead, the guy with Mahinder both looked and sounded Latin American. It just didn't make sense.

Jasmine called out from the living area, where they'd left her on the hardwood floor. "Are you awake, Suzanne? Are you okay over there?"

Suzanne grunted in acknowledgement.

Jasmine carried on. "My watch just signaled an alert. You get anything on yours?"

No alarm had sounded, but Suzanne checked the watch for messages, just in case. "I've got nothing here. What's happening?"

"I've had false alarms before, but Serge has all the security team's watches programmed to detect a digital Multima identification code. It sounds when it detects another Multima security watch within a range of about 100 hundred yards."

"Are you serious?"

"Like I said, I've had false alarms before, so let's not get our hopes up too high, but the alert light is still illuminated on my watch."

Within seconds, the electrical power returned to their suite with a sudden surge that saw the lights, heating, and fans all activated at once. Before their eyes adjusted to the new light, they were once more startled by what sounded like an explosion from the basement below them.

The loud boom sounded again and again, now more distinctly—someone was firing gunshots inside the hotel.

Sixty-Seven

Wabush, Labrador, Tuesday December 26, 2023

It was only a few minutes after the team had installed him in a wheelchair they'd found at the Wabush Airport that a louder-than-usual ring from his phone startled Serge. He'd set the ringer higher before Majorie Laplante—the RCMP officer assigned to watch over him while the team did its work in town—had plugged it into the wall socket to be sure there were no service disruptions or communication failures while they awaited news from the hotel. It was she who retrieved the nearby phone and passed it on to Serge.

"Some complications here." It was the calm voice of Constable Gagnon. "The first stage started fine. We sent the first two in, wearing Labrador Hydro uniforms. They followed the utility staff's instructions, and the power returned as expected. A few seconds later, a nearby boiler malfunctioned in the basement and exploded. Our guys weren't hurt, but one of the bad guys with them panicked and drew a gun on them. We had to take him out."

"Are they firing on our guys?" Serge asked.

"No. It's now a hostage situation. We've lost contact with our guys in the basement. I've set up a ring around the perimeter of the hotel and tried to establish communication with whoever's inside. So far, the phone in the hotel rings, but no one responds. I've just sent in two heavily armed officers to see what they can find. I'll keep you posted as I can." Gagnon hung up the phone.

Marjorie Laplante looked as worried as Serge felt. He pressed another button on his phone. "James, we have a problem here in Wabush. There were gunshots, and the local police are investigating the situation now. Have you heard anything from the guys in Vietnam?"

"Nothing yet. Would you like us to try them?"

"Yeah. I know it's evening in Ho Chi Minh City, but get one of my guys to call. See if they have any news out of Inuvik. Then, get someone to patch me through to Floyd in South Florida."

Marjorie Laplante scrolled through her phone for text messages or updates as Serge waited for his security guy in Palm Beach to respond.

Floyd was short of breath when he came on the line. "I just got back to a safe area. To monitor incoming communications, I must get myself within a hundred yards of the guy's office, and he's been busy. Throughout the night, he's been receiving and making calls almost continuously. Clearly, he's dealing with some sort of crisis."

"How many people are watching him?" Serge asked.

"It depends on the time of day. Mornings, he rarely leaves the complex, and from outside, it looks like only two or three resources monitoring him. Afternoons, when he often plays golf, I've counted up to a dozen. In the evenings, there might be three times that number."

"All Secret Service?"

"No. I'm guessing here, but I imagine he has a basic detail of two, maybe three Secret Service agents in the evenings. To me, the others all appear to be private contractors."

"Have you got any photos of the area close to the compound that you can send me?"

"I'll text them to you as soon as we finish here," Floyd said.

"One last question. You've been going all night, at least. When did you sleep last, and how much longer do you think you can operate at peak efficiency?"

"I snoozed for a few hours Christmas Day, when there was less happening here. I'm good for another couple hours."

"Get some coffee and your weapon. Keep it concealed, but ready," Serge instructed.

Moments after he'd finished the call with Floyd, another phone rang. He heard Marjorie say that there was no one around to overhear the conversation, and she was putting the call on speaker. Serge glanced behind him to be sure she was right.

"Things are now stabilized in the main power room in the hotel's basement. When another potential shooter saw our guys' badges, he pulled back while our men brought the situation under control. They've arrested him and left him in the basement. So far, no one else has intervened, but the guy doesn't speak English. Russian only, it appears. He had a phone conversation with someone in Russian before he surrendered."

Serge digested that bit of information before he replied. "Sounds odd to me. Be sure your guys are careful of a possible trap. I'll warn Antonio and the boys as soon as we finish here. What's your next step?"

"We've positioned resources on all three floors. Your people are on the second and third floors, and my team is combing the ground floor. We found the master digital code that opens every room door, and the teams have just started checking the rooms, one by one. It may take a while." Constable Gagnon's tone betrayed more than a touch of concern.

Serge commiserated. "I share your apprehension, but I've got four key people confined somewhere in that hotel. I want us to rescue them all, and we're running out of time. Keep me posted, Guillaume."

He'd never used his former colleague's given name in a conversation before. The change was intentional, conveying both appreciation and subtle pressure for the guy to produce the results they so desperately needed.

It was Serge's phone that rang next. James Fitzgerald had Archie Begat from Ho Chi Minh City on the line and offered to patch him through.

"Thanks, James. And stay on the line—you need to know this information as well."

From the moment Archie started to speak, his discomfort was apparent. He spoke slowly, choosing his words with care, using a tone they had to strain to hear.

"I just heard back from Nunavik. The Russian-speaking woman managed to review the tapes from five different calls, and they all had a common connection. Each call dealt with Multima. One confirmed that Russian resources are holding Suzanne Simpson and a woman named Jasmine. Another talked about transferring massive amounts of money to all parts of the world. Yet another said they'd captured Natalia and a lawyer named Alberto Ferer. They've got Natalia and Ferer in a hotel in Wabush, Labrador."

"There's nothing in those calls to confirm where they're holding Suzanne and Jasmine?" Serge asked.

"The woman made no mention, and she was very thorough." Archie sounded defensive for some reason.

"Okay," Serge reassured. "We're quite sure they're both in the same hotel. We've got people over there searching for all of them. Now, do we know who is directing all the traffic with these people?"

"No one has used a name, first, last or otherwise, but the woman is sure of one important detail. This entire exercise is designed to raise five hundred million dollars for some participant to run in the next election to become president of the United States of America."

Sixty-Eight

Wabush, Labrador, Tuesday December 26, 2023

They told Natalia they'd be back for her answer in just a few minutes, but over one hour had passed with no communication. She read their cursed agreement several more times to determine if there were subtle implications in the meanings of words or expressions. It was hard to imagine they truly wanted her to serve as a pliable minion who showed up for corporate events.

She had a growing sense that she was in danger. What might happen the moment she signed the document? Might they order her to sabotage some part of the company or someone in the company? The entire exercise seemed poorly thought out, entirely impractical, and destined for failure. Was failure what these people wanted for Multima?

With growing anxiety, her attention switched to her personal safety. She wore the digital tracking device provided by the security team despite her doubts about its value. It was small, strapped to her waist, and she normally forgot all about it throughout the day. Yesterday, she'd tucked it inside her underwear in case they searched her clothing.

She remembered that first day, when the security folks had asked her to start wearing the tracking device. They'd laughed when she asked if it would still work inside her vagina.

"It will still work inside your body, even if you swallow it," the technician had boldly proclaimed.

She'd carefully removed it from her panties before relieving herself each of the two times it was necessary, both on the flight and after arriving at the hotel. There was no way to know whether it was still functioning. Curious again, she moved into the bathroom to check on it once more.

She wiped it with a tissue after removing it and held it up to the light. No part of the simple device looked like it might serve some other purpose, like an on/off switch or a control device one might find on a phone or flashlight that might accidentally shut off. On impulse, she squeezed both sides of the flat surface between her thumb and forefinger . . . twice. Amazingly, for the first time, one of the device's surfaces gradually brightened from its normal, dull silver exterior to a warm, green glow, indicating that it was still working. Satisfied, Natalia re-inserted it just inside her panties, pulled up her jeans, flushed the toilet from habit, and washed, then dried her hands.

As she stepped out of the bathroom, a loud click at the doorway caught her attention. When she looked in that direction, she saw a parade of people filing into her room. Their mood seemed somber, almost like a funeral procession, before they spread out around the room and made way for Mauro Alvarez, who pointed her toward a comfortable chair beside the sofa.

"Who did you contact?" he growled, puffing up his chest to project authority, "and when?"

"No one," she replied. What was going on? If she hadn't contacted the outside world, was it possible that someone else in the group had, and they blamed her? "Where is Alberto Ferer?"

"None of your business. Answer my question. Who did you contact?"

"I've had no contact with anyone. I have no phone, no computer, nothing. You've—"

Before she could finish the sentence, Alvarez launched a rock-solid fist at her face with the intensity of a baseball pitcher releasing the ball. It hit the right side of her jaw with enough force to partially throw her over the armrest of the chair, leaving her head hanging toward the floor, and her teeth both loosened and broken in her mouth. She tasted blood and gagged. The intense pain caused her to sob onto the floor, blood oozing from her lips.

As she tried to push herself upward, someone kicked her arm away with enough force that she heard a crack as she fell back to the carpet. She grabbed her injured arm with her other hand, blubbered like a baby, and curled into the fetal position to protect herself.

That was when she heard a loud voice inside the room yell out a command. "Freeze where you are!"

Two gunshots exploded. One of the Russians screamed in agony before crashing to the floor only feet away from her face.

"I said, freeze!" the voice yelled again, even louder. "Freeze, or I have enough bullets here for everyone!" A few seconds later, another command. "On the floor!"

Bodies joined her on the floor, each of them stretching their arms out in submission, wearing expressions of either shock or defeat. Two or three of the people searched the prone bodies for weapons. When they found them, they slid them across the carpet away from their owners with brisk kicks.

Satisfied, one of the rescuers tapped Natalia's shoulder gently and asked, "Are you able to speak?" It was Bernie Perez, the guy who'd accompanied the woman who'd first brought her the tracking device many months ago. He turned her body and helped her into a sitting position.

"My face, mouth, and right arm are all injured." She spat out a mouthful of blood. "I think I swallowed a tooth, too."

"Relax. Take this with some water. It will help you through the next few hours."

As she cupped her hands around the water bottle and

popped the offered pill into her mouth, she started to feel dizzy, her vision fading. Before she could place the water bottle back on the floor, darkness set in.

Sixty-Nine

Montreal, Quebec, Tuesday December 26, 2023

James's conversation about the information received from the translator in Nunavik was interrupted by the female RCMP officer stationed with Serge at the Wabush Airport. He had been away from their call for a few minutes. When the security chief returned to the call, the relief in his tone was immediately evident.

"They found them all. Suzanne, Jasmine, and Alberto are all fine. Natalia has some injuries, non-life threatening, and they have a doctor on the way to the airport as we speak. We'll try to bring him on the corporate jet with us back to Montreal, and we should be in the air within the hour."

They chatted for several minutes as Serge described the takedown in Natalia's suite, how they'd discovered Suzanne and Jasmine a few doors down the hallway on the same floor of the hotel, and where they found Alberto, bound and gagged on the ground floor under a stairwell near an emergency exit. Serge provided a quick overview of Constable Gagnon's arrest of Abduhl Mahinder and Mauro Alvarez, together with five Spanish and Russian-speaking thugs. Then, their conversation took an unexpected twist, one James never would have guessed.

"There's little point in contacting the police down there. The man responsible for all this owns them. Has for years. The information out of Nunavik is damning, and there's little doubt the bastard is up to his ears in this shit, but bringing law enforcement in now probably won't even produce an arrest. If they do take him away, it'll only be for a few hours before he's waddling back to his complex. We need something else. Any ideas?"

James took a long moment to reflect. He did have an idea, but how much could he prudently share with Serge? "I have a special number I can call. I think we can achieve the results we desire. What I have in mind is marginally but not blatantly illegal, but could harm Multima's reputation if the wrong people find out. I won't cause him any physical harm, but I think I can scare the shit out of him. Scare him enough that he'll abandon this grab for ownership or scheme to raise election funds or simple protection bribe— whatever it is."

"I must let Constable Gagnon do what he wants with the gang here. After the sacrifices his team made over the holiday and putting their lives at risk, he'll surely want Suzanne and the others to testify if the case goes to court. Does that complicate your idea?" Serge posed the question as a caution, his tone carrying no hint of judgment.

"I doubt it. The scoundrel thinks only of himself. He'll let the Russians and even Mahinder or the hoodlum from Argentina fend for themselves, confident none of them would dare divulge his role in this fiasco. I'm comfortable moving ahead, and I'll leave Multima for good when Suzanne and you are home. If the guy tries any retribution, it will be directed toward me, and I'm willing to take that chance."

Serge mulled over the information for a moment or two, no doubt searching for an alternative. When he was satisfied he had neither questions nor objections, he replied with a heartfelt, "Thank you, James."

The call finished, James leaned back in the swivel chair to think it through once again. Were there any gaps? He squirmed and rubbed his hands together. Was he subconsciously washing his dirty hands, even before he'd committed the nasty act?

For the call, he moved to Serge's office. It was better if

no nosy ears heard bits of the conversation. It was also better if there were no witnesses. Calling from the landline in Serge's office made it impossible for Multima's security team or anyone else to record the conversation. Everyone knew the director of Multima's security had installed scrambling technology to prevent anyone from tracking calls from the dedicated line.

Seated behind the massive walnut desk, James pulled his mobile phone from a pocket and called Floyd Desmerais. He described the plot, careful to imply that he had Serge's support without actually using as many words. When Floyd understood his role and agreed to perform the task, James asked three last questions: "Is your weapon ready? Are you close enough now to complete the mission? Is your vehicle close enough to escape within a minute?"

"All affirmative, James. I've also made all the arrangements at the airport. The pilots are in the plane and will start the engines when you give the word."

"Call them now." James waited for Floyd to return to the line to confirm he'd reached the pilots, then unleashed their plot. "I've got you on speaker. When you hear me use the code word, execute the plan, then kill this call on your mobile, and get out of there."

James cleared his throat before dialing the next number on the secure landline. He wanted his voice crisp and clear. It took longer than expected and required three different conversations before someone finally agreed to put through his call without knowing who was trying to reach their boss.

"Heads will roll if I'm not speaking with him in thirty seconds," James had declared to the last screener.

The guy he sought used his usual dismissive tone when he finally came on the line. "Who's threatening my people and disturbing my morning coffee?"

"I have no intention of identifying myself, and there's no point pushing the record button. This call is scrambled.

Should you record it, it will be worthless. Let me say only that we know all about your scheme to steal Multima. We know all about the Russian involvement. We're aware of all that the Yakuza did to help you create the upheaval. And we're aware that your insidious plot failed. The RCMP in Wabush, Labrador, currently have Abduhl Mahinder, Mauro Alvarez, and five Russian thugs in custody. Have I made myself clear?"

The scoundrel's only response was, "What do you want?"

"We know you're doing all this to raise money for next year's presidential election campaign. We know the Yakuza promised you five hundred million dollars if you helped them recover their lost investment in Jeffersons Stores from Multima Corporation. We also know all about your intention to compromise Multima's management team. Call it all off. Immediately." James emphasized the last word, then waited for a response. It took only a moment.

"I don't know who you think you are, calling me up and making threats like that, but I'll do whatever I fuckin' please, whenever it pleases me to do it. So, fuck off."

James sensed that he was probably about to terminate the call, so he shouted, "Wait—don't hang up. If you think me and my people aren't serious about this, duck down now!"

The next sound he heard was glass smashing in the background. It sounded as if many windows had shattered. There were screams of fear, shouts for people to lie on the floor, feet scrambling, and multiple orders issued in abject confusion.

"Are you still there?" James asked calmly into the phone.

"Yeah. Yeah, I'm still here." His tone was barely above a whisper, his breathing labored.

"Order the Secret Service people and your own security

detail to stop all pursuit. Yell it out now." James waited for a response. When he heard his order executed as instructed, he carried on.

"For the last time, call it all off now. The plot. The Yakuza interference. The Russian mafia thugs. Any intentions you might have about running for president. Do you understand?"

It took several long seconds before the scum answered. His voice was barely above a whisper. "I understand."

"Tell me not only that you understand. Tell me that you agree," James insisted, his tone threatening.

"I agree."

The guy had a reputation for changing his mind, so James delivered one last warning. "If you disregard this warning at some time in the future and run to become president of the United States of America, the next shot won't simply be a warning."

Seventy

Montreal, Quebec, Tuesday December 26, 2023

Suzanne found Serge's security team at the hotel was remarkably well-prepared. Immediately after discovering them, they wrapped Suzanne and Jasmine in wool blankets snatched from the closets, helped them hobble down the hallways in the awkward garb, and physically carried them from the hotel rear door in the two-foot-deep snow to waiting SUVs.

It was impressive watching one of the officers from Constable Gagnon's detachment lead the hastily assembled convoy to the airport, with lights flashing and sirens blaring as the vehicles following veered from side to side on the slippery, snow-covered road. Although they traveled at a relatively high rate of speed, there was no cause for alarm, as the drivers appeared both conditioned and comfortable with the circumstances. The very few oncoming cars pulled to the right of the roadway, well away from the advancing convoy.

At the airport, the police escort SUV guided them through a gate held open by a sole guard, who offered a half-hearted salute to the passing cars before pulling it closed again immediately after they passed.

The pilots had already started the engines. Serge's team lifted Suzanne from the SUV while Jasmine waited for her turn. Both were still barefoot. Suzanne offered a gentle touch of encouragement on Jasmine's elbow, letting her know it wouldn't be much longer before the burly pair hoisted her up the stairway. The floor inside the jet was still cold, but the instant Suzanne saw Serge, she threw off her blanket and dashed across the few steps to where he sat facing her in the first seat.

The guys had already told her Serge was unable to walk or even lift himself on his own, so she wrapped her arms desperately around his shoulders, drew him tightly against her breasts, and held him there as their tears gushed. Neither said anything for more than a moment. Finally, she managed to expel the words, "Thank you so much, chéri. So much!"

That was all she could get out. She bent forward until their faces met and kissed him with every ounce of passion she could muster. She gripped his shoulders once more and pulled him tightly toward her.

To make room for the team streaming in, Suzanne took the seat across the aisle next to Serge and had a good look at him. He seemed barely awake. His pallor was more extreme than she'd ever seen, and his eyes struggled to stay open, blinking tentatively every few seconds as he tried to gaze back at her. He attempted a smile, and although his eyes sparkled for a fleeting instant, the intention never quite materialized.

She reached across the aisle when no one else waited to pass and squeezed his arm. "Rest. I see you're in pain. We'll talk later."

Airborne mere minutes after, Suzanne unbuckled her belt and stood in the space beside Serge's seat, using the armrest for balance as the jet continued its upward climb. She hovered over him, looking for signs of his current condition as he dozed fitfully. As soon as the turbulence reduced enough for safe movement within the cabin, she waved to the doctor treating Natalia two seats over. The security team had won his agreement to make the unplanned trip to Montreal with them after a promise of five thousand dollars cash and a return flight on the same jet within three hours of landing in Montreal.

"He's drowsy, in pain, and still suffering from a

concussion he incurred almost three days ago. If Natalia doesn't need you immediately, can you check on him?" To make her case, she held his gaze, pleading but not begging.

The doctor woke Serge and checked his vision, mouth, throat, and ears. From her seat, Suzanne couldn't hear the questions the doctor posed, but he asked several. After some minutes, he turned toward Suzanne, then took a step or two before leaning over to speak.

"I suspect internal bleeding, but it's impossible to know for sure without a scan. Please ask the pilot to arrange for an ambulance to meet us at the aircraft upon arrival. I'm going to give him an injection to induce sleep, so his movements will be limited. Let the pilot know that he should descend slowly and without sharp drops in altitude if possible."

She followed his instructions after knocking on the cockpit door. Before returning to her seat, she walked over to Natalia. Her face was bruised with tints of black and blue on the right side of her jaw, and her mouth was stuffed with either gauze or an absorbent sponge to ease the bleeding. Still, she managed a tentative smile when Suzanne looked down, then leaned toward her.

After a greeting and the expected pleasantries showing her concern, Suzanne said, "We have a lot to discuss."

Natalia's eyes darkened before they dropped downward. Was it shame? Fear? Disgust? Suzanne waited for her president of Supermarkets to respond. She deftly adjusted the dressings to the side of her mouth with her index finger so she could talk.

"I don't know what they've told you, but I'm at a loss to explain what happened. One of the security guys smashed his partner, Jack Smith, on the head, then physically dragged me to a meeting with an Argentinian, a guy named Alvarez. I'd never heard of him until he told me they planned to make me the CEO of Multima. They said you'd be leaving and they'd pay me the same salary and bonus as you. The next thing I knew, they'd hustled me onto a private jet, and I had no idea where we were headed or why."

She looked down again, clearly uncomfortable with the conversation and the pain and gauze in her mouth. After drawing a breath of resolve, Natalia continued her story, mumbling, and clearly trying to keep it as short as possible.

"We landed in Erie, Pennsylvania, of all places, and I expected to disembark and learn more about their intentions. Next thing I knew, Alberto Ferer climbed into the jet, and we were off again without a word from him. No greeting, no conversation during the flight. Only a brief glance in my direction before he took a seat in the back of the cabin. We landed in Labrador, in the middle of nowhere. They hustled me to the hotel and locked me away in a room without food or water for hours. Later, Alberto arrived with the other two, Abduhl Mahinder and the Argentinian, Alvarez. He handed me an agreement to sign, and I begged for time to read and study the document. They agreed and left me alone for a while."

She paused to wipe some blood dripping from her mouth with an absorbent sponge, then carried on. "Sometime later, they came back. I told them I wouldn't sign. Alvarez's men beat me before the security team arrived and rescued me."

As she spat out the last words, Natalia burst into tears.

Suzanne elected to say nothing. Instead, she reached down, gently squeezed her colleague's shoulder and held her hand there for a moment until Natalia raised her head and their eyes met. Suzanne met her gaze with a simple nod of understanding and a facial expression designed to convey little more. When an appropriate amount of time had lapsed, she moved two seats further back in the plane.

Alberto Ferer made eye contact for only a second, then his gaze dropped quickly to some imagined crisis in his lap.

It might have been comical under different circumstances. Rather than lord over him, standing, she chose a vacant seat across from him and swiveled to face him before starting carefully. "Are you willing to share with me what happened?"

He shrugged without looking up immediately, as though hoping she'd just go away. Instead, she chose to let the silence hang and wait. After a moment or two, he glanced up, but seemed to look over her left shoulder at someone as he spoke, although no one was there. "I'm a lawyer. The security guys already threatened that the RCMP will be meeting us upon landing to arrest me. I'll have nothing to say until I'm with my lawyer."

She struggled to maintain a neutral expression to mask her surprise, but remained determined to seek some engagement. Suddenly, her brief telephone conversation with Serge from the SUV on the way from the hotel to the airport popped back into her mind.

First, Antonio Primavera had passed her his mobile without comment. Then, Serge had taken a moment to inquire about her health and physical condition, but he'd switched quickly to the subject of law enforcement. She struggled to remember the exact words he'd used, but it was something like, "Don't talk with anyone about the incident. Law enforcement likely won't take any action for several reasons. I'll share everything with you in person, in private, when we meet."

Now, her guy was sedated, and her chief legal officer refused to speak. She quickly resolved that wouldn't continue. First, she glared at Alberto and started with a command. "Look at me!"

He raised his chin slightly and made eye contact, so she continued. "I know there was a plot to replace me as Multima's CEO. You must have just seen me speaking with Natalia. She suggested that you created a legal document they wanted her to sign, and I can only assume you created a similar agreement they expected me to sign, with or without duress."

He squirmed uncomfortably in his seat but said nothing. She decided to risk disobeying Serge's request. "There won't be any law enforcement waiting for you on the ground in Montreal, I can promise you that. But I won't promise they won't eventually get involved. Tell me your story. Now."

His legal mind seemed to struggle with the dilemma for more than a minute before he spoke. "Abduhl Mahinder first told me you were in physical danger if you didn't cede control of Multima Corporation. He promised to do everything possible to restrain the forces working to take over the company. Said he had contacts who could influence them if we made the process easy. Promised me ten million dollars and a job with Bank of the Americas if I didn't want to stay with Multima. When I told him I wasn't interested, he threatened my family. Eventually, I acquiesced."

A somber shiver jolted through her body as the realization took hold. One of her closest advisors and a trusted colleague for over a decade had been forced to "acquiesce." Her fingers and toes suddenly felt numb. She found it necessary to breathe deeply and was tempted to check her pulse. Never mind the probable expression portrayed on her face in the shock of the moment. She could understand his need to protect his family first, but it underscored her own vulnerability.

Still, she had a corporation to run, and the sorry excuse for a lawyer facing her was essential until she could be certain of her control of the company and its direction. She swallowed deeply before speaking.

"Eventually, I'll need to know the entire story, all the details, no matter how difficult that might be for you. In the meantime, you're my chief legal officer, and I have a company to run. I forgive you for the decisions you've made, no matter how horrendous you might feel about them at this moment. Now, tell me: what steps must I take to protect Multima from a recurrence of this nightmare?"

His advice proved limited. He really didn't have time to organize his thoughts, so perhaps it wasn't fair to expect a clear picture so soon after the trauma the guy had experienced. Still, she needed more insight. After two less-than-satisfactory conversations, she pulled back the curtain separating the security team at the back of the cabin from the other travelers and gestured for Antonio to follow her.

In the main cabin, she motioned for him to sit in a corner chair. She assumed the one in front and swiveled around to face him, her lips pursed, her expression stern. "What went down back there that I don't know about, Antonio?"

He claimed to know nothing more than he had already relayed to her. When she rephrased a question or homed in on specific details, like who the Russians were working for, he either feigned ignorance or actually didn't know. She couldn't be sure which, but after the fourth question, he finally volunteered one morsel she could work with.

"The only additional detail I know that I haven't already shared with you is that Serge gave the order to enter the hotel after he had a conversation with James Fitzgerald. He told me James had a lead on who the real culprit was behind it all."

The Russians had stolen her phone, so she motioned for Antonio to cough up his. He complied, and within seconds, she heard ringing as she waited to connect to the security center in Montreal. A moment later, they had located James Fitzgerald.

"It's wonderful to hear your voice," he said with a mixture of relief and satisfaction in his tone. "I hear things were a little rough for a while there in Labrador. Is everyone all right now?"

She answered his question as succinctly as she could under the circumstances. Within a few minutes, she shared information about Serge, Natalia, and Alberto's current physical conditions, and took pains to keep her tone factual and non-judgmental.

As she wrapped up the summary, she shifted her tone and choice of words. "Now, James, without any filter or bullshit, tell me exactly what you engineered from that cozy office in Montreal. And don't you dare leave out a single detail."

For a few seconds, he remained silent and she waited. "Sure, Suzanne. You deserve to know everything. Let's get together with Serge as soon as you arrive in Montreal and, together, we'll fill in any details you want."

"Nice try. However, I don't have a second more for 'nice.' You're my friend. I respect you more than any other colleague, and I value your judgment. But you work for me, not Serge, and I want to know exactly what took place, with whom, and why. We have about thirty minutes until landing. Use as much of that time as you need."

He caved. After swearing her to total secrecy, he reviewed his conversations with Serge about the translations out of Inuvik and the rich information those intercepted and translated calls had provided. He helped connect the dots between the Russians, the Yakuza, and the good-for-nothing in South Florida behind it all.

His pace slowed measurably as he recounted his advance preparation with Floyd, organizing the electric golf cart for a quick escape, the private jet fueling, then starting the engines at the airport fourteen minutes away and synchronizing devices and speakerphones to trigger the blast that had shattered the windows of the resort complex.

She couldn't help herself—she laughed. As James

continued to relay the information that Floyd had indeed escaped undetected in an electric golf cart with its standard speed controls deactivated, then drove himself to the jet waiting at the nearby airport, her laughter increased uncontrollably.

James stifled his satisfaction with the story better than she, because he was also able to squeeze in his final threat to the reprobate about more to come should the good-for-nothing change his mind again and try to run in any US presidential election.

"I'm confident this would-be tyrant will leave you alone in the future," he assured her with quiet confidence.

"You're missing one important detail. You already told me the scoundrel was *not* the forty-fifth president of the USA, as I'd expected. So, who was it?"

"Believe me when I say he's worse than that degenerate, but I will never share the tyrant's real name."

On that note, Suzanne knew there was no more to come from her loyal subordinate.

Instead, she would simply have to force herself to recover, refocus, recalibrate, and reorganize Multima Corporation to become ever more successful. When that was complete, she'd probably pass on the baton when the time was right.

Suzanne could always change her mind. At the moment, though, it looked as if Natalia remained the best-positioned candidate.

The End

Acknowledgements

This is my ninth novel in the Multima Saga since *Three Weeks Less a Day* launched in 2016. I want to again thank all readers around the globe for reading my stories. I write to entertain you, and your positive feedback confirms that I succeed on that level.

As you may already know, I always start off with an outline of a story I think readers will enjoy, and tell it as effectively as I can. Once a manuscript draft is complete, two excellent writing professionals tell me all the mistakes I've made! I listen to them.

For this story, Elise Abram and Val Tobin have worked separately, but together, to help me deliver the novel you're either about to read; or have just completed. They did much more than detect mistakes. Both provided valuable suggestions that improved my story meaningfully, and I thank both for their expertise, dedication and patience.

To catch those nasty little typos and errors that try to work their way into every book, Deborah Armstrong of Terrahill Publishing carefully proofread the final drafts and pointed out her discoveries. However, if you find any remaining errors or shortcomings, they are entirely mine.

Early in the review process, I asked Cathy & Dalton McGugan and Heather & Dan Lightfoot, to read the story and share their thoughts about the characters and plot. Each provided excellent suggestions that added significant value to the story, and I thank them for again for helping with beta-reading.

Sharon Brownlie of Aspire Book Covers designed the impactful cover and pleasing book layout. I thoroughly enjoyed working with her across continents, and hope we can do it again in the future.

To each of these excellent collaborators, I express my heartfelt thanks and appreciation.

ABOUT THE AUTHOR

Gary D. McGugan loves to tell stories and is the author of Three Weeks Less a Day, The Multima Scheme, Unrelenting Peril, Pernicious Pursuit, A Web of Deceit, A Slippery Shadow, CONTENTION, and When Power Fails.

After a forty-year career at senior levels of global corporations, Gary started writing with a goal of using artful suspense to entertain and inform. His launch of a new writing career—at an age most people retire—reveals an ongoing zest for new challenges and a life-long pursuit of knowledge.

Home is near Toronto, but Gary thinks of himself as a true citizen of the world. His love of travel and extensive experiences around the globe are evident in every chapter.

Follow Gary D. McGugan

Author Gary D. McGugan Website:
www.garydmcguganbooks.com

Facebook: www.facebook.com/gary.d.mcgugan.books

Instagram: Authorgarydmcgugan

Threads: Authorgarydmcgugan

LinkedIn: https://tinyurl.com/rmbhfzer

BlueSky:
https:/bsky.app/profile/authorgarydmcgugan.bsky.social

MeWe:https://mewe.com/authorgdm